THE LAST WARRIOR

THE EPIC JOURNEY OF JACK GEORGE

ANDY DICKINSON

This book is dedicated to Liz my wife, and to all of the Parkinson's Warriors like me who just keep on moving forward.

As warriors, we do not ask for the easy way, we demand the hard way, because that is what we do. We rise above the self talk, choosing the higher ground, where champions take their place. We live for the chance to prove ourselves, in combat.

— JACK GEORGE

CONTENTS

1

AYLESBURY

Things were beginning to change at home, and it scared me.

We lived in middle-class Aylesbury on Wendover Road, and from my mother's perspective all appeared normal. But I caught my mother crying, which was strange as I had never seen her cry before. I started to cry and hug her leg, willing her to stop crying. At these times it felt like my world was collapsing. I would imagine a world without my family. Hell for a five-year-old. I felt lonely, isolated and craved love from my parents; a simple hug that never came.

Mum did her best to cover up how devastated she was and protect us from the painful truth. I learned much later that my father, after getting home from a long day at work, dropped a bombshell. He was leaving and emigrating to Australia. It was 1969. So off he went, leaving his wife, his mother and five kids between two and thirteen.

I did not understand why we packed up our brand-new house on Wendover Road and moved to a much smaller, old townhouse in Chaucer Drive, on the other side of Aylesbury. My mother had a knack for being able to clean a house and make it quite liveable, but this house was definitely a step backwards. Living in a brand-new house in Wendover Road and then moving to a rundown townhouse was a fall from grace, but from the beginning my mother made it feel like it was all an adventure.

I think my mother was depressed but back in the Seventies mental health was not a roaring trade like it is now. You were told to grin and bear it, soldier on or just plain cheer up. I could not show my emotion or the pain that I would suffer as a young boy. I yearned for my mother to hold me, but I was expecting too much. Always busy and always complaining, my mother would scream, "Get out of the kitchen, go and play with your brothers." She would even threaten to beat us, which terrified me. I felt like she did not love me, which in my mind was worse than dying.

Looking back now, my mother's unpredictable mood swings were probably bipolar in nature. Not knowing what to expect made me very anxious. If I was out, I would telephone home to see what mood Mum was in, and just hope that she did not pick up the phone. If one of my brothers or sisters answered, I would quickly ask, "What kind of mood is Mum in?" Even though I knew that her moods could change in an instant, I still had to get the heads up from my brothers or sisters.

If she did answer the phone, the interrogation about where I had been would lead to her screaming into the phone, "Just don't come home, you are not welcome here." The idea of having no place to go, without a home, would devastate me! So I'd sneak into the house best I could and hope she did not see me. Maybe she had changed her mood. Sometimes, I am in luck. "Hello love," she says as I walk through the front door. She is now a different person. It is these times that I yearned for.

Mum was brought up in a small council home in the beautiful country town of Amersham about forty-five minutes north of

London. The house was small with a living room and dining room downstairs and three small bedrooms upstairs, it was always warm in winter and cool in summer, and there was always something delicious cooking on the old stove.

My mother was by no means an elegant, sophisticated or well-educated woman. She wore her working-class upbringing like a badge of honour and would enjoy embarrassing us all by getting drunk and obnoxious whenever we would go out as a family. It would make me cringe when we were in social situations and Mum would make a scene. I'd try to justify it by remembering that my mum's family were all so poor; my mother left school at thirteen to assist her mother who was working in the local laundromat.

My mother's older sister Dot met an American airman in England soon after the Second World War ended. He was a rear gunner in the lumbering Lancaster bomber. This position was the most dangerous; quite often the rear gunner would, as they called it, 'go mad'. Or, in modern terms, have a breakdown.

Marwin and Dot got married and quickly fled the destruction and rebuilding of post-war England. Or was it my grandmother they were fleeing from? I heard years later from my cousin Kody, who lives in America, that her mother also suffered from extreme fluctuations in her moods. It was probably also depression.

My grandmother's side of the family were grave diggers, road workers and labourers. Typical working class. I saw a photo of my grandma's younger brother sitting back in his chair, his uniform too big for him, but proud to be included and to do his part, resigned to what is about to happen. I put myself in his position and I cannot imagine the thought of going to war. He seems so calm about it, yet so young. I dread to think how he died. He was only seventeen years old. Killed on the Western Front, my grandma never heard from him again.

My mother's father Albert, a veteran of the infamous Somme in the First World War, was lucky to survive. So many of the new recruits were slaughtered; entire towns of young men, some just teenagers, ceased to exist in an afternoon of carnage. They had a misguided belief that they were somehow embarking on an adventure. As they formed up lines in the heavy rain and got the first whiff of the dead being loaded into waiting vans, the smiles were wiped from their faces. *This was not right, I did not sign up for this.* It was all too late. Many sobbed when the realisation dawned on them that they were probably going to die that day.

The barrage of the cannons was enough to make them all crazy. The mud was thick under their loosely fitting hob nailed boots, making it difficult to walk. They found their place on or beside a ladder that would propel them up and across no man's land, where they were told great glory awaited them. Given a tot of rum they waited for the bombing of the enemy lines to finish, and then came the haunting sound of the whistle. They hesitated, wetting themselves in a panic. The first line of men torn apart by machine guns, their bodies collapse back into the trench. Yet somehow these young men find the insane courage to step forward up and into no man's land, only to postpone their death by a couple of metres.

The hours of bombing to soften up the enemy was like a flea on a bear. Thousands upon thousands of young men lost their lives on the Western Front in what was a tragic stalemate between the German and Allied forces. The total irony of this war was that the trenches were at the same position at the beginning of the war as the end of it.

My grandfather Albert survived the slaughter in the trenches. It was pure luck. But the gas, a deadly fog, would silently creep over them, shredding their skin and suffocating them, there was just no escape. The gas masks were their only protection. Caked in mud and blood, the gas masks were bulky and awkward to put on. The mad rush to get the masks on, the simple fumbling of the mask strap, was the difference between life and a painful death. It would creep up in the night, a deathly shadow that would infiltrate the resting soldiers, catching them totally by surprise.

Albert somehow made it home but died a lonely death at thirty-five. He was sick for many months upon his return from the Great War. His skin not healing from where he was touched by the gas, it would peel and fester into infected ulcers. My grandmother had no intention of looking after him and kicked him out, much to my mother's disdain. He ended his life in a small upstairs bedroom, alone. My mother used to say that her father was never the same after he tried to stop a bolting horse and carriage. It went back further than that though. He left part of his soul on the Western Front, he could never reconcile why he survived while so many of his friends perished.

———

When my mother was thirteen, she developed severe gum disease. Rather than treat the infection, the dentist said it would be much cheaper to pull all the teeth out. So from thirteen years old, my mother had no teeth. She hid it by having well fitted dentures her entire life. She adapted well, making an artform out of wearing and juggling her dentures. I remember, she used to take them out and leave them in a small bowl of water when we all sat down for dinner. I hated it. She would ask one of us to clean her dentures and the thought of it still turns my stomach to this day. I loved my mother – I think – but I wonder now if I only loved her for the security of a home. After being threatened so many times with "you are not my son" and "you can go and live in a boys' home" I was so scared that one day I would be shipped away from my brothers and sisters to some kind of home. It was no wonder I was so shy, I was just shit scared of getting on the wrong side of my mother's temper and losing everything. No child should have to go through that kind of abuse.

My grandmother was the same as Mum. She was an angry, aggressive woman. Grandma Gertrude was a lady about town. Though poor, she managed to have four husbands and at least one child to each husband. She worked in an old laundromat, making mere pennies as she turned the roller to squeeze the last remaining drops out of the sheets.

"Don't stand so close," she barked at my mother. "Feed it faster."

As she tugged on the sheet, my mother's hand went into the roller. She let out a scream as her tiny hand was pulled between the two main rollers.

"Now look what you have done," Grandma sneered as she pulled the hand out and clipped her on the back of her head in one swift motion.

My mum used to say to me, "You never had it so easy, Grandma was cruel, but I know she loved me – even though I broke all my fingers in the laundry roller that day. Look, my fingers never fully recovered." She would show us her hand with permanently bent fingers.

My mother's side of the family had no formal education. The men were hard workers loyal to their bosses. Grandma carried the mantle of poverty, she could not help it, always complaining about her hard life. It was naturally perpetuated again by my mother in her life. When I was growing up, I always dreaded going to visit Grandma. At that time, she was married to her fourth husband, Nigel.

"Hello Uncle Nigel," I would shout as I passed him where he always sat in the kitchen.

He would pull his tweed cap down and push his round John Lennon glasses up on his nose as he rushed to finish his cigarette. "Be a good lad," he would say and then without another word head down to the pub for several pints and try and find a way to cheer up. He was a miserable sod, but who could blame him. That generation survived the Great War and subsequently the depression. They knew real hardship.

———

Olivia Shippley was born in 1901. She was my grandmother on my father's side. I can remember quite a lot about her as she would visit us whenever she was in town. Mum would put out the best teacups and cotton napkins. I was always so happy when Grandma came over, she would hug me and kiss me on the cheek. She always brought over a bag of cakes from the most expensive bakers. She loved being the life of the party, dressed in the finest clothes, long blonde hair that fell down her back and always wearing a magnificent fur coat. She would entertain us for hours with stories of her travels She would often say that she loved her lifestyle but she loved us all so much more.

"Grandma was quite a performer," Mum would always say. Olivia loved a crowd to play up to, it didn't have to be anyone in particular. From a young age, she was always dancing, singing, and performing. Growing up, she lived with her sister, mother and father in Hertfordshire, north of London. Education was not an option as the family was so poor, and as she got older, she craved a better life for herself.

Her father worked long hours at a printing press, responsible for keeping the machines greased and working. Her mother was a kitchenhand at the local bakery. The bonus of working at the bakery was bringing home the shortbread and flapjacks that had not sold.

Olivia, tall and blonde, stood out from a young age. She loved singing with the local church choir and taught herself tap dancing.

At eighteen she got a lucky break. "I saw a poster on the wall in the local community centre," she would recall excitedly. "Magic was coming to town, and they were looking for new employees." As we all sat and listened, her voice grew to a crescendo. "Magic shows had gained a huge amount of interest since the great Houdini! Everybody loves the magic shows," she would sing out. "And being part of a magic troupe was exciting and fun, a great lifestyle with prestige."

She turned up at the arranged time and was met by the troupe manager, Edith Smith. Edith was an uptight woman, never smiled, smoked constantly and topped up her glass of neat gin throughout the interview. She fired off questions that Olivia did her best to answer, there was no telling how she was going. Edith suddenly stood up and barked "wait here".

All of a sudden, the room filled with people and the centre of attention was a rather large man, who seemed to envelop the rest of the group with his charisma. It was 'The Great Clyde', the world-famous magician. He looked directly at Olivia and asked, "How would you like to join my troupe as one of my assistants?"

Olivia went on to be one of the greatest magicians' assistants of her time. Nicknamed Wong, as she starred in a Chinese themed part of the show, going on to hold the world record for being sawn in half. When she was twenty-five and living a glamorous life, rubbing shoulders with comedians, actors, and wealthy businessmen, she was approached by an up and coming star who was making a name for himself in the new silent movies – Charlie Chaplin.

He made it very clear to Olivia that the future lay in movies and she should join him in America. Olivia flatly refused. She was at the height of success in the magic game and playing to packed theatres all over Europe. This was and would always be the future of entertainment. So she declined. Little did she know her life was about to change in a way she never would have expected.

The troupe were performing in Berlin in the Summer of 1929. Germany was resurrecting itself as the new cultural centre of Europe. The German people were excited about the new fervour and just plain fanaticism of the promises being made by the Nazi party leader, Adolf Hitler.

There was no doubt that Germany was lifting itself out of the once crippling sanctions that were punishing the country for its blight on humanity in the First World War. Hitler was driven by a pathological hate of the Jews whom he blamed for the defeat of the once great German nation. This drove him and it in turn drove the German people to rise up.

Berlin welcomed shows and acts from all over Europe and the famous magicians were treated like royalty. The after-show parties were swimming with champagne, fine wine and an exquisite selection of food from the best chefs in Europe. It was understandable that the parties were well attended by high level members of Hitler's National Socialist Party, and members of the police force that would go on to become a ruthless group of murderers: the Gestapo and the SS.

Olivia attracted many suitors and was often the centre of attention. She was twenty-nine, single, glamorous, and now pregnant with my father. She had her suspicions as to who my grandfather was, but she was just not sure.

She acted quickly and arranged for Mummy Mac who ran a foster home called Sunny House in Amersham to take Charlie in, even though he was still just a baby. Olivia would drop in to visit in between exotic trips all over the world. She would always take a gift for him. Whenever the magic troupe performed in England, she would pick him up and seat him in the front row.

I remember sitting with Dad as he was dying. "My only regret is not getting to know my mother better," he would cry.

I found it hard to cry, as there had been so much history between him and the rest of the family. I was just blank. So I would sit there and play his favourite music. He spoke of the times that he spent with his mother with softness and love. She was his family. Though the other children at the foster home were also like his family, his mother was the only real family that he had. He had no aunties or uncles, no brothers, or sisters. It could be quite confusing;

he would call the other Sunny House residents his brothers and we referred to them as uncle. I learned much later that they were not my real uncles.

———

My parents lived in very unhappy homes as they were growing up. They were unsettled and lacking in even the most basic love that you would expect from a parent. That and a deep desire to get away and find a new life propelled them towards each other. Every Friday night they would both go down to the Sycamore Club, which was just a plain hall used for social functions and a place where young people could meet. It was bright and airy, the modern looking gramophone belting out Bing Crosby and other top hits. Charlie was in a corner sipping on punch, getting ready to join the band with his piano accordion. Margery was on the other side of the hall, chatting with her choir friends.

Charlie was not a big man, quite short actually, but he had a sense of confidence that made him appear larger than he was. He made his way across the hall to Margery; he had been keen on her for a couple of weeks now. "Fancy a dance?" he asked.

She blushed a little, but no one would have noticed. His voice was posh which she did not expect, perhaps it was from his education. Regardless of his situation at Sunny House, he graduated from King Edward's High school, where he was on a scholarship. King Edward had set up a fund for disadvantaged students to attend this prestigious college.

So they danced and that was the beginning. They were almost inseparable from that day onwards. They were both twenty-four years old and desperate to leave, to get away from the lives they were living. But I think back now on the upbringing they both had, devoid of any deep emotion, any real depth of feeling, and love was just dished out to manipulate. Yet they both yearned for family. But neither of them was prepared for what was to follow. They left home together and got married.

————

Fast track thirteen years and they now had five children. Dad was never at home. My mother would say, "Why can't you spend a weekend at home?" It was not that she needed his help with the children as my older sisters did most of the work helping in the house. My two brothers and I were well controlled from an early age. We were all basically happy and just blended in. The fights between us started a couple of years later.

Dad was an engineering salesman. He sold machinery parts and oils to large factories which took him initially all over England, and then overseas, so he was away a lot. I think he craved the silence so did what he could to get away from the complaints from my mother and the constant noise from five kids. I loved the postcards he would send. I still have one that he sent me personally from Australia. I had no idea he was having thoughts of moving to Australia. I couldn't wait to see the colourful baggage tags every time he returned home, wondering what great adventures he had been on.

As I was growing, I felt the need of a father figure intensely. I got a pat on my head from Dad occasionally. He was very sparing on what affection he doled out. I would just hang out for the scraps of attention, only to be severely disappointed when he would cancel at the last minute or even worse, not show up, blaming everybody but himself, refusing to take responsibility. He never learned and although it hurt like hell, I learned to live with it.

I was beginning to resent my father; his lack of attention made me misbehave. I felt like I wanted to hit something or someone. It was a feeling that stayed with me for many years. My mother called it anger; she was the only person that I shared these feelings with.

She had enough of her own problems going on to really notice what was going on with me.

On the one hand, Dad would say, "I just love my family and am working hard for you all." On the other hand, he loved his space, a classic wanting your cake and eating it. My mother rode my dad fairly hard, but he was aloof and distant. I would hide up in the bedroom with my pillow over my head, just wishing the arguments would stop.

I think my mother suspected my father was having an affair, she felt a shift in him for a while but could not put a finger on his newfound aloofness. This was a familiar feeling for my mum, as my father had many affairs during their marriage. *Why?* She would think. *He has a great home with five loving children, why throw all of that away?*

I remember Mary Green who lived down the end of Wendover Road. She had an interest in my father. Mary was married with two children. She was quite an attractive woman with long brown curly hair. Her husband was a shift worker that often worked at odd hours.

My mother knew that Dad would leave if she confronted him, and she loved life in her bubble no matter how much it hurt.

I used to ride my cool three-wheeler bike past the Greens' house on my way to the park with my sisters. I would notice Dad sometimes in the front room as the curtains were hurriedly pulled shut. "Why is Dad there?" I would ask my sisters.

"Ohhh, don't worry about it," they would say.

I had an inkling that something was not quite right. What was my father doing at Mrs Green's house? Why is he hiding? Kids just have an instinct. My sisters were old enough to know what was going on. "Dad and Mary are friends," they would say. "Just try not to worry about it." My sisters knew I worried a lot, so were always looking out for me.

Why do men and women have affairs? A question that I would

ponder repeatedly as I too initially found it difficult to commit to just one person. I could easily blame my upbringing, but for me it all came down to I simply had not met the right person, so more is better. I often thought about how my life would be with a wife and children. Some people are best to leave it alone.

When Dad was away, we all got on and Mum made it as much fun as she could. But even back then, my mum had an anger which we all tried hard to avoid. She was an awesome cook; we all loved the treats she would cook up over the weekend. She always baked our choice of cake for our birthday. I would look forward to this all year, counting off the days to my birthday, when I would have to make a choice. "I will have the chocolate mud cake please." I would say in my best voice.

When I was in infant school there was one teacher who would help herself to the yummy homemade cakes in my lunch box. I just let her, not knowing how I should be handling it. I felt so powerless.

Craig Thomas, my mate, would ask me, "Why do you let her take it?"

Her name was Mrs Crawford. I figured years later that I would get in trouble if I mentioned it. But that also felt really strange because I knew she was doing the wrong thing. Basically, I was a coward, and I hated myself because of it.

We had an old Vauxhall Viva. It was dark green and my mind boggles at how the six of us would fit, with bags. One weekend in spring, Mum loaded us all into the car and we drove all the way south to Chichester. It was a two-and-a-half hour drive and then a short drive to West Wittering by the sea. The squall of the seagulls and the smell of the seaweed have stayed with me my entire life. I was only five years old, but I remember these times and how happy I was. Sea and salt represented an age of innocence for me. A time when things didn't seem to matter. I was free to let my mind just roam. This is the feeling of being content; maybe this is what being happy feels like.

Even now after all these years when I hear seagulls or the smell of the ocean I slip back to the seaside and feel like a happy boy again.

2
SYDNEY

One morning six months into our new life without my father, I was sitting on the carpeted staircase whilst my mother talked on the phone to Dad in Australia. The conversation was not an argument, my father was simply saying he wanted the family back together again. "So, pack up the house and migrate to Sydney." And how my mother managed to do that alone with five children amazes me. It all happened so quickly.

I could see that my sisters were not happy. They were in their early teens and were well set up with schools and friends. But we all had to go. I often wonder how my life would have been if we decided to stay in England.

Dad's mother Olivia took it hard. We were the only family she had. She wept and wept when we left. She went back to her London apartment and became a recluse, staying in bed all day, day after day, swigging vodka and tonics continuously as she reminisced about her glory days when she was a star, talking to no one in particular.

She had her husband, Percy Shippley, suave and debonair, a

smoker of thin cigars but he was too interested in being seen about town with Wong on his arm.

I remember the day when Percy called our house. "Wong has died. She called me into the bedroom on Monday morning and said, 'Oh Percy I have wet the bed.' I told her to not worry about it. So I fetched a clean sheet and some fresh towels and went in to the bedroom. I found her with her head on her chest. She had died then and there. It was so sudden, and there was nothing I could do."

Apparently, she had been hiding a heart condition for years. Nobody knew about it. My mother told my father and he said he wished he had known she was sick, he would have made more of an effort to find out who his real father was. But like the great magician's assistant that she was, that was one secret she preferred to keep to herself.

———

My mother just did not want to go, leaving all of her dear friends and family. But she did what she thought was good for the family.

What a rush. All the hard plastic suitcases were packed into the back of Ivan's car. My mother, brothers and sisters all found some space in between the cases. Ivan drove an old Cadillac which was huge. He was my Aunty Gillian's boyfriend. Aunty Gillian was my mother's younger half-sister, her father was Uncle Nigel. Ivan was always keen to help.

I remember asking him, "Will we be able to see kangaroos in the city?"

"No. Don't be stupid."

So the journey began. First stop was Southampton, where the ship we were scheduled to leave on, the Shaw Saville *Southern Cross* waits.

We emigrated to Australia with my mother, two brothers and two sisters. We never had an extended family, we were quite alone.

All the grandparents and cousins were in England, now on the other side of the world.

The move from the frigid winter of England to the stifling heat of a Sydney summer took six weeks on the ship. This was a real adventure and me and my brothers made every nook and cranny ours to find new adventures. I still remember vividly the deckhands diving into the water from the main deck in Trinidad. The smell of the pineapple and melon in the air in Fiji and the beat of the kettle drums in Panama.

Each place we stopped intrigued me. In Fiji, Mum bought me a really cool wooden model of a traditional Fijian fishing boat. I loved running my fingers over the smooth teak and playing with the small canvas sail. Imagining skimming across the waves, singing along with the other tribesmen, without a worry in the world. There were so many things to see, hear and touch, I was mesmerised by the entire experience. Luckily, I was the only one of us that did not suffer from sea sickness. The ship seemed huge to me, but it was very small compared to modern cruise ships. It would roll up and down as it crashed through the waves. My brothers and I would watch the flying fish and dolphins in the wake of the bow seemingly racing the ship. What fun they were having.

Every morning the cabin attendant, Richard would bring us in a cup of tea and sweet biscuits. *What a luxury*, I thought. There was no fresh milk, so they used Carnation milk or dried milk. I did not mind. Richard was from the West Indies. He had the whitest teeth and his smile beamed such warmth. He would often sit and talk about his family.

"I love the life on the ship," he would say, reminiscing as he recalled his young family, whom he missed terribly.

I was watching the ship from the mid cabin as it squeezed its way along the Panama Canal. The water in the ship pool turned a muddy brown, the same as the water in the canal. There were all kinds of activities on the ship. We would join the bingo, and one day

I won a Mars bar. How delicious, the chocolate and the caramel. I had never tasted one before, what a delight it was.

As we prepared to arrive in Sydney, I was getting quite anxious. I would be going to a new school. New school means new friends. When my friends came over, I had to tell them to say, "Hello Mrs George, how are you today?" If they didn't say hello properly, my mother would blow up. I was so embarrassed. It was no wonder I was so shy. My mother shamed me.

From a young age I did have a sense of right and wrong, so I rarely got into any real trouble. My shyness attracted the bullies, but I was strong for my size and had a short temper. I was beaten up a few times, as the bullies thought I was any easy target. It was strange, because I would be so hard on myself thinking I was a coward for not fighting back. But the thing is, no one ever taught me how. I carried this victim mentality around with me for years, believing it was all my fault, until finally someone took a real interest in me, and taught me how to treat bullies.

———

Arriving in Sydney was spectacular. It was 26 January 1970. The day was crystal clear, and we were all awestruck as the ship that had been our home for the last six weeks eased its way past the building site of the Sydney Opera House and under the wrought iron steel structure, the iconic Sydney Harbour Bridge, famous all around the world.

At last, we docked. We all made our way from the dock in Pyrmont and found our way to Town Hall Station. What a sight it must have been. A woman and her five children, traipsing with their heavy suitcases and bags to who knows where. All of our main luggage was packed away in timber caskets and would arrive many weeks later. Dad sent the details of how to get to the house by post but could not be there as he had work commitments. I think we would have believed anything he said back then.

He had known for six weeks when we would be arriving. We all felt it, but that was how it was going to be with Dad, just one disappointment after the next. It was in these early years that my father taught me so much. I knew by watching his actions that I could never rely on him.

We took the old red train which rattled and shook. You had to really push to open the door. We had to be quick for all of us to get off safely. We were heading all the way north to Hornsby.

"This train is terminating here," blurted out the loudspeaker. It made us all jump.

"Quickly, take the suitcases." There was a distinct tension in my mother's voice. Who could blame her. She left her life in England in the middle of bitter winter to arrive with family to a blistering hot summer's day, only to be yelled at by a loudspeaker.

We changed at Hornsby for Berowra; this journey was taking hours. We lugged the suitcases up the stairs across the walkway and down the stairs to the correct platform, or at least we hoped it was.

What an adventure, I thought.

My mother and my sisters navigated us all the way from the city to the outskirts of northern Sydney with a tiny map. Berowra really was in the 'bush'. It was at the end of the world.

I would ask my father many years later why he chose Berowra.

"Because on a map it appeared close to the beach."

How strange, I would think, *it is nowhere near the beach*.

Finally, we had made it. We all got off the train at Berowra, and sat on our suitcases on the deserted platform. The silence was deafening except for a loud shrill of the cicadas. I had never heard or seen a cicada before, a large insect that had names like the Green Grocer, Yellow Monday and Black Prince. They were harmless, spending many years underground then digging their way to the surface, shedding their skin, mating, then dying. All in a day or two.

Where to from here? I wondered.

We had instructions from my father to telephone the real estate agent from the pay phone on the corner of Berowra Waters Road and the Pacific Highway.

It was 10 cents for a local call. Dad had posted $20 for expenses so we had enough. Not that it did us any good. The pay phone was not working. Now clearly distressed, Mum let out a huge sigh and put her head in her hands.

3
ARCADIA CRESCENT

The woman opened the door to the florist and kiosk on the corner. "Dear, dear me. You poor things you must be thirsty and starving. Let's get you out of this sun. My name is Elspeth." She had a thick European accent. "Now, where are you heading?"

I could tell my mother warmed to her straight away. "To 23 Arcadia Crescent."

"That is not far from here. I will take you there." She strode out of the shop. So much for resting and having a drink.

Elspeth Menka always seemed old. She came looking for us when she heard through others there was a new English family that was migrating to Australia. Elspeth was Jewish, and I learned much later that she was a holocaust survivor. She would tell us stories of her time in Nazi-occupied Europe. She was in the Warsaw ghetto, in Poland and her story of survival is incredible. She ended up in Auschwitz, where she only just survived.

"They packed us into these tiny carriages, far too many of us. My mother and father were old," she would say, "these carriages were not fit for pigs. Day and night we waited then moved, stop start, stop start. The Nazi troops would turn hoses onto us and would yell, 'Drink up, you Jewish pigs.'

"At last, we arrived at a long station. The door flew open and there was absolute chaos. The men dressed in grey striped baggy clothes were encouraging us to leave our bags. We could get them later, they said. The dogs, my God, the dogs were in a frenzy, vicious German Shepherds. I tried desperately to stay with my parents, but they were ripped away from me. It was heartbreaking. The last I saw of them was when they were made to walk down the pathway past the small orchestra, then they just disappeared forever, reduced to dust. So sad. I was lining up with other women when one of the workers in the baggy clothes leaned in and whispered to me, 'Say you are a seamstress and you will survive.' So I did, and he saved me.

"I walked up to the tall man in dark leather knee high boots, and a spotless SS uniform, and he said, 'Do not be afraid my dear, what do you do?'

'I am a seamstress,' I said.

'Very good, take the far line.'

"And that was it. I worked in the large clothes factory with hundreds of other women. Luckily, I could sew. We re-made thousands of clothes into usable garments that could be re-worn by the German people. Of course, there were rumours going around about the gas chambers and crematoriums. And there was no missing the smell or the ash coming from the large chimneys. Where did all the people go? My mother, my father?"

Elspeth would go into another world. It was clear that she was still very much affected by her experience. But I felt there was always more that she wanted to say. We think that she probably was a woman that provided 'special services' for the camp leaders. Who could blame her.

"You did what you had to survive," she would say. "I ran from the camp as quickly as I could once liberated by the Americans. It would have been much worse being taken by the liberating Russians as they were not much better than the Nazis. I just did what I could to survive, I guess."

Once out of the death camp she returned to Poland. "Warsaw was completely decimated. It would take years to rebuild. I saw that many countries were taking refugees, and one of them was Australia. I chose here because it was the furthest away from Europe and spoke English.

"I met my beloved Hugo on the ship. His family has also been wiped out and he was also a survivor of the death camps. We settled down here, life was good. We were free, the air was clean and the water drinkable. Then we had Herbert, we were so happy. But Hugo carried a deep wound. My God, how he suffered. Then one day Herbert and I got home from a walk and we found Hugo hanging from the garage rafter. That was a number of years ago now. I miss him terribly but at least I have my darling Herbert."

Elspeth always seemed her happiest when she was around family, including my own family. She lived with Herbert. He fascinated and scared me a little. I remember clearly, he was a tall, powerfully built man who wore thick black-rimmed glasses and carried pens in his top shirt pocket. He wore shorts that came down to his knees. He never talked much, and always left whenever we arrived. When my mother used to take us to Elspeth's house, a small but clean weathered fibro house close to the railway, I would sneak into Herbert's room and was fascinated by his model railway. The detail was incredible. I never had the courage to turn it on so I would just run my fingers over the silver carriages. Elspeth lived close to the station so Herbert could see the trains.

We took a short cut across the oval. The magpies were noisy as they watched and waited ever protective of their nests. I would have many battles with the dive-bombing magpies. At first, I was terrified, but then after a while they got used to me.

We soon arrived at Arcadia Crescent, the road was not sealed, it was gravel just like a bush track. I would have many battles with this gravel road, taking quite a few falls when riding my push bike. I tended to go too fast, forever challenging my limits, racing my brothers. A barefooted figure wearing baggy pants and a strange looking loose top strode up his driveway towards us, a bottle of VB in his hand. He appeared quite gruff and had a mop of curly hair and a beard in need of a trim. What a sight we must have been, an old lady, my mum, and five kids, sweating and tired.

Vic coughed, one of those raspy, not so good for you coughs. "Well, who do we have here then? My name is Vic." He came straight to the point. "I like it quiet around here, so we will get on fine if you stay on your side."

Vic, short for Victor, was a bit of a lonely figure and silently suffered from shellshock or what came to be known as PTSD, after his experiences against the Japanese in the Second World War. He lived alone and strangely enough taught mindfulness at the local community hall. He lived on a massive ten acres that ran from the front of his house to the valley behind our house. Behind all the gruff and attitude, he was very kind man. And he really helped me during my time there.

———

Growing up in Berowra was what you would call a normal, even somewhat subdued life in the suburbs. We were the archetypal family. Mum, Dad and the five children. The highlight of my father was the new company car that would appear often. The Ford Falcon 500 and the silver Kingswood were favourites. He would take my brothers and me on long drives to the Blue Mountains and we even went to Canberra where we camped and went to the War Memorial. We loved that as it was all about war.

My mother stayed at home and made sure the food was cooked and the house clean. The closest she had to a job was loading her sandy coloured rucksack with the local post and heading around the streets of Berowra. She did not have many friends, so this was a great way for her to interact with people and it kept her busy.

We were quite self-sufficient. My mum made sure we always had enough by growing our own vegetables, baking our own bread, we would even make our own lemon cordial. She made an awesome pumpkin cake with sultanas that lasted for a week or more.

These were things I loved about my mum, but as I got older, things gradually got worse. My sisters left home as soon as they were old enough.

"Please don't go," I would beg.

"We are just sick of Mum's moods," they would say.

Being the second youngest of five children, I don't remember much of my older sisters living with us. But I do remember the arguments between my mum and my sisters; raging, swearing affairs that upset us all. My two brothers and I would just dissolve into the thick Australian bush our house backed onto. We spent hours playing spies and soldiers; learning to move and be silent came naturally to us. We would sneak up on the frill necked lizards, the tawny frogmouth owls and rock wallabies.

Quite often we would creep so quietly, with the smell of the bush on us so the fauna would have no idea we were there. We learned and felt the rhythm of our natural surroundings. The bush had a pulse of life to it, a natural order where everything had its part, all interwoven as it had been for thousands of years. I felt a deep connection with that order, hard to explain. I would just close my eyes and breathe deeply as a cacophony of sounds and life slowly absorbed me into its space.

I was the king of the road on my blue dragster, I loved it. I had freedom and used it. There was huge bamboo patch beside a flat dusty track. I would ride my bike right into it. It would creak and groan as I pushed my bike further and further away from everything and everyone. It was like it was moving. I would sit for ages just listening and feeling the breeze. It was the beginning of a love for bamboo that would stay with me for many years.

My buddy from school, Glen Brightly, and I were riding through the bush and stopped to look out over our favourite valley. He had a wry smirk on his face as he pulled two Viscount cigarettes from his pocket. I loved the thought of doing something naughty. I felt quite rebellious. I was not caring at all what my mother might think. Glen had lifted them secretly out of his father's packet. Wow, I was ten years old and all in. I did not think twice about puffing on the smoke, all I knew was I was doing the wrong thing and I loved it. That was the beginning of a habit that stayed with me until I was twenty-one.

4
BULLY

Every time I arrived home from the bush, I must have had cigarette smell all over me, but no one, including my mother, ever said anything. On one of our rides into my favourite bamboo patch, Glen and I ran into Peter Duggan and the Cornwall brothers. These boys were the worst bullies at school and best avoided. They had not gone as far as the edge of bamboo, and they had no idea how to get inside.

They came out of nowhere, like they had been sitting and waiting for us, pushing their bikes into our path. The Cornwall boys had fancy chopper dragsters and they thought they were pretty hot. So I blurted out, "The only muscle that you have got is between your ears." That was the best I could do, and I thought it was pretty funny.

Duggan threw down his bike, which did not matter as it was a rusty heap anyway. He was much bigger than me and a couple of years older. I sat there and watched as he walked up to me and without any warning 'whack', he punched me right on the jaw. I was shocked, it came from nowhere. But I was more shocked that it did not really hurt. It simply felt like someone had pushed my face to one side.

"Gimme your smokes," he scowled. I was still sitting on my bike. The Cornwall boys went quiet. Smash! Duggan hit me again.

I smirked. "I hope you hurt your hand on my jaw." Now I *was* scared, petrified, actually.

This sent him into a frenzy, he punched and punched until one of the Cornwall boys told him that I had had enough. He picked up my cigarettes, about half a pack of Wild Woodbines, spat towards me, picked up his bike and the three of them walked off. My jaw was a little sore, but that was when I learned that I had an iron jaw.

Glen came out of the bamboo. "Are you right? I saw everything."

I felt ashamed, I cried and cried. I had just sat there and copped it. I made no attempt to fight back. I started to cry again, I was so ashamed. I turned my bike and rode home.

It was just getting dark by the time I got back. Vic was putting the finishing touches on his lawns. He could see that I was upset. "What's the matter, Jack?"

I wheeled my bike past him. "Nothing," I muttered.

But he could see the red welts that had come up on the side of my face. "Who did this to you?"

I did not want to say anything as I would get into trouble for smoking. So I just put my head down and walked the short distance home.

The following morning as I left for school, my mate Ronnie Sibton dropped in on his way past my house so we could walk to school together, swapping sandwiches that were supposed to last until lunchtime.

Vic was waiting on his driveway. "Oi, Jack, gotta minute?"

"Okay," I nodded. I called out to Ronnie to go ahead, then met Vic on his patio and sat down.

"Looks like you copped a beating last night, who would do that to you? I won't tell anyone if you don't want me to."

I was trying to put words into the feelings I was having, which is hard for a young boy. "I feel sad."

"Just relax," he said. "Sit up straight, put your hands on your knees, close your eyes and take a deep breath in, then breathe out and say to yourself 'relax'. Now do this five times. Don't worry about your thinking, that will just continue. What I am doing with you is just dropping into the present moment using your breath. Try and do this as many times as you think about it during the day."

"Thanks Vic, I am feeling a little better." I hitched my school bag on my shoulder and ran to catch up with Ronnie.

That afternoon, Duggan was waiting for me by the rear gate of the school. He was talking to a girl, Lucy, who was Katie's older sister. I had a crush on Katie. Duggan looked at me and I lowered my gaze and stared at my feet. I was scared, and I walked a little faster.

Too late to get away, he shoved me over pushing me in the back. I hit the ground with a painful thud, he was standing over me. "Got more smokes?" he sneered.

"No," I cried.

"Too bad." He launched a swinging right punch to my face. It made a loud smack sound. I rolled over onto my side and tried to cover up. I could feel something inside, my face flushed and what I can only describe as a rush feeling went through my body, my legs and my arms. I felt like I was ready to explode.

Is this happening, I thought. *Just breathe.* The words of Vic reverberated inside me. So I took a couple of deep breaths and felt this feeling of power inside me slowly disappear.

Lucy was pulling Duggan off me. "Leave him alone."

I watched as he walked off; he turned and shouted, "You better have some smokes for me on Monday."

I was so embarrassed and ashamed. I wet my pants, I was so scared and totally humiliated. Other than Lucy who helped me up, no one else helped me.

"Are you okay?" she asked.

"Thanks," I squeaked and quickly walked away, desperately trying to avoid any eye contact. I now had the weekend to try to buy some more smokes.

I went straight to Vic's front door and knocked. "Go away" was all I heard. I knocked again and this time Vic opened the door just enough to be able to look and see it was me. "What do you want?" he barked.

"I got beaten up again today," I cried.

He opened the door and let me in. "Oh, no, are you okay?"

The front room was clean and smelt sweet. There was a picture of an old Indian man with long hair and beard, funny beads and strange burning sticks.

"Who is that?" I asked politely.

"That is my guru." He motioned as he gave me a glass of water. "Sit here on this stool."

"What is a guru?"

"Don't worry about him, let's talk about you." Vic sat quietly.

So I told him about Duggan and how he was trying to get cigarettes from me.

Vic listened patiently until I was finished. "I have met many men that want to hurt. I have seen men do the worst things to each other. I too have dealt out misery to many men in war. You never recover from killing another man, but that was my job.

"After the war, I went to India to try and recover from the many things that I saw and did. That is where I met Papaji, an Indian spiritual teacher. He taught me how to forgive and heal my anger. The one thing that I learned was that the peaceful solution is always the best as it will not carry the burden of negative karma."

I did not really understand what he was saying so I just listened to the flow of his voice.

"But sometimes boy, you must fight back. No matter how scared you are. You have to channel that anger you felt, take a deep breath, close your fist like this and just strike out, hitting the bully so hard that he will never ever touch you again. Can you do that, Jack?"

"Yes, I think so, but I don't want to get into trouble."

"This has gone beyond that and will only get more violent unless you take matters into your own hands. You must be brave and act with courage."

Vic's words of conviction really resonated with me. I was able to relax over the weekend as I had a clear plan of action. I was scared, but as Vic said, *be brave.*

Sure enough there he was, with his mates the Cornwall brothers standing like vultures at the gate waiting for their feed. Jake, the younger of the two was there. He told Duggan to back off the last time we all met. I was not sure if he would act in the same way today. Either way he was not to be trusted.

"Do you have my smokes?" barked Duggan.

I continued walking. I could feel something was rising within me. It was the same feeling that I had last week. It was pure untethered anger. I clenched both fists, took a breath and turned to face him. I stood there, a deadly mixture of fear and anger was slowly consuming me. "No, I don't!" I said through clenched teeth.

Duggan was furious. Without any notice, he smashed his fist into my jaw. It was not as hard as it had been before and I barely flinched.

What happened next was incredible. Quite a crowd had now gathered and were shouting "fight, fight, fight" trying to goad us into a brawl, just like the ancient gladiatorial days. I stood there staring at Duggan. Then, all of a sudden, he turned and walked away.

"Come on," he called to the Cornwall brothers, "let's get out of here."

I watched him go. I had won the day. I controlled my temper and was so ready to unload on him, and he could feel my intention without me ever having to throw a punch. Duggan and the Cornwall boys never bullied me again.

———

I continued to visit Vic and learn as much as he could teach me. Vic was a troubled man, but he did his best to hide it from me. He did not talk about the war much, but he laughed and made fun of me and my brothers as we played wars using brooms for guns and running around the house making fake guns and bomb sounds.

He fought on the Kokoda Trail and lost many of his mates on that muddy impassable track. When I asked Vic to tell me a war story, his eyes would glaze over as he quietly talked about the Japanese soldiers.

"Although my orders were to kill as many Japs as I could, I realised that they too were just young men following orders, and they were damn good soldiers. Many times when the Japanese attacked they would do what we called a 'banzai charge'. In effect it was an all or nothing charge, a suicide mission and they would dive into the Aussie bunkers armed with swords and bayonets. The hand-to-hand fighting was vicious, I was stabbed and gouged several times." He would still recall them getting so close that he could smell their stale breath, and feel their incredible strength. Many of them were suffering from malnutrition and surviving on meagre rations of boiled rice, but regardless they were strong and took a lot to kill. "It was a damn shame, and senseless killing. I would go through their pockets and find photos of the dead soldiers smiling with their young wife and children. They were just like us."

He found solace in the bottle. But he had enough strength to study the ways of his guru, Papaji. Vic would tell me incredible stories about his time in India. How religion plays such a large part of their life. He taught me some strange songs and he called them mantras. We would sit for hours and burn what he called incense and repeat the mantras.

"Always remember, young Jack, breathe gently and count your breath from one to five, see the thoughts come and go and just focus on the breath." Vic taught me to do this simple exercise from a young age. I think he enjoyed having someone that he could teach. But then I forgot about it and lost it for many years. He would often say it is important to be here and now. I never really understood what he meant by that, and little did I know what a huge part of my life that would become. One thing was for sure, I felt calm and peaceful after my time with Vic.

For two or so years I met Vic in his front room at least once a week. My mother did not seem to mind, she would say he was a good role model for me, then proceeded to say insults about my father. "I bet your father would never spend as much time with you."

My father was best described as a part-time father. He would drop in at random times, stay for dinner and maybe the night. The extent of his affection towards me was a pat on the back, saying "be a good boy" and that was it. Not much had changed from when we lived in England. He was away most of the time, so he had no influence on my life whatsoever.

He continued to have his affairs. I could see he was upsetting Mum. He finally left us for Joanne, a prissy spinster with two Siamese cats. He met her on one of his business trips and my mother was distraught.

My father would insist we three boys spend every second Sunday morning with him. We would go to Sun Valley, a cheap amusement park out west. There were pinball machines that we loved to play; Klondike and the Six Million Dollar man were my favourites. We also enjoyed the trampolines and swimming in the pool.

All the fun that we may have had was soon wiped out by my mother upon our return. She would question us for what seemed like hours, "How can you trust him?" she'd demand. But my brothers and I would retreat into ourselves, just waiting it out.

My mother's life seemed to implode on top of her. Her grief was endless. Seeing my mother sobbing, and being the one that she would ask questions of that a boy could not, or should not, be expected to have an answer for.

"Why would he do this to me?" she would ask, which pushed me further and further into myself. She would often threaten to leave us. This, for a young boy that looked up to his mother, was devastating. To lose my only source of stability, as shaky as that was, and to have a father that had already run for his life, it is no wonder that the deep wound I carried throughout my life – of not being able to trust, commit and feel – was created in my childhood.

One afternoon, I got home from school and my pristine life that I had been able to create a semblance of order after my father left, had been shattered by a huge bulldozer. My father was standing on a huge earth mound that had been created exactly where the gateway to my freedom was; the bush. The bulldozer had rammed its way through rock and dirt creating a driveway between our existing house, Vic's driveway border then clearing an area the size of a basketball court in what used to be our bush backyard.

I was shattered. My brothers were not overly concerned as they quickly sought out the biggest chunks of dirt and hurled them at me. Then it was on, we had found a new way to play wars, clod fights. There was an old, corrugated water tank that sat on the edge of the clearing. My brothers and I were still small enough to lower ourselves down into the empty tank. Two of us would take a position in the tank whilst the other one would collect the largest rocks that he could find, and pelt them at the tank. It was a game to see how long the two of us could put up with the ear shattering scream of the rock finding its mark on the tank. Then one day the tank was gone.

My father told us that he was building a new house. I just assumed that it was for the family, and was so excited, the idea of the family being back together thrilled me. So when my mother told me that we were moving and my father was moving into the new house at the back of our home with Joanne, I was so upset. How could he do that? I hated him for doing such a despicable thing.

Leaving Vic was especially difficult, he had been like a father to me. I would miss him. I felt a grief that I had never felt before.

"Go on lad," he said. I gave him a hug and buried my face in his shoulder and got in the car. I could not look at him as we drove off.

My father shunted his five children and my mother into a filthy, unrenovated deceased house on the corner of a main road in Normanhurst. He then sold our home in Berowra and proceeded to move into the newly built house with his new wife, Joanne. To top it all off, Joanne despised me and my brothers, demanding we took our shoes off when entering their new house then complained we had smelly feet. She would say, "You have to take your shoes and dirty socks off."

"No," I would say.

"You must or else you can't have dinner."

"Suits me fine," I would stammer.

"Don't be so rude."

"You are not my mother, I don't care what you say." And that would finish it.

We left so much in Berowra, it was a huge part of my life, I felt like I was in a cocoon, and had built my life around Vic, Elspeth and the bush that my brothers and I would disappear into.

This was to be my next adventure. I was nervous but also keen to explore my new life.

5
NORMANHURST

The new house in Normanhurst was on a large corner block. It was an old, rambling fibro house with two separate grassed areas. A deceased estate, and boy was it in a mess. It may have been big, but it was very old. There were cobwebs in every corner and along the cornices. The walls were painted a dirty dark green, which made the place darker than it seemed. And in every corner just below the ceiling were large round mirrors. I had no idea why they were so numerous, but the old lady who lived in it before us lived there alone – maybe the house was haunted, but I tried not to think about that.

Mum fixed up the place as best she could. We took down the old mirrors, and we all chipped in to paint the walls a light-beige colour. We ripped up the old carpet and found pristine newspapers lining the floors under the carpet. The newspapers were from 1945 and gave a snapshot of what it was like at the end of the war. All in all, the house shaped up quite well.

Soon after we had moved in, one afternoon, we heard a stone hit our front window, but the window, thankfully, didn't smash. When

I looked outside, I saw a group of local kids all standing around on the street.

My mother pushed past me and headed out the front door. "What do you want?" she demanded of the kids, hands on her hips.

One of the largest boys, Cam, yelled back, "You've taken Duffy's bike, and we want it back."

I then piped up behind Mum, "No, we didn't! It's my brother's bike."

Cam shrugged his shoulders, and I could tell that he didn't like to be in the wrong.

Then I blurted out, "Why don't you all just go home. You'll find Duffy's bike."

The kids didn't look convinced, but they meandered off.

Then Cam turned to me. "You and me have some unfinished business."

My eyes widened. I couldn't believe it, another damn bully. But I looked him straight in the eye. "Okay, bring it on."

The next day, I saw them all playing at the park down the road, including Duffy, who was riding his own green bike.

Cam passed me at school the following morning surrounded by a crew of younger boys. They all looked up to him like he was some kind of god. He did not waste any time. "This afternoon, 4 pm at my park."

"Sure," I said, and did not give it another thought. It seemed that I was a bully magnet, but I had come a long way since warding off Peter Duggan and the Cornwall brothers, with Vic's help of course. Cam was a couple of years older than me, and he looked bigger and stronger. Apparently, he was the tough guy around here and the boss of the park.

I was there at 4 pm and he was late. 4.30 pm came around and there he was with his group of no hopers closely behind.

"What are the rules?" he said.

I didn't have any as I launched a hard right punch to his jaw. He dropped hard and fast and did not get up. The other boys just stood there with their mouths wide open. They could not believe what had happened. "The park is here for all of us to use," I declared, and walked up the hill to home.

Cam still walked around with an attitude, but he never said anything to me ever again. The public park was now enjoyed by all the kids. I enjoyed the swings and climbing the large willow tree. It was a great source of pleasure for many years.

My brothers and I found a large valley of bush and a creek that ran right through it down the end of the street. It extended from the end of our road, all the way over to Fox Valley and to the back of the old Loreto Convent. There was an ancient grave site that fascinated me, a place they buried the old nuns. We discovered every nook and cranny of this large bush playground, and we even found a cave that was a great hiding place for our smokes.

My mother would drive me and my brothers hard. She had what we called the weekend chore list. This included mowing all the lawns and clipping the edges and bushes. We had to finish what was on the list before we could go and play. There was no cutting corners, as this would set Mum off and make it a living nightmare for the entire weekend.

Every Friday night my brothers and I would go down to the Hornsby PCYC. We would wear our light blue PCYC T-shirts and play British bulldog and other games. It was great fun; I would sometimes go to the boxing class but got put off as I was used as a punching bag by the older boys. Some Friday nights we would finish early and sneak next door to the billiard room where all the local toughs used to congregate.

They ignored us as we were so young. But I recognised Gary Vice who used to be a friend of my mate Glen Brightly in Berowra. Rumour had it that Gary broke into an old church and vandalised it quite badly. He had spent some time in a boys' detention home, but was now free. I met him briefly one afternoon. Glen and I were on our bikes and Gary turned up in a water carrying truck that he had taken from the local depot, without permission. I said hello then got out of there as fast as I could.

The manager of the PCYC was an older, fit man who we called Constable Gil. He always offered to drive us home from the PCYC on Friday nights after the session. We sped along the roads and we were tossed around the back of the small bus that he was driving. It was great fun. When we arrived home, Constable Gil would come in and my mum would feed him and give him a cold beer. I would hear him driving away early the next morning.

There were quite a few men who would come over to visit my mother. Stan who had a shock of white hair, lived a couple of suburbs away in a caravan park and did shift work on the heavy vehicle toll gates. He was nice enough, but I got the feeling that he only put up with us to get close to Mum.

Nev, a short mousy-looking man, was a nasty piece of work. He had two kids about the same age as us; Stefan and Julieta. Apparently, Nev's wife walked out their front door one day and walked straight in front of a train. Stefan used to drink from the small bottles of liquor and smoke cigarettes that he had pinched from his father's alcohol cabinet.

Oh, and Mr Pfister. Yes! We had to address him as Mr Pfister. He was an older man who carried his small yappy dog with him wherever he went. Our big tom cat Dillon, who we had rescued from a feral cat's nest when he was a kitten, was one angry cat. We used to set Dillon onto Mr Pfister's lap dog, and it was not a pretty sight.

Then there was Dick, a real sad sack. He had lived a rough life, and he wore the wounds of his life on his face. His eyes drooped and were constantly streaming. He did not say much.

Ben De Groot was a tall strong Dutchman, who loved a smoke and a drink. He drove a brown Kombi van and worked for a company making prototype toys. An angry man with a short temper, he screamed at his three kids in his thick Dutch accent. But he always treated me well. At first, I liked him.

Ben had a daughter, Suzanne, who was drop dead gorgeous, at least to me as a fourteen-year-old with no experience with women. She was a year older than me and would tease me with a not so innocent look on her face. She started to crawl in beside me in my single bed, and we touched, explored, and fumbled as two young teenagers do. Her dad would have killed us both if he ever caught us.

Ben's anger and boozing were slowly getting the better of him and he was not a good drunk. At first, I thought it was just my mother poking the bear, for she also had a terrible temper and could not hold her liquor. One Christmas Day, Ben and his kids all came over to our house for Christmas lunch. Mum asked Ben if he would carve the turkey. Ben literally ripped the turkey to pieces with his hands. He stood there smiling, thinking he had done a great job, my mother exploded, saying he had ruined the turkey. He picked up his gifts, got his kids and quickly left. Another perfect Christmas ruined at our household. I stood there shellshocked at how quickly it had all fallen apart. My mother turned on Ben in an instant. Her mood swings were relentless.

Things only got worse after Christmas. Ben was getting agitated and had started threatening to beat my mother. He was at our place one evening, he and my mother had been drinking and were now arguing. She screamed, "Get out or I will call the police." But it was too late, he raised his fist to strike my mother. I knew he'd been hitting her by the bruises on her face and arms, but she always denied it. This time he did not hide it from me. So I hit him. I grabbed one of my mum's heavy cast iron pans and with one movement I hit him across the side of the head. He struck his head on the corner of the table as he went down. He fell hard and was out cold.

"What have you done?" my mother yelled as she turned on me.

One thing I have learned about myself is that I will only be pushed so far. I was not sorry, for Ben or my mother. He soon woke up with a thumping headache and did not remember a thing, or so he said. Ben did not come over so often after that. I missed Suzanne.

There was often a new man sitting in our kitchen when I came out to have breakfast. Mum deserved a little tenderness in her life, but I would not tolerate them disrespecting her in any way.

About the nicest of the lot was Bob. He was an engineer who lived a simple life in Wollongong. I went down there for a week and dug up his backyard to install drainage pipes. To be honest I had no idea what I was doing, but it felt good being outside with my shirt off doing some hard manual labour. Like all of my mother's relationships, it did not last long.

Then finally, there was the one-armed cockney, Gordy was his name. He worked as an engineer at a popular confectionery factory. He pursued my mother relentlessly. It was kind of weird, him opening up and telling us all, "I am going to marry your mother." He seemed like a nice enough man but what was the hurry, I wondered.

My mum married Gordon in a cute ceremony in the side yard under the large tree next to our house. She sold the house and that was the end of an era, or so we thought! Mum moved up to Mooney Mooney into Gordy's old shack that looked over the water. About the only cool thing was his yellow speed boat.

Within a week, he had turned nasty. My mother called me in tears, begging me to pick her and her things up. He was beating her. And that was the end of that.

These times that my mother was sorting out her boyfriends, I slipped through the cracks as to which high school I was going to attend. I was left alone to decide, and had no input from my parents. I chose the selective high school that my brother went to. What was I thinking? There was a perfectly good high school at the end of our road. All my friends went to the local high school, it was the obvious choice. Instead, I was selected to attend James Ruse High School, one of the top academic schools in the state.

I fronted up at the beginning of term and knew no one. *What have I done?* I thought. I tried my hardest to keep up with the academic load but in the end, it just burnt me out. So I left the first opportunity I got.

6

LONDON CLUB

I bought myself an old truck and was getting labouring work and gardening. I made enough to pay the bills and I rented a spare bedroom at my father's house. Why did it not surprise me that my father charged me full rent?

I was also going to technical college and doing photojournalism a couple of nights a week, for something different. I was sitting down for a scheduled break when Terry, a friend I had made, came and sat down beside me.

"What have you been up to, mate?" I asked.

"Not much." Terry looked a little older than me, he had a dark, rugged complexion. "In fact, I have been doing some training."

"Oh?" I said, just to fill in the silence.

"Yes, have you heard of taekwondo?"

"No, I haven't."

Terry's face lit up. "It's a crazy martial art, there are these guys from Korea that fly through the air and break stuff like timber with their bare hands and feet, they look super-human."

That was enough, he had me on super-human. "Where do I find this taekwondo?"

"It's all over the place, just look it up in the yellow pages to find a class near you."

I had no idea why I was so interested. I had seen all of the Bruce Lee movies at the old Hornsby cinema. I loved them, but not ever enough to want to train in martial arts myself. There was just something about the name taekwondo, that drove me to find a local school.

That night, I parked my old ute on Hunter Street in downtown Hornsby. I was on my way to a new Turkish restaurant that was getting rave reviews. I was walking along Bridge Road when I happened to glance up and see a poster in the front window of a hairdresser. It was of an asian-looking man, flying through the air smashing timber with his feet. It was just as Terry had described. On the poster were details of the classes in a church hall in Waitara. I was to learn that there were hundreds of martial schools in various church halls throughout Sydney. There were only a few that taught their martial arts in dedicated studios.

I headed up to the church hall at the scheduled time. Two of the senior students; Paul and Graeme, greeted me at the door. They invited me to join the class which I immediately accepted. I had a surge of what I can only say was sheer power. As I was taught the various stances, blocks and punches, I felt a deep connection with the moves. It was as if I already knew them and was just relearning them. I let a breath out, *Ahhh, I am home.*

I was dedicated from then on. It became a huge part of my life. It underpinned everything I did. I trained hard and eventually earned my black belt. I soon set up my own school, teaching taekwondo at the old gym on Crown Street in the city. I had all kinds of students, some young, some older, and I was having a great time.

I approached James Street Nightclub for a job as a doorman, as they were called back then. Mark, the manager, interviewed me and wanted me to commence immediately, so I started the following night. I was under the impression that James Street was a tame club. Oh, boy, was I wrong! I started on a Tuesday night and on Tuesdays it was called London Club.

At 10 pm I was joined by Paul and Robert, two more doormen. They were a couple of characters. Paul was an ex-Mossad operative, or at least he said he was. He looked the part and had the accent, but I soon realised that he could not fight. He prattled on about being a Krav Maga self defence expert, which is taught to the Israeli special forces. But I saw the way he moved when under pressure. He was all talk, but I liked him anyway.

Robert on the other hand, was a tall good-looking model/actor with chiselled features. He made no bragging claims about being a great fighter or a martial artist. He just had a fierce temper and was very quick to punch the lights out of anyone that provoked him. One thing though, he is a very talented actor and I have since seen him in many movies and series. Quite often I could not tell who I was working with, Robert the actor or Robert the person. Either way, they were both very entertaining.

Both Robert and Paul had their own way of dealing with conflict. Paul would schmooze them and talk in a really calm voice, put an arm around them and walk them to the front door. Robert's eyes would roll backwards, and he would start shouting. We all knew to quickly take cover, as Robert the beast would soon appear. He would go right up to them, putting his face in their face. He would turn bright red and start frothing at the mouth.

At this stage I would gently tap him on the arm and say, "It's all good mate, they have gone, take a deep breath with me, and let's go inside for a moment."

So, you see I had to manage the other doormen as much as the club clients. It took me only a couple of nights to learn about how the door operated.

The club was a huge warehouse-like building with high ceilings and a large mezzanine that had its own bar and dance floor. It could take well over a thousand patrons. We as doormen always tried to do things in twos. Two inside the club, one on the door, and one made the club circuits, as we called them, as brief as possible. But the club being so large it was easy to miss a bad situation rising. But all in all, with the help of the bar crew we were able to quickly knock situations on the head before they escalated into something of major proportions.

There were two doors, one at the front of the club and one at the counter. Sometimes if the counter staff could see that we were under pressure on the door and things were heating up, without any warning the counter staff would shut the door, leaving us at the front door to deal best we could with the confrontation that was going on. The counter staff would then call the police and let them come and sort it out. Sometimes this put us under intense pressure. Luckily, between the three of us, we could usually divert any major fights on the door. All the aggro was usually because we had denied a group of drunken bums access to the club.

On Tuesday nights at the London Club the line ran up the side of the building. My place on the door was just behind the thick rope that acted as a barrier between me and the people. I would control this rope and at the same time I was in charge of who I let through into the club. I took all kinds of bribes from the queue of people waiting their turn to get into the club, and made quite a bit of money charging a fee for people to jump the queue.

Club Members could jump the queue and walk up to the front of the line, flash their member ID and go straight in. This created a lot of arguments as for the uninitiated it seemed that there were people just jumping the line. They would then push to the front of the line and demand to get let in. "I have been waiting an hour and these people just push in to the front of the line" was a standard complaint.

"I understand your frustration sir, but as the notice says," I would say, pointing to the sign on the wall, "members get priority."

Robert would pipe up, "Go and wait your turn."

What happened next was the grey area that had the propensity to get violent very quickly. They would either back straight down and go back to their place in the line; turn and go away brooding, and swear at us as they rambled on about returning with their brothers, cousins and mates; or on the rare occasion launch themselves at us, whereby we would grab the thick rope barrier and slam the front door closed behind us. We would then wait it out, or would stay as long as necessary for the antagonists to run out of bluster and take their aggression somewhere else.

Getting a membership was not easy. You usually had to know someone that knew someone; quite often Mark the manager would give out memberships like they were cookies to children, and in my opinion they were usually to the opposite of who we would allow in the club. He would show his disdain saying it was a request from the owner.

I, on the other hand, would be quite stingy about whom I would give out memberships to, as I knew that some of these turds were just being friendly in order to get a membership. I learned the hard way about giving out memberships to people that I did not know. Quite often they would change completely, brag about how they were now a member, demand free drinks only for me to drag their sorry drunk asses out the front door, removing their memberships from them. Mark would always back my call remaining stoic, just watching and not commenting as they screamed, "But I am a member!"

Lovell from the Bronx in New York controlled the carpark. He would do the negotiation and they would pay me. Lovell was also the access point for the sale of ecstasy and cocaine. I was smart enough to never get involved with drugs in any way. "How are you buddy?" he would greet me with a hug. I loved Lovell, he was always smiling and happy, we were great friends. He never touched the drugs at work but enjoyed himself when out socially.

One night when all the employees of James Street went out to celebrate Christmas, we ended up at another well-known club, the Cave. Lovell was really out of it. I looked after him and took him back to my place, settled him down on the couch and he slept it off. He could never thank me enough. Lovell was a great fighter, both in and out of the ring. He always had my back when there was trouble on the door. We had a mutual interest of martial arts.

I heard some years later that Lovell had died. That made me very sad. He fell in with a rough crowd and was beaten up quite badly. Apparently, he never recovered.

The James Street Nightclub was a hot spot for all kinds of interesting characters. Mark was always getting upset with me for letting in a couple of trouble making trannies, but they paid well. I always denied letting them in and they were harmless enough. But Mark always had bigger fish to fry.

I caught him ushering in big time organised crime figures who were always packing guns. Then the drug dealers would just happen to be there on the same night, followed up with the local licensing police. It was quite a group, and I stayed away from it all. They still got to know me by name; I used to think this was the cool part of being a doorman. But it was toxic, and I wanted nothing to do with that side of life. I knew right from wrong and that enabled me to set my boundaries very clearly.

I met some great people on that door, and I met some real dickheads. The alcohol and drugs changed people. Regular faces that I would get to know and become friendly with, I would help to become a member. If they had to wait in line for five minutes and would get aggressive towards me and start making demands, I would soon shut them up by reminding them who organised their membership.

Sometimes we would have to evict a drunk patron, especially at the end of the night when we were getting ready to close. They would be my best friend at the beginning of the night and by the time we closed the club, they would be my mortal enemy, swearing and abusing me, full of booze and drugs.

One night I was working the door by myself. The club was being rented for the night for a private function. I get to work at 6 pm and the counter staff opened the doors. There were about fifty businessmen and I recognised a few of them, they had been to the club before and caused trouble. They all worked at the stock exchange over the road, a high pressure job. But they thought that if they paid extra to hire the club for a party, they could take liberties. Right from the get-go they were annoying me and it was obvious that they had already been drinking.

I was polite as they walked into the club. One, whose name I remember as Davo, turned towards me, prodding me in the chest as he spoke. "This dim wit got me thrown out last time I was here."

"Let it go," some of them were saying.

But Davo just had to make a point. "Say sorry, dim wit."

I acted straight away, I grabbed his prodding finger, held it real tight and bent it right back; it made a terrible cracking noise and I knew I had broken it. He dropped to his knees immediately.

"No one has the right to touch me, not even you, Davo."

The other businessmen helped him up and sat him in a chair. One of them said, "No worries, mate, he started it, and he is a bit of a bully, so he had it coming."

Mark, the manager had seen the whole thing. He put his arm around me and asked, "Are you all right?"

"Yeah fine, I acted in self defence."

"I know."

Davo sat there complaining it hurt and asked a couple of his colleagues to take him to a hospital, so they did and all because one man got drunk and thought he could take out a bouncer. But I had news for him, and it was all bad. Don't ever touch me again.

I loved those days and the camaraderie with the bar staff, waiters, dee jays and the male strippers that worked on girls-only

Friday nights. Many of them were out of work models, actors and singers, all had interesting stories. They were always friendly, and respected that the doormen and the counter staff ran the club.

During the long winter months between 2 am and 4 am, when we were freezing our backsides off on the door, one of the bar crew would bring us out hot chocolates with a smile and a pat on the back, and spend time with us, sharing stories of their lives. And when the shift was over and the club was getting ready to close at 4 am, once all the patrons had left, the bar crew would pour us a Drambuie on the rocks and we would all enjoy each other's company after a hectic night.

7
HOKUTO RYU

The first time I heard of the secret art of hokuto ryu was when I was working at James Street nightclub.

I used to enjoy talking with Gav, one of the regulars at the club. He was about my height and a little lighter than me. He would hang by the front door during the bitter cold winter nights and I would get him coffee. I think he was lonely and appreciated the company.

One night he was looking up into the sky. "Do you know what hokuto means?"

And with that one question, my life would change forever. Though I had studied a bit of Japanese, I was not familiar with this word. "No, what does it mean?"

"It means northstar and sits directly above the north pole. It leads the way, giving direction. There is a very famous school of martial arts called hokuto ryu. They disappeared decades ago, closing their doors and have not been seen since. I believe that they are now in a secret valley in Japan where they train in mind and body. That is as much as I know. My ninjutsu teacher told me about the hokuto ryu years ago."

I did not know if I should believe him. I thought it sounded like a whole lot of rubbish. So I listened then parked it.

After that night, I never saw Gav again. I continued to work there for a while, but people just got worse. And I did not like what I was becoming. I was getting more and more aggressive. I would be quite rude to the clientele. It was only a matter of time before I would start assaulting people. The club was not what it used to be. It used to be fun when I started and had great music. These days there was more and more police and undesirables regularly entering the club. Then when Mark the manager left, I knew my time was up. So I also left, and commenced my research into the hidden dojo in Japan.

I was quite happy with my life in Sydney. I lived with my two brothers, and we moved house every six months. I first moved out from my father's place into a three-bedroom house on the leafy upper north shore suburb of Lindfield. We would go on epic runs down to Tryon Park. It was always competitive between us, especially when we challenged each other with the 400 metre sprints around the oval.

Lindfield was no doubt a party house and we held some enormous house parties. I relished this time with my two brothers. When the lease was up at Lindfield, the real estate agent was pleased to see us go. We moved to the inner west suburb of Annandale. This was an old terrace house with three large bedrooms at the southern end of the iconic Trafalgar Street, close to the buses on Parramatta Road and close to the city.

In the 1980s, retro music boomed. The live music venues around the city were thriving. Our party life increased, as we bopped to the latest pub bands INXS, The Flowers and Cold Chisel. Not to forget the Angels, and the Machinations. The live music era was at every pub and wine bar, it was a memorable time, and has never been repeated since.

I rotated through a few brief relationships. Of note were the two daughters of a high court judge, who I dated at different times. But I was not interested in falling in love, I was having too much fun.

I kept having a nagging thought. It seemed to be calling out to me. Was Gav's ninjutsu teacher telling the truth about the mysterious dojo in Japan or was it just a pack of lies?

I had plenty of work as a taekwondo teacher, a budding photo journalist and a part-time gardener. I loved my jobs and loved my lifestyle. I was free, as I kept my own times and schedule. I once had a dream of being a flight steward, kind of like Adam Sandler and John Turturro in *Don't Mess with the Zohan*. They were mortal enemies, and highly trained assassins, Adam was Jewish and John was an Arab. Yet all Adam wanted to do was to be a hairdresser and all John wanted to do was be a shoe salesman. Very funny. I soon got over wanting to be a steward, it would not suit me. I got a job with the popular publication *Australasian Martial Arts* and through them I was approached to do some writing for the American publisher, Rainbow, who published several martial arts magazines in the USA.

In the beginning, I wrote a couple of articles on local martial artists that were excelling in competitions overseas. I learned very early that martial artists love talking about themselves. The key was learning how to guide them to get to the gems, and not letting them just ramble on about mindless bullshit. As it happened, I usually had to rewrite the article in my own words, and this managed to add to the intrigue. What was really funny was that when they read the proof, they never questioned the new content, in fact they seemed to love it regardless of the fact that it was all in my own words and not theirs.

Kelvin Brown, the owner and publisher of *Australasian Martial Arts* loved the articles and asked if we could meet for lunch. This was quite the occasion because Kelvin was notorious for being elusive and not answering his messages and generally avoiding all face-to-face interaction. He rang me out of the blue and I got quite a shock when he said, "Jack, can we meet?"

"Sure."

"How about we meet at The Boathouse at Shelly Beach. Next Wednesday 12 noon?"

I was thrilled and at the same time wondering what this was all about.

————

Kelvin got right to the point. "The readers love your column. In fact, it is the most popular in the magazine. Have you thought about taking your skills and traveling through Asia? I so wish that I had done that."

"Well, I have thought I might travel, but have really been enjoying my life doing what I am doing here in Sydney."

"You are talented in martial arts and have a knack for writing interesting and somewhat controversial articles. I have thought about going to Japan whilst it is still not completely ruined by the influence of western culture sweeping through their country. But the kids are still in school, and my wife has not been well. My neighbour's daughter lives in Tokyo; she would be a really good place for you to start. I also have the name of a long-term expat that has a lot of knowledge about traditional Japanese martial arts. He is American and his parents have lived in California for many years. He is also fluent in the language. He could get you a firm foothold and introduce you to several masters. It would be a great read and I would pay you well for the articles and photos."

"I will give it some serious thought." I took down the numbers of Kazoku and Mr Sumisu.

"You do that Jack, I will get the bill."

————

When going anywhere new to train, it really helps if you have an introduction to where you intend to train from your teacher or an ex-student. A short while before, I had had the pleasure of meeting Raynor Fernandez. My mate Joseph, who was working at a popular martial arts shop, suggested, "I should introduce you to Raynor. His old master in the Philippines might be able to guide you to where it is that you want to go."

"Great," I said as Joseph handed over his phone number and at the same time slipped a couple of martial arts books into my bag. Joseph was what I call a rough diamond. He walked a very fine line and could easily have lived a criminal life.

Back in the early '80s there was no internet, emails or social media. Raynor answered the phone with an infectious jubilance. "I would love to meet you for lunch and help you out." So we made a time to meet in the city the following week.

We met at a Japanese restaurant near Wynyard station.

"They have a really nice lunch bento box here," he said.

Raynor carried an assortment of knives tucked in around his body under his suit. I asked him why he carried so many.

"Well, you never quite know when you will need them. The real art is in just slicing someone up, and not killing them."

I remember thinking, *Maybe this guy is a maniac!*

Raynor was born and grew up in the Philippines. He told me about the time he first met Michael Rickard. He, along with Tony Diamond and Romeo Mac, were the senior students of Grandmaster Listro. Michael had a nasty temper. "The first time I met him, he immediately challenged me to a fight. Even before I accepted, he struck me in the face and then kicked me to the ground. Then he continued to kick me in the head over and over again." Ray was still traumatised from this assault.

When I asked him why, he simply shrugged. "That is the way."

I wondered if the same was waiting for me. Before I left, I asked Raynor if he had heard of the hidden dojo. He giggled as he told me that Grandmaster Listro had mentioned the hidden dojo a few times. "You should ask him."

I decided to start my Asian journey in Manila. I had not been to the Philippines, in fact other than emigrating to Australia as a boy, this was my first trip overseas, and I was looking forward to the experience.

Planning my first adventure overseas was very exciting. My brothers and sisters were quite proud of me. None of them except for Kit, the youngest, had any idea of my quest to find a hidden ashram in Japan. He thought I was nuts, but he also knew that I was no fool and knew what I was doing. It felt like an honour then to be able to take this noble path when most people my age were heading overseas to Europe for skiing or Bali for surfing.

I was on a strict budget, as my funds would not last long if I was not careful. I was planning on working my way around Asia; I was not sure of exactly where I would be going. I was planning on visiting as many Asian countries as I could. What I did know was that I was starting in Singapore and ending in Japan. I had a couple of contacts, but I was quite prepared to do it alone.

First stop Singapore, where I was planning on catching up with Margaret, an ex-girlfriend, then Hong Kong to see where Bruce Lee trained and finally catch up with my Irish mate Derek.

8

MY JOURNEY BEGINS

I could not believe that all my brothers and sisters came to the airport to see me off. They looked concerned but I felt loved. It had been quite a journey for us over the years. But against all odds we came together and were there for each other. We said our final goodbyes and I marched off towards immigration. I did not turn, I wanted to, but I had to be strong. I had been refining a stoic attitude of late. I had a tendency to hide my emotions, and I could appear somewhat cold. Stoicism is a philosophy that flourished in ancient Rome. I had always admired Julius Caesar and Marcus Aurelius, two of the greatest Roman Emperors.

Wow – I was really doing this? It was quite cramped in economy class and the flight was packed. I was thankful that I was not in smoking down the back of the plane, though the waft of cigarette smoke drifted throughout the entire cabin. I watched the crew go about their service and it was bedlam for them. As all drinks and food were free, it reminded me of pigs at the trough, people just going for it, eating and drinking as much as they could. Of course, what follows the drinking frenzy is all the aggression from the drunks.

The poor girls were really doing it tough. Some of the stewards came in to help but their mannerisms were quite feminine, so weren't much help. The drinks were stopped, the window blinds were lowered, the lights turned out and a movie was put on. That was okay at first but then the call lights lit up and they were constant. There was a persistent call for bourbon and coke and Bundaberg rum and coke. In the end the drinks ran out, so they had to stop any service. The passengers were very aggressive to the crew, but the crew kept their resolve and remained very professional. Note to self, make sure that I make enough money so I never have to fly economy ever again.

At last we landed in Singapore. What a culture shock. The airport is called Changi airport and I remembered Vic mentioned Changi prisoner of war camp. He said that it was synonymous with the suffering of Australian prisoners of war at the hands of the Japanese. I never asked more as Vic only gave just enough information. I always got the feeling that he suffered every time he spoke about his experiences. Changi airport was impressive, modern and state of the art. I quickly cleared customs and immigration and as I was walking out, there stood Margaret. Tall and dignified and she had not aged a day since I saw her last.

Margaret had lived in Sydney's eastern suburbs. I met her at the gym on Crown Street where I taught taekwondo. We hit it off and dated for about six months. She was a devout Christian and really lived the Christian life. She was so kind and forgiving, the living manifestation of an angel, a saint. I loved my time with her, she showed me how to have a loving, forgiving relationship. Margaret left Sydney to look after her mother who had developed a nasty breast cancer. It was a no brainer for her. She packed up and left very quickly. Though I was quite sad, I knew that this was something that she just needed to do.

Her parents were divorced many years before. Her father owned a timber town in Borneo and was very rich. At least, that's what he tells Margaret. He still supported the entire family, including their housing. Why? Because he could.

And now, there she was.

We briefly hugged. "So nice to see you."

She smiled. "Likewise."

I was staying at her place as a friend. The road to downtown Singapore was straight and fast, no traffic. The bright lights of Singapore city were very impressive.

"This part is called Orchard Road. It is the best area for shopping."

We continued for another five minutes, then passed the botanical gardens and turned into a wide driveway. "Here we are."

What a great spot, so close to the malls of Orchard Road and the botanical gardens, which I ran around every morning. Her apartment was on the top floor of six. Luckily it had a lift. The weather was so hot and humid. Margaret had fans but no air-conditioning. The apartment was huge. It rambled on forever.

"Don't worry, my father pays for the rent. This is your room. Would you like to have a shower and clean up? We are meeting my family for dinner at the number one seafood market in Singapore."

"Great, I will freshen up."

What an introduction to the wealth of Singapore. Margaret's father was treated like royalty. He was a tall slim man in his mid-sixties. Next to him sat his new wife, who was a Singapore Airlines air hostess. She worked in first class and met Margaret's father on board. I heard that as part of the process to get into Singapore airlines they had to walk on a catwalk, where they paraded in evening wear and swimwear.

Next to his new wife were twin boys, his sons. They were looked after by the entire extended family. Margaret's brother was also there, he was an international lawyer working for a top multinational legal firm. He was educated at Oxford in England. Margaret's mother and auntie were enjoying eating, drinking, chatting and laughing. And then there was me. *What am I doing here?* I wondered. I drank the cold Singha beer, it was on tap which I loved, and ate the fine seafood. I just dropped below the radar and tried not to bring attention to myself – which was not difficult as the entire conversation was in Chinese. Margaret and I avoided any unanswered questions about our relationship. She was the perfect hostess, and we enjoyed our time together, no pressure.

The next day we headed out to the headquarters of Master Hun. He had published a very good book, an encyclopaedia of kung fu. He was well known worldwide as this book is a wonderful reference on kung fu and its history. He had a large chain of schools throughout Asia and Margaret was a popular black belt in his system. Master Hun said to drop into his office anytime in the afternoon.

"We have some time so let me take you to a shop that you might enjoy." Margaret suggested. So we set off to Orchard Road again. We headed into the carpark of the Far East shopping mall and made our way up to the third floor and entered a very plain looking clothes shop. It was the kind of shop that had old dusty mannequin dolls with clothes from the fifties hanging off them.

The shop manager looked up. "Hi, Margaret."

"Hello Mr Wu. This is my friend from Australia, can you please show him what you really sell?"

"Sure." A couple of larger men kept guard by the front door. Mr Wu slid a false wall to the side. "Please, go ahead."

We walked down a very narrow corridor to a door. Mr Wu knocked lightly.

What is this? I thought. *Oh no, I hope it is not drugs.* Singapore was notorious for executing foreigners who were caught even with a very small amount of drugs on them. I stopped dead in my tracks and turned to Margaret. "I cannot go any further. Is this drugs?"

She could feel the tension in my voice. "Oh, no! It's not, no way." She touched me on the arm. "It will be okay."

We entered a dark room and when the light came on, my breath was taken away. "Wow!" I exclaimed. There was an incredible array of designer watches, designer shirts, belts and jackets and the most beautiful selection of designer bags. Row after row of the most expensive brands of bags and clothes from all over the world, in one place.

"They are the best copies money can buy," Margaret nodded.

I was stunned. How could this incredibly sweet and mature woman be caught up in all of this? It just goes to show that you never really know what drives people, deep down. Apparently, the police were keeping an eye on this place. And it was one of hundreds throughout Asia. As long as they received their monthly share of the money taken, the police were happy. The two henchmen out the front standing guard were not on the lookout for the police, they were on the lookout for petty thugs that want to rip Mr Wu off. Though making copies was – and still is – technically illegal, it was so popular and with the police involvement it was a thriving business. I could not resist; I bought a blue Rolex, it looked incredible. We then dropped in next door to buy some cassettes of some of my favourite music, all copies.

"That was awesome." I turned to Margaret. "How did you get involved?"

"It was through my father. He loves the copies and invests money into their production. So we often come here to check the quality."

I was really surprised as Margaret was so matter of fact, quite relaxed about it. We walked down another floor and came to a small café.

"Have you ever had chendol?" she asked.

"No, I have no idea what that is."

"It is a Singaporean delicacy. And here is the best place in Singapore to buy it."

It was sweet and crunchy then sour and slimy. A taste sensation. Chendol with ice-cream, pandan jelly and delicious toppings is one of the most common Southeast Asian desserts. We finished our chendol and headed to Master Hun's office.

When we arrived, the place was busy. And in the middle of the chaos was Master Hun. He was completely out of control, damn this, damn that, he was really angry. *How hard can it be to run a large martial arts school?* I wondered. But then I saw this so-called master with no idea of what he was becoming or creating. His office staff cowered away and removed themselves from his attention. I have never forgotten the contradiction that was standing in front of me. In fact, I would go as far to say he was a bully.

He caught Margaret's eye and stopped for a second, shaking his head.

"Master Hun this is Jack George, the journalist from Australia," Margaret said.

"What do you want?" he bellowed.

"Absolutely nothing from you. I have seen enough." I walked out of his office, Margaret following closely behind me.

"Jack, stop," she shouted.

"No, let's get out of here." We walked back to her car.

"Are you okay?"

"Yes, fine, I just don't want to be around that man."

"Shall we go for dinner?" she asked. "The Sofitel hotel is just off Orchard Road. They do a really good Thai buffet. Are you hungry?"

I love good Thai food, and this buffet did not disappoint. There was Pad Thai and Pad see ew, as well as my favourite chicken larb salad, chicken mince infused with lemongrass, garlic and chilli. I also loved the cold beef and lemongrass salad. The satay beef and peanut sauce was divine. I ate so much. You could eat as much as you wanted, so I made a bit of a pig of myself.

The following morning I was leaving Singapore to travel to Hong Kong. "Margaret, thank you, I had a great time."

There were no issues that we needed to sort out. She was dedicated to the health and recovery of her mother, and had found peace in her spirituality. But she still found it hard to say goodbye.

I found out that Margaret's mother had later passed away.

9
HONG KONG

It was a short flight to Hong Kong. I arrived at the Kai Tak international airport around lunchtime. I was not expecting the tight landing. I felt you could almost reach out and touch the buildings either side. The flight crew really earned their money landing the great 747 EUD safely.

I took a cab to downtown Kowloon. Hong Kong was in sharp contrast to Singapore, I was taking it all in. I decided to splurge by staying in The Langham hotel near Kowloon Park. That evening, I walked the streets looking for a good Chinese restaurant. I chose one which had the most locals in it. The fried rice and wonton noodles were excellent. I was quite upbeat considering I was spending so much time alone. I was really enjoying all of the new experiences.

The following morning, I was awake at 6 am, so while it was still cool decided to go for a run through the streets of Kowloon. I made my way up, choosing the longest staircases and steepest hills that I could find. I ended up in Kowloon Botanical Gardens. What a treat that was. There were so many masters all with a large group practising different kinds of Chinese martial arts. I was mesmerised particularly by the tai chi and chi gong. I had not seen a great deal of tai chi; this was the first time that I got to watch a master in action. The moves and forms seemed to go on forever, I marvelled at the way the master delved deep into his being and expressed his heart through his movement of his hips, arms and legs.

The master could tell that I was interested. In fact, I was fascinated. He motioned for me to join the back of the large group. So I did, I just followed on the best I could do. The master said something to the group in Chinese and the girls giggled. He then came right up to me.

"I said you are very handsome," he whispered, as he moved my arm in a circular fashion, then pushed my hip in and touched me on the shoulders. "You very strong but your ki is weak. What is your name?"

"Jack."

"Well Mr Jack, my name is Dr Chen. I am always here in the mornings, come and find me when you are ready to learn the way of softness. But first power off, move your weight like this, bring your arms to your hara, your centre, push them out on the breath."

I completed the movement with the group, thanked Dr Chen for the incredible lesson, saying one day I would return. But I knew I first had some serious things that I needed to do.

Dr Chen brought his hands up to his heart. "Yes, Jack, I can feel you are going on a great journey." And as he walked away, he said something that stunned me and stopped me dead in my tracks. "I hope you find the hokuto ryu, Jack."

But how did he know? I had never met this man before and meeting him was totally random. I turned to ask him, but he was gone.

That afternoon I met up with my old buddy, Derek. He and I had been friends for many years. I originally met him when I was studying at the technical college. He was from Ireland and moved to Australia many years before. He met a Chinese woman and moved to Hong Kong and had been teaching English ever since. Talking with him, it sounded like he had well and truly settled down. I reminded him of a story he told me after I met him for the first time, which I had never forgotten.

He was walking down the platform at Central Station. It was still quite early, and Derek had left the old drinkers' pub on George Street with a gut full of Toohey's Black, the closest drink he could find to his favourite Guinness. He had been there all afternoon and into the evening, steadily downing more and more beer. He knew he had had enough when he mistook the ladies' restroom for the men's. Stumbling his way out saying what kind of a pub doesn't have any urinals, he made his way to the door and the barman shouted out to him "Oi, Derek, shall I call you a cab?"

He ignored him and waved as he left. He had reached a bench on the platform and was happily waiting for the next train.

Two teenagers walked up to him and asked if he had a smoke. He just stood up and walked away. The teenagers were dressed like your regular thugs and were quickly joined by three more teenagers.

"Give us your money," one of them demanded, and pushed Derek over.

And that's where it gets interesting. I remember reading the news the following day about a drunk Irishman who beat the crap out of five teenagers.

"I took everything that they did to me. I got knocked to the ground and kicked in the head, but I just kept on getting up. There was no way that I was going to give them any money. I smashed them, Jack."

The funny thing is that Derek had never been in a fight before and had never done any martial arts or self defence training. It was pure fighting spirit and willpower to survive no matter what. He thumped them and kicked them wherever his shin could find a soft target. He bit into them, removing an ear, or half a nose. He dragged them along the curb and gutter, stomping on them until they begged for mercy. They got the shock of their life, Derek told me.

"No more!" they pleaded.

But this only angered Derek even more. He was covered in blood and had a couple of red welts on his face. He smiled and exposed a bloody smear across his teeth. "You picked the wrong fella." And with that, turned his back and left a scene of carnage behind him. He broke legs and gouged eyes, the teenagers were lying about the platform stunned. How did they get this so wrong?

Derek walked to the police station and gave a statement. They then called an ambulance and he was taken to Royal Prince Alfred Hospital where he was treated for minor cuts and abrasions.

I have always believed that even the most unassuming person should never be taken for an easy target. You should never underestimate even a white belt because you never know what they are capable of.

That night Derek and I laughed as he recalled that day. Though his face lit up retelling the tale, he said they were different times. He gave up drinking a few years ago and was happy and settled as a married man and respectable English teacher.

"Have you been to the Bruce Lee statue?" He asked, still with that glint in his eye.

"No, that will have to wait for another time as my flight leaves in the morning."

10

MANILA

I landed in Manila in the afternoon, I watched the older men fuss over their younger brides as they were getting off the plane. Some had children, most didn't. The Filipino bride is very strong and would do anything to escape the poverty and find someone to support their family, usually on the back of a horny retiree. But they appeared happy so who was I to judge. I passed customs and immigration without any fuss and walked straight into a waiting taxi.

I was off to the Novotel, a comfortable five-star hotel with a large pool and all-you-can-eat breakfast. I checked in then went down for a swim. I was blown away by the number of girls hanging by the back entrance, trying to catch the eye of the first sucker they could snag. It did not take them or me long, I was soon caught in their snare. I innocently ushered one of these beautiful ladies onto the premises.

"What is your name?" I asked.

"I'm Ruby."

Ruby was very friendly. I had in my mind that we were going to just chat but we spent the evening enjoying each other's bodies. I did not think for a minute that this was going to happen, but I was naïve. She was a hardened, experienced prostitute, and I was like a bug caught in her web.

She really enjoyed a sleep in the king size bed.

"Good morning, shall I order some coffee and some breakfast?" I asked politely. "You can order what you like." She ate and drank so much the night before, like she had not had a decent meal for a while.

She looked at the clock and then looked at me. "Sure, that will be great."

We ate a good breakfast, and I asked her when she was going to leave.

"Oh! You will need to escort me out to the front." As Ruby was getting herself together, she wrote down the telephone number of a friend in Bangkok. "Look up my friend when you get to Thailand, Lecky, she will look after you."

I had to escort her through the lobby to the taxi stand. I could feel the critical eyes and giggles but kept my head high and opened the door to the taxi. She jumped in and waved as she left.

I made my way down to the carpark, not really knowing who I was looking for. He'd told me over the phone that he would find me. So I waited and waited and before I knew it I had been waiting for an hour.

That can't be him, I thought. But it was. Romeo was a short and powerful looking man with a full head of jet black hair which actually looked a bit like a cheap wig. He was Raynor's teacher, who I'd met briefly for lunch back in Sydney. Raynor recommended Romeo above all his other teachers of the Filipino martial art – Arnis – that uses swords, machetes and knives.

He was full on. He brought out what looked like a towel and wrapped up in it were fighting machetes and knives. Romeo said that he kept his sharpened weapons close by, as he challenged any man who slandered him and he might need them in a hurry. Apparently, these challenge matches happened regularly.

"If you have time, I would like to take you to meet the grandmaster and other top teachers of arnis."

I jumped at the invitation to meet the grandmaster and Tony Diamond, one of his top students. So we headed out into the traffic and made our way deep into the heart of this fast moving city. Every time we pulled up, the car was surrounded with beggars and street kids. Quite sad actually.

We turned right and I could see that we were at the entrance of Smokey Mountain, the infamous Manila slum city.

"We will have to walk from here," Romeo said.

What a culture shock, such poverty! I found it hard to imagine the grandmaster living in a slum. We seemed to be walking forever, accompanied all the way with the stench of raw sewage. We turned down a narrow pathway and into a small shack. Romeo and I sat on an old brown vinyl couch. Tony Diamond walked in right after us. Tony has both the Asian and Spanish features and he looked strong. Like Romeo he had thick strong arms from training with the heavy machete for many years. I was wondering where the boss was when a younger woman, maybe forty, entered the room from a side entrance.

This was Mimi, Listro's wife. She was carrying bottles of a cool soft drink, a generic brand, that looked like orange fizz, and small packets of savoury biscuits. We had arrived when Listro took his morning nap. He was almost ninety years old and not only was he champion with the machete, surviving many challenges and fights to the death, he was also a champion pistol shooter. He moved into the room like a sleek cat, taking up a position on the hard mud floor. Romeo and Tony moved the couch and the old lino from the floor to make room. The old man, fondly known as Tata, started a routine with Tony. Romeo was explaining the moves, they switched between knife, sticks and the heavy machete. They were so fast. The knives were sharp which made it even more exhilarating. The incredible thing was, Listro was legally blind.

Tony stopped after a while and turned to me. "Do you want to try?"

"Absolutely."

This was a perfect time to learn about knife fighting and defence. A few weeks before I left for Singapore, I was set upon by two knife-wielding thugs on Crown Street, across from the Hard Rock Café. I managed to dispose of them with the martial arts I knew, and not get cut.

I learned so much from that one lesson and organised to spend as much time as I could with Romeo, Tony and Listro, though I did get the shock of my life when a large black rat ran through the middle of us and out the door. It was all part of living in a slum.

The sun was setting as we got back to the hotel. Romeo asked me if I would like to do some more training. I agreed, so we found a spot in the garden overlooking the bay and practised just a single cut with the machete. This was a gruelling workout as my hands were already blistered and my forearms burning. I could understand why he wanted me to practise this one cut, it was quite traditional and very similar to the katana cut in Japanese styles of Kenjutsu. I didn't think it would be any use in Sydney as it was not something that I could keep in my pocket.

The following morning, Romeo picked me up and we headed to meet some more of his friends and masters. First stop, Edgar. He was the founder of a form of Arnis. He had become quite popular in the USA and now spent his time between Manila and LA. Edgar was quite proud of the fact that he had been in real knife fights and wore the scars like trophies.

Edgar was a fast mover. He had put his own take on the traditional style of 'Listro Arnis' but to be honest, I couldn't tell the difference. I was lucky to get to meet Edgar, as I found out a number of months later that he passed away. Cancer.

"Next stop, Michael," said Romeo.

I had been dreading meeting Michael ever since I heard Raynor was beaten up by him. "He takes on whoever he can," Romeo confirmed. "But you should be okay, he has heard how fast and big you are."

"That's a relief."

We arrived at a real estate office in downtown Manila and walked up the stairs to the second floor where there was a lot of grunting and the sounds of bodies being thrown. The second floor had been converted to a martial arts studio. Michael was a smallish man but was very intense. He walked with a limp and was quick to show me the scar on his lower leg where he was knifed, cutting his Achilles tendon. I could see and feel that he was angry and impatient, as he took his two training partners on, striking them freely. I was wondering if this was supposed to impress me. It reminded me of the bullies I used to work with in security.

My attitude changed completely, I wanted to fight him. I asked Romeo, "When is it my turn?" I was twice his size, and my fighting skills were the best they had been.

At last there was a break and Michael ignored me. Romeo stepped forward. "This is Jack George from Australia, he is Raynor's friend."

"Stuff the etiquette," I blurted out. "Is it my turn?"

He did not blink an eyelid, which surprised me. He certainly was brave, but he had a lot of openings that I intended to drive a kick or punch through. We faced each other and I nodded my head, which was meant to be a bow. I just stood there and waited, he came swiftly across the floor and before he could get close to me, I sent him flying with a hard front leg side kick that knocked all the wind out of him. He stood straight up; I was impressed as that kick would have knocked over an elephant.

Back then my fighting was raw and violent. I had very little concern for my opponent. Most people I fought were plain inexperienced and could not fight. They were all talk. So I would call them out. Most were bullies, and I had the greatest pleasure in taking them out. I remember all of them. We fought, we bled, some I won and some I lost. But every so often a real hard nut would cross my path and I would find myself in the fight of my life. This was one of those times. I soon saw by the way he moved that Michael had trained in some sort of martial arts. But the real giveaway was his steely gaze. I could just move away, it was not too late, no blood had been spilt. I knew that this was the better option. But I was driven. Who was the better fighter?

"Stop posing your kicks," he only just managed to say as he adjusted his top and pants.

I ignored him as he came charging into me again. I went high with a front leg turning kick. Now that shocked him and wobbled his legs, I followed up immediately with a hard turning kick with my right shin, taking him down, where he stayed.

"That was for my mate Raynor." I scowled at him as I walked off out the door.

Romeo followed and laughed as he told me that Michael had intimidated many people with his aggressive attitude, and it was good to see him get some of his own. There is nothing more humiliating than being beaten up in your own dojo in front of your students.

The old adage is that you now live to fight another day. I recognise now that the voice compelling me forward had no real interest in my well-being. The ego is a slippery beast.

The following morning, Romeo picked me up and we headed back to the slum. It was hot and humid, the sweat soaking my shirt. There were so many street kids. They so needed a good bath and a good feed. But regardless of how they looked, they seemed happy. We made our way along the narrow walkways, careful to avoid the human excrement sprinkled along the path. The deeper we went the darker it became.

At last, a reprieve from the smell that had walked with us all the way from the car. Tata was pleased to see us. He had been warming up with Tony. As I entered the shack Tony blurted out with a giggle, "I hear you met Michael yesterday."

I did not know whether to be embarrassed or proud.

"Don't worry," said Tony, "he has had it coming for a while."

I relaxed with relief.

"Let's train," said Romeo.

The moves got faster and faster and they praised me on my speed and power.

"Let's break," said Tony.

As we sat Mimi brought out plain biscuits and orange fizz.

"Can I ask Tata a question?" I asked Romeo.

"I will check." Romeo translated. "Tata said, 'No problem, go ahead.'"

So I plunged in. "I understand that you spent time training in some of the elite samurai schools in Japan." Tata shook his head. I didn't know whether that meant yes or no. So I pushed on. "Did you train at the hokuto ryu?"

Tata took a sharp breath and his usual happy demeanour changed quickly. It was as if a dark cloud had suddenly descended on him. He barked something in Tagalog to both Romeo and Tony. Romeo touched my arm and said Tata has finished for the day. It is time for us to leave. I shook Tata's hand which was clammy and weak. He looked like a different man, like he was beaten.

Tony disappeared further into the slums. Romeo and I made our way back to the car.

"So sorry," I said, as we climbed back into the car. Romeo was silent. *Well, I really messed that up,* I thought.

Romeo did not talk to me, he drove all the way back to the hotel in silence.

"I will pick you up tomorrow at 9 am." And Romeo left.

I was quite down. I had come all this way, and it was wasted. I went back to my room, showered the smell of filth off me, changed into a clean pair of linen pants and a loose polo shirt then headed to the nearby taxi stand. I had never been to the red light district so it was all a new experience. I chose to enter the Pink Pussy Cat. I sat at the bar and ordered a beer and was immediately surrounded by several beautiful women. They were perfectly behaved and jostled between themselves in what appeared good natured fun. Pouring my beer and rubbing my leg. All the while I was watching the stage show, girls dancing around poles and slowly removing their clothes. This was getting a little uncomfortable for me. One of the girls was becoming quite pushy, asking me to release her for the night by paying her bar fine, then she is mine for the night. On a whim, I paid for the beers and snacks and rushed down the stairs into a waiting taxi. *Wow that was close*, I thought as I relaxed back into the car seat.

Suddenly, there was a motorcycle beside my window honking his horn. To my surprise the bar girl was sitting on the back of the motorcycle dressed in plain clothes screaming out for me to pay her bar fine. We soon arrived at the security gate of the hotel. And the motorcycle pulled up beside us. *Damn it*, I thought, so I paid the bar fine and in we went. At least I could let her have a shower and a good meal. But that was just the beginning of the night. She quickly got undressed and invited herself into the shower. She came out of the shower wearing only a towel and dropped it to her feet. So ready and waiting, she just stood there. As she walked towards me, I took off my shirt, she unzipped my trousers and soon had them off. I gently eased her back onto my bed and enjoyed the night.

———

I walked my friend to the front lobby of the hotel and watched her drive off in a taxi as I patiently waited in the shade for Romeo. I did not really think that he would show up after yesterday's disaster. But at 9 am on the dot there he was, as cheerful as ever.

"We are going back to see Tata today," Romeo said.

"That is great news," I replied, "I may get a chance to get some information."

When we arrived at Tata's place he was sitting on the couch, talking with Mimi. He shook my hand and patted me on the back as he spoke with Romeo.

As Tata spoke, Mimi translated. "He apologises for yesterday, he says he has not heard those words for many years, and it brought back so many memories. Tata had made many Japanese friends when they occupied the Philippines during the Second World War. They were fascinated with his sword work and Tata shared his knowledge freely. For that he got many favours for his fellow villagers. One night, a group of men from a neighbouring village entered Tata's village demanding to know why he was so friendly with the Japanese. Tata was and is a warrior and the Japanese colonel was also a warrior who came from a long line of warriors in Japan. These villagers threatened to kill all of Tata's family and friends if he continued to maintain a friendship with the colonel.

"Tata took his sharpened machete and with one clean strike took the head off the leader of the other village. There was screaming and crying for Tata's head. He quickly ran to the colonel's villa and explained what had happened. The colonel said his name was Nishio Fujita, and he would protect him. He was a good man. All he wanted was for the war to end and to go home.

"'There will be a boat that will take you to Japan,' he said. 'Once you arrive go to the fish markets at Ueno and ask for Toby Kano. He is half Japanese half American but has lived for many years in Tokyo. He will take you to my home. A very special place hidden in the mountains. Stay there and I will come for you after the war.'

"Tata stayed there for ten years. From what I can make out the training and lifestyle were brutal."

Tata looked me squarely in the eyes and said, "Do not go there."

He was obviously scarred by his time there. But that did not put me off at all! In fact, it made me even more determined.

Mimi finished by giving me a name and phone number. It was a Tokyo number. I did not know then, but it was the number for a Stanley Morgan.

That was the last time I saw Tata. Many years later, I heard he had passed away. He almost made one hundred years old. I also heard that Tony Diamond died of cancer. I cherish the time that I spent with them. I did hear that Romeo is well and burns the flame for Listro teachings worldwide.

———

It was time that I headed to Japan. But first I went for a holiday in Thailand. My late buddy Lovell always said to me if I get a chance, I should visit Bangkok. I was so close, being in the Philippines, so now I had my chance.

For some reason, I had only recently come to realise, trouble seemed to follow me. I learned many years later that if your Ki; life force, is not good, you will attract negative energy to yourself and this can manifest in many ways. It will continue to happen repeatedly, until you realise that there is something fundamentally wrong with you and what you are doing. Most never have any idea what I am talking about. They live and die never realising that if they had taken a deep look at themselves, they would have seen how their misery affected every aspect of their lives.

Even just a glimpse of themselves and they would have seen how their misery manifests and what was causing it. Unfortunately, I still had a way to go before I would learn this life changing lesson.

Saying goodbye to Romeo was quite difficult. He was a very interesting character. He would arrive by suddenly appearing, and leave the way he came, by simply disappearing. There was something mysterious about it and when I asked Romeo, he just looked at me with a wry smile and a sparkle in his eyes and said, "I have no idea what you are talking about." Nevertheless, he drummed to a different beat. One minute the warrior, hell bent on fighting in challenges, the next minute the philosopher espousing everything from the Bible to the *Tibetan Book of the Dead* to references from the Bhagavad Gita.

I will never forget the times we spent together after training. Not much was said as we sat in silence, so much was shared in that silence.

I was on my way again, heading off to the next adventure. What an adventure it was going to be.

11

BANGKOK

I cleared customs and found a public phone, dialled the number Ruby had given me and wondered what to expect. The voice on the other end was a little abrupt. She told me to get a cab to Patpong Road at the Silom Road end, on the corner.

Waiting for me as I arrived was Lecky. It was very kind of her to meet me and escort me to a hotel. Lecky was a tall, slim woman, with long straight jet-black hair, quite elegant. Some would say she was stunning, and I must agree. All that mattered was she was my only connection here in Thailand and I needed help. Lecky spoke a kind of pidgin English and Thai; it was enough for me to understand.

"Shall we get a taxi?" I asked. "I am going to stay downtown in the Khao Sar Road or Sukumvit area."

"Ah, no, you stay at my place." Lecky said.

Great, I thought, *just what I wanted.* How could I say no? It would probably be good for a couple of days while I got my land legs and set a plan for training.

It was a busy, bustling area. The oppressive humidity was already taking its toll on me as I lifted my backpack onto my back. I followed Lecky down a one-way laneway, and turned left into a mid-size building. There was no lift so the stairs it was. I followed her up the stairs and finally we arrived on the third floor. Her apartment was very small and hot and I noticed all the noise from the market place seemed to funnel up the staircase and into the apartment. It was the size of a small bed sitter, the only bed in the room was separated by a sarong.

"This is very small." I looked around. "I am happy to stay at a hotel."

But she would not have it. "No! You stay here." Lecky grabbed two cold beers from the bar fridge, and we sat next to each other on a small sofa.

After finishing the beer, she got up. "It's so hot. Do you mind, I get changed?"

"Of course not." I expected her to do so behind the screen. She slipped out of her dress and just stood there in a black lacy G-string and no bra. I was shocked.

Lecky was a beauty. She came towards me and asked, "You like?" as she unzipped my jeans and quickly removed them. My boxer shorts were next to go and before I knew it, I was literally stripped naked. I was hot and had not showered since that morning, I felt like I needed a shower.

How lucky am I? I thought. I just sat there.

Lecky laughed but made me feel comfortable. "Another beer?"

Lecky was not fussed, she just carried on half-naked without a care in the world; totally comfortable in her skin. I must remember she is likely a prostitute. I wondered what I was supposed to be doing. I covered myself with both my hands feeling slightly self-conscious.

"I still hot." She deftly removed her G-string and I got the shock of my life. It stood there, rock hard. She is a he!

I pulled away, chuckling. "I am so sorry, I had no idea."

"You will like," she insisted. But in a blink of an eye, I was fully dressed and sitting, a little embarrassed, back on the sofa.

Lecky had been an elite escort for ten years. She held herself so well that only a very few got to sleep with her. I would probably put her at around thirty years old, but was surprised to learn that she was in fact thirty-five. Now she was working as a manager at the Queens Castle Bar on Patpong Road, no longer working as an escort.

———

At 7 pm, I walked down to Patpong Road. It was bustling with locals and tourists, I grabbed some Pad Thai and a beer at one of the street vendors, then walked the short distance to the Queens Castle. Lecky was standing at the front, talking to a couple of the girls who had taken a break from the pole dancing. I sneaked past her and made my way inside.

What a place, full of foreigners – mostly older foreigners – and the women flocked to them. The music was blaring Rick Astley's 'Never Gonna Give You Up'. I positioned myself where I could get a good view of the stage and ordered a bottle of beer. I was quickly joined by two of the bar girls who were keen for me to buy them a drink. So I did. It was pleasant. The whole bar girl thing can be quite controversial, many say that it is exploitation of these poor girls, women. That may be true but a lot of them seemed to be having a great time. And they earned enough to send money back to their family.

The show started with a man and woman having sex on the stage. They looked quite bored and it ended sooner than they planned.

I had heard all about the ping pong balls being launched across the room by these girls, and I was quite astonished seeing what they could do. I made my way back to Lecky and said goodbye. "I am tired and it is getting late, I'm gonna head back to the apartment, where shall I sleep?"

"You can sleep in my bed."

I was too tired to argue and just wanted to crash out. I was fast asleep when Lecky and another girl came home late that night. They turned on the music and had more beers. Lecky was quite drunk. "Get up and enjoy the party," she laughed as she slipped out of her short skirt. I ignored her and pulled the pillow over my head.

The following morning we made our way downstairs to the café. I asked Lecky to help me locate the Taekwondo Association, I had heard they are a large powerful organisation.

"No, No," Lecky blurted out. "First of all, we go sightseeing."

We jumped in a tuk tuk, a three wheeled taxi that is like a cross between a motor bike and a car, and made our way to the king's palace. The king was a very popular monarch and had reigned for many years. The grounds were so beautiful and well kept. "The king is only a figurehead and has no real power, other than head of the armed forces," Lecky told me as she gulped down a bag of coke and ice.

I was lucky I was with a local. The tuk tuk drivers have two prices, one for the locals and one for everyone else. When walking around the tourist spots, friendly men would just appear and help with directions, they would provide a really good idea of when and where to go sightseeing. They would even hail a cab or tuk tuk for you. Having no idea what direction we are going in, the cab or tuk tuk driver would appear to innocently pull up at a clothes factory and suggest we go in to have a look. It is by about this stage that you realise that you have been scammed. The friendly man is in on the scam with the particular tuk tuk and cab drivers who work for the clothes factory. They then dump you out the back of nowhere and the entire process repeats itself over and over again, until you buy something. Very sneaky; I got trapped in this scam, not once but twice.

12

TAEKWONDO

We arrived at the Thailand Taekwondo HQ at 1 pm. They had been expecting us. Lecky insisted on coming along. She was intrigued as she had never seen anything like it before. The studio manager was a woman by the name of Mrs Yong. She was warm and welcoming. The chief instructor Master Nam was in Korea until the end of the week. She motioned for us to sit. The studio was on a large block that sat way back from the road. There is a lush garden either side of a narrow path that you followed until you reached two large warehouses. One of the warehouses had a large training area, fully equipped with every type of punching and kicking bag used for various training drills. Off to the side was a small office and kitchen.

"Tea?" Mrs Yong suggested.

I was relieved that she spoke quite good English. "Yes please," I replied. I love a good cup of tea, I guess it is the remnants of the English in me. We all sat down and one of the office staff brought out a pot of hot tea with freshly cut mango.

"So, what can I do for you today?" Mrs Yong asked.

"I would like permission to come and train here." I deftly

avoided the elephant in the room, the other large warehouse. It was spotlessly clean and had incense burning to clear the hot and humid air. It appeared to be well used. I was also wondering why it was hidden from view from the main road.

"Yes, you are welcome to train in classes on Tuesday and Thursday from 7 until 8.30 pm. Anybody from any style is most welcome to train at those times."

Wow, I wondered, *what was this place used for the rest of the time?*

As if she read my mind, she told me the other hall was hired out to other regular groups. The second room had a rough square taped out on the hard mud floor and set out around the taped square was a number of small grandstands where there was enough sitting for a smallish event.

But what was it used for? Obviously, it was their main source of income.

———

The next evening, I strolled along Patpong and ate dinner at my favourite street vendor. I had already eaten there a number of times without bringing it all back up. The food was fresh, plentiful and delicious. Lecky had left for work early.

She had brought a tall athletic American guy home last night. I was relegated to sleeping on the couch. They were at it all night.

Come morning I was angry with Lecky, which was totally out of line. We argued, she said nobody owned her and she was free to sleep with whoever she liked. I was feeling a little weirded out by the whole thing and realised that I was probably feeling a little jealous.

She went off in a huff, and I did not see her all day, so I walked down the road to Queen's Castle, and soon spotted her infectious smile. I walked towards her, she saw me and smiled shyly. She seemed pleased to see me, which made me happy.

"Jack, there is someone I want you to meet."

"Okay." I blindly followed her into the back of the club.

"This is Shultz. He is the owner of the club." From the instant I laid eyes on him, I knew he was trouble. I should have walked out of the club right away and run as far away from Shultz as possible. But then there was Lecky, and I really didn't want to upset her. Shultz spoke English with a heavy German accent. He was small and wiry with grey hair tied into a simple ponytail. He was a heavy smoker, which was obvious by the yellow nicotine stains on his fingers.

"Nice to meet you, Mr George. Lecky has told me so much about you. You are a fighter?"

"A martial artist." I corrected him.

"Are you interested in earning some good money? The studio you went to yesterday doubles as an illegal fighting venue."

I knew it, I thought, *there just had to be more to it.* The venue was perfect and there appeared to be plenty of exits in case of a police raid.

"This is the only way that the taekwondo club can survive. In fact, it is thriving. They have the best fighters. Will you be one of my fighters? What do you think?"

"Who do you answer to?" I blurted out.

"I have some close colleagues that are business men that fund my fighters."

"Mafia?" I asked.

"The mafia are in all levels of business here in Thailand. It is best to be on their side as the police are hopelessly understaffed and under paid."

"How much will I make?"

"That is a great question. Initially you will fight on a retainer, or how do you say, just for turning up. Once we establish you are a reliable source of income, as with my other top fighters, you can make between $1000 and $5000 US per fight, depending on your popularity."

"Can I sit on it for a day or so?"

"Sure." He rubbed his hands together, knowing that he was poised to score a top fighter. All I could see were the dollar signs lighting up in his eyes. I felt very much like a commodity, like a prize fighting cock.

"How long do I have to prepare?"

"The fights are every Wednesday and Friday night. So I will slot you in as soon as you agree and I get the final approval of my colleagues."

The following morning whilst having coffee with Lecky, I mentioned casually about the proposal Shultz had offered.

She looked at me and her tone turned serious. "Shultz is not a good man, Jack, he can get quite angry, I have seen him hitting my girls and most of the girls are afraid of him."

"Wise words. But it is good money, and I will be able to pay you for your kind hospitality."

"Jack, you must be careful, Shultz is connected to the local mafia gangs so he does not keep good company. The only winners of these terrible fights are the mafia. I must go to work now but can we talk about it tonight after work?"

We sat down that evening. Lecky looked at me with concern in her eyes. "Jack, you are heading into danger. Money never comes easy, it takes a lot of hard work. If you do this, you will be inviting the dark side to enter your life. They are all involved with drugs and other crimes, you will be a part of their web of pain and suffering. You are a nice boy, Jack, and I would hate to see you get hurt."

I was moved by her caring and I said so. "But I just have to know."

"Know what, Jack?"

"Who is the best!"

13
STREET FIGHTING

"Okay, Shultz, I will do it." I was excited.

"That's great."

"But there are a couple of conditions. I want $500 per fight against two average opponents. Then from there I will take on more experienced opponents paying a minimum $1000 per fight."

Shultz shrugged. "This may be hard; I will need to discuss it with my partners."

I met him two days later. I sat down opposite him in the bar and sipped on an ice water.

"Okay, my partners agree on your terms, but they might ask you for a favour at some stage."

"And what kind of favour might I expect?" I queried.

"Don't worry, it's a standard comment from these business men."

I wondered what I was getting into. My first fight was scheduled for the Friday after next, so I would have to fine tune my fitness and conditioning.

I ventured down to the Taekwondo Academy where all this originally started. It was a training night, so I was quite pleased to see so many people training. Not only were there taekwondo fighters preparing for the up-and-coming championships, but there were also many thai boxing fighters getting the edge by adding in the devastating kicks from taekwondo into their already lethal repertoire of strikes. Then there were the range of other fighters that were all shapes and sizes trying to make a quick buck while on holiday in Thailand. I thought that maybe they were trying to do the Rambo or Gladiator thing and hold some misguided notions that there was glory in any of this.

I couldn't afford to look at anyone and attempt to predict their experience or ability, so I just minded my own business and got down to skipping and doing rounds on the kicking and punching bags. The bell would go off every three minutes simulating a round, with a thirty second break between rounds. I managed twelve rounds of skipping, shadow fighting and bag work. Then finished with push ups, chin ups, and burpees. I did a short stretch and that did me. *Not bad for a first time,* I thought. I will jog in the morning and do some sprint work, that way I will cover all bases.

Lecky didn't agree, but was still supportive of my new venture, though she constantly warned me to be careful. She still persisted in walking around the small apartment with nothing on. I must admit, she had a cracking body, tanned skin without a blemish. She would watch me watching her and run her hands down teasing her nipples, I had to remember she was a professional call girl and this was what she was best at, the art of seduction.

The fight night came around quickly. I made my way to the small stadium. It was packed with people and the betting was frantic. Shultz nodded his head towards me as I made my way through the crowd and into the change room. All the scheduled fighters gathered there and made small talk. I could tell there was a mixture of fear and anticipation. I checked the evenings draw that was taped to the wall. I was fighting in an early fight against a tough taekwondo fighter from the middle east. His name was Ali, a nice enough chap, he was really strong and aggressive which made up for his lack of height.

"Looks like it's you and me mate," I said.

"Yes," he sneered, knocking away my extended hand. "I hope you are ready to give me a good fight."

I got into my thai boxing shorts and took off my shirt. It was humid and I was already sweating. I was nervous but did not show it. It was essential that I controlled the fear, which was like a knot in my gut, sitting there waiting to consume me. There was a voice inside my head, begging me, pleading with me to run as fast as I could from this place. But I could not. Where would I go? I took solace in the fact that all warriors experience fear. It was normal, the fight or flight response to the unknown. It is the exact same response that our ancestors the cavemen would experience to help them stay alive against predators like the sabre tooth tiger.

The key here was to not let it cripple you. The age old saying, feel the fear and do it anyway resonated right through me. I let the thoughts come and go as I focused on the blaring music. I was ready.

This was my first time fighting in an unsanctioned street fight. There were no gloves, and no rules. The centre referee controlled the fight and it was he who would determine when a fighter has had enough. The only way to win was by knock out or submission.

My name was being called. "Jack George, you are next up."

I put in my mouthguard, took a deep breath and left the changing room. The noise and heat hit me like a wave. It took my breath away. I walked to the edge of the taped ring, bowed my head and walked to the centre, where Ali was waiting. The referee announced our names, Ali had a record of three wins and two losses, and I had a clean slate, no wins and no losses.

"Start!" The ref shouted.

Ali came at me hard. His intensity shocked me, I had to get with it. *Move*, I said to myself, *just move*. In a blink of an eye, I kicked Ali in the side of the jaw with a strong, focused roundhouse kick. Thwack. He dropped onto the hard packed mud floor; he was out cold his eyes rolling back in his head. It was all over in ten seconds. The crowd was in a frenzy. In movies you see the actors getting hit over and over again all over the body and the head. But in real life, a hit to the head or face will end the fight very quickly.

The last I saw of Ali was him on a stretcher heading out into an ambulance. He should have shaken my hand was the only thought I had of him. I pushed my way through to Shultz.

"How was that for you?" I asked.

"You did well, Jack." He passed me an envelope.

"Five hundred US dollars?" I asked.

"Of course."

I picked up a beer from the ice bucket at his feet. "I can go again next week."

"That will be great." Shultz was cool and distant, I found him hard to read.

I made my way to the Queen's Castle, to see Lecky.

"Good to see you survived," she smiled.

I took $100 out of the envelope and gave her the rest. "I won," I said with no fuss. Taking a seat at the bar I downed a couple of tiger beers as I watched the bar girls do their stuff.

———

Friday fight night soon came around again. It was now the Thursday night before the fight. Shultz was in the bar smoking a large thick Cuban cigar. He loved this life. From what I could make out he was a bit of a no hoper. I thought because of his name that he was German. No. In fact, he was Romanian. I could not pick his thick accent, German, Russian or Romanian, they all sound the same. He had fled his homeland and was making good here in Thailand. I asked around among some of the other expats about

Shultz. They said he was an aggressive sleaze bag and I should not get involved with him. He used to be a policeman working for the Romanian government but was arrested himself for prostitution and extortion. Apparently, he bribed his way out of gaol and fled from Romania to Thailand where he had been ever since.

He had set up a number of dummy companies and owned nothing, on paper he was completely clean. But I knew he got his hands dirty, and it might only be a matter of time before he ended up in a Thai gaol, taking everyone that worked with him to the same fate.

He motioned for me to come and sit with him. I didn't like the way he used his two fingers to beckon me to go to him. But I let it go.

"Jack, how lovely to see you. Have a seat, my boy, and let's chat. You are getting quite a name for yourself, the way you easily knocked out Ali. There are fighters lining up wanting to take you on. You see, Jack, you are becoming quite the celebrity and very popular with the betting. The other fighters see a large payment coming their way if they can dispose of you. Your next opponent tomorrow night won't be such a push over."

———

It was very humid. The heat in Australia is a dry heat and a lot more bearable. But I still don't like it, I prefer the cold. I just had to grin and bear it. I arrived at the fight with plenty of time to spare. I made my way through the crowd, it was very difficult for me to keep a low profile, a cheer went up and there were plenty of well-wishers patting me on the back. The atmosphere was light and between the beers and shouts to secure a bet it was quite jovial.

I checked the draw pinned to the wall. My next fight was against a tough fighter from Croatia, a top Australian karate champion, trained in Japan. His name was Tomislav Zobec. He and I were about the same size. As I was doing my stretches he bounced in front of me, giving me the evil eye, huffing and puffing, trying to intimidate me. I just smiled and did my best to ignore him. I had watched his fight the last time I was fighting, he came in with a low stance, very strong and stable. He kept his hands down on his hips and feinted with the left and fired off the right reverse punch with great power. I had a plan and was looking forward to putting it into action. From my experience, when you take a long sideways stance against a fighter that wants to fight you square on, you can lean back away from their long reverse punch, leaving their mid-section and head fully exposed. To my advantage, he did not look really fit, he was a bit flabby around his hips and stomach.

We stepped into the taped ring as they removed the last fighter out on a stretcher. The crowd was lusting for blood and there was already plenty in the ring. And then it was on, but I did not feel ready, I needed time to centre, it was all happening too fast.

"In the blue corner with a record of one fight and one win by knockout: Jack George. And in the red corner with a record of three fights and three wins by knockout: Tomislav Zobec. Fighters ready… Start."

We shook hands and began. Zobec bounced on the spot with his hands low, just as I thought he would. Why not? It had worked for him in the past. I was just a little slow to get into my side stance and he grabbed the opportunity and thumped me clean and straight to my nose. Ouch! With blood pouring out of both nostrils I countered immediately with a punch directly to his nose. Whack! It knocked him off his feet.

So the count began. One, two, three … there was some movement … four, five, six. Zobec stood, blood pouring down his face. He smiled at me and spat blood in my direction. He went back to the bouncing with his hands low, he shot in again and caught me in the nose. This one really wobbled me, but I did not go down. I calmed myself and waited for him to attack again. Sure enough, he could smell a win, but I was not done yet. As I had planned, I stood side on, when he lunged towards me I leaned back and he ever so slightly overbalanced, I lowered my stance and launched a ferocious right cross. All those years of doing hard labourer's work on jack hammers and sledge hammers had helped me to hone a lethal right punch.

I connected with Zobec's nose and face and I felt nothing, it launched him off his feet knocked out cold. The last I saw of Tomislav was the medical team trying to revive him by putting him on oxygen. Another spectacular win, I did not feel bad, we were all adults and knew exactly what the risks were. I just took it a little further. Whenever I left to go to a fight, I made sure all of my affairs were in order, bills paid and my Will put clearly where it can be found. I was willing to put my life on the line, and if my opponent was not also committed to do the same, I found their cracks and I exploited them ... *This is the warrior way.*

I made my way to Shultz and held out my hand. "You cost me money, Jack." Shultz sneered as I waited for the envelope.

"Well, you should not bet against me."

He passed me the envelope, I grabbed the customary bottle of beer and made my way out of there. Note to self, be careful of Shultz. Once again, I handed Lecky $400 US. She really appreciated it; my fight money was more than she earned in a month. She was great the way she looked after me, kept the apartment spotless and the fridge well stocked with ample food and beer. I would never have imagined that I would be sharing an apartment with a stunning tranny model in the hub of Bangkok, making my living fighting in unsanctioned street fights.

———

The next six weeks went by with ease, I was quite settled in, living the life of a fighter. I was careful to not get too comfortable and made sure that I stayed away from Shultz as much as possible.

There was a nasty element that lingered around Patpong Road. They were the types that were just looking for trouble. They were bullies and took great pleasure in goading the innocent holiday makers who were just wanting a good time. They would hang around in certain clubs, and while the foreign patrons ordered beer after beer, their bar tab would increase significantly. The price for a beer would increase without them knowing it.

When it came time for them to leave, the thugs would block the doorway, the only way out, and demand the payment. The drunk men, usually Brits or Australians, would refuse and try to barge their way out. It would get really messy; knives and pipes would appear as they were thrown down the stairs. The thugs would then attack them, eventually the police would appear and just make a nuisance of themselves. By that time the thugs had usually managed to disappear into the crowded streets looking for their next victim.

I won my next three fights by knockout. In fact, no one had even come close. The worst injury I had had at this point was a swollen nose, courtesy of Zobec. I was beginning to think that I have a rubber nose; it had been whacked so many times but never broken. I was now making good money, $1000 per fight; I was giving the crowd a good show.

Apparently, they ran the same sort of fights at the famous Lumpinee Stadium. These were run on the dark side in between the thai boxing nights. The two stadiums were attempting to get the top fighters from both stadiums to fight off for the 'King of Bangkok'. I was one of those fighters. They wanted two fighters from each stadium, the winners of the first round will then fight off against each other in a super bout. At first, I was not really keen on the idea. Lumpinee was a hot bed of betting and criminal activity.

But on the flipside, I could possibly retire from fighting if there was a large enough payout.

As usual, Lecky was against the idea, but she was always against me doing any fighting. She didn't talk about her family very often, but for some reason that night after a couple of drinks, she shared details about her younger brother who was sold to a thai boxing stable when he was ten years old He spent eight years training and fighting in horrific conditions in traditional thai boxing, or muay thai as it is called by the locals. Her family was so poor; not only was her younger brother sold but the younger sister was also sold as a prostitute to a club in Phuket when she was twelve. I could feel Lecky's pain as she broke down talking about it. Lecky left her home when she was thirteen and made her way to Bangkok to work as a prostitute. She used to send money to her parents, but once they found out that she was becoming a transsexual, they disowned her. Lecky always said she would try to make it better with her parents and intended to look after them as they got older.

Her younger brother became a heroin addict, and his life ended sadly one night in a back room of a Bangkok bar when he was found with a needle deep in his arm. It was obvious that she was still hurting and had suffered so much pain. Tears streamed down her face. "You make me so happy, Jack, I would hate it if something were to happen to you."

Over the months that I stayed in her apartment, we had become quite close. She still walked around with nothing on and tried to tempt me. She knew that there would never be anything sexual between us, but she was stunningly beautiful, body and soul, of which I reminded her over and over again. I also made sure that she got a huge pay packet from me once every two weeks.

I could feel that it would soon be time for me to move on. But first I needed to have two more fights. The first super fights were set. I would be fighting the tough and experienced Tony Bowman. He was from country New South Wales in Australia and had been living in Japan for many years. He flew over to Thailand to compete for the big money in Bangkok. He was two times world karate champion and had a record of twelve wins, twelve knockouts, two losses. He was a couple of years older than me but we were the same height and same weight. Tony and I were always friendly towards each other. He was a down to earth kind of guy and appreciated my no bullshit approach to martial arts. In the hard packed mud ring, we both agreed to not take it easy on each other. No quarter asked for and none given.

He was a typical brawler but had the finesse of a trained martial artist. Most of the fighters in this game were driven by fear, they had no strategy and just came out as fast as possible, brawling. Tony's only strategy it seemed was to brawl better than the brawlers. That could be a hard style to counter, especially against someone fit. Usually the brawler type fighter would punch and kick themselves to fatigue fairly quickly. All you had to do was wait them out and then unleash on them with an assault that they have never experienced before. The key here was to be superbly fit yourself.

It was the day of the super fights and the bookies were running hot. My odds were ten to one that I would win. Tony was the favourite simply by the fact that he had fought so many more fights than me. His odds were two to one.

I was quite relaxed, I always recall the words of my friend and first teacher Vic, he would say, breathe it in and breathe it out. Focus completely on the breath, just let the chatter of thoughts fade away as you become present here and now. I consider him my teacher so much more than any of the teachers I had at school. The biggest gift that he gave me was to be able to channel my emotions. The self-talk and emotional highs and lows in the lead up to the fight can sap your energy and cause you to crash out energy wise early in the fight.

———

On the day of the fight, I lazed around at the apartment most of the day, doing a light stretch and being rubbed down to keep all my muscles loose. I drank weak tea and water to stay hydrated. Lecky was out, I instructed her to put $1000 US on me to win the fight. It was a mark of how much I trusted her. I was also testing out the reliability of the book keepers, and planned to place a larger bet on my next fight. I also told her to cash in the betting slip as soon as the fight finished.

This was my first fight at Lumpinee Stadium. It was a vast step up in intensity from the smaller taekwondo stadium. The crowd was at least five times larger than the one I was used to.

I was at the edge of the ring, facing Tony. He would not hold my gaze, but that meant nothing. He wore a blue tradesman's singlet, his hands were taped and his mouthguard ready. He looked calm but I could smell his fear. I enjoyed the stillness just before a fight. The stillness was the mind. I had learned my lesson when I fought Zobec. I must be ready and focused the moment I stepped into the centre of the ring. I would always say a silent thank you to Vic, then I would go into myself, the mind was settled and calm, I was totally ready for any outcome.

The ring announcer made his introductions, the crowd was in a frenzy, jam packed to capacity. I heard nothing, all my focus was on Tony. The referees hand came down with a resounding "Fight!" at which Tony closed the gap immediately. We stood toe to toe for the best part of thirty seconds literally pounding the stuffing out of each other. We punched whatever we could lay our fists on including the neck and back of the head. All illegal shots but I did not care. We smiled at each other as we both knew we were committed to a lethal outcome.

I refused to take a step back, and launched a terrible elbow to Tony's forehead. The elbow opened up a deep gash. As soon as he went to wipe the blood away, he came at me with a sloppy back leg roundhouse kick, followed by a left right punch combination, I stood up straight and counter punched him with my hard right cross. I caught him off balance and he was down. I could hear the crowd; "Jack, Jack, Jack" they chanted. Tony immediately stood, and waited with his hands on his hips as the medic cleared him to continue.

He was in no rush to engage, I picked up on his hesitation, feinted with a low front kick and was close enough to him to do a jump spinning back kick. I landed the kick right on his rib cage. It was such a sweet kick. To his credit Tony remained standing, but he looked like he had had enough. But I was not finished, I blocked a couple of feeble kicks, switched my left leg from front to back, and brought down an axe kick from the heavens. It slammed him on the side of his head, he went all wobbly on his feet, stumbling over, hitting the mud ring where he remained. The centre referee stepped in and pushed me to the side. The medic was right there too. At last, Tony sat up. He was dazed and confused, and I would also say just a little concussed. The referee raised my hand, there was no doubt, I had won.

Tony was now sitting on a stool, and he looked alright. I went over to see him. "You okay?"

"What the heck hit me?" he mumbled.

I smiled. "Good fight, mate."

We shook hands and I left the ring. Luckily for me my odds on winning went to twenty to one, just before the fight. I guess a lot of people lost their money. There was a lot of pushing and shoving and I could feel the tension in the crowd, so I pulled my cap down and I got out of there as fast as I could.

I heard my name being called as I left the stadium. "Jack, Jack over here." Lecky was waiting in a tuk tuk. I climbed in and she placed a large bag on my lap and kissed me on the cheek. "Well done."

I made $20,000 dollars from the bet and $1000 from Shultz for winning the fight. All over in less than three minutes. Lecky and I set off in the tuk tuk towards home, where we had some champagne and beer on ice waiting for us.

After my fight, you would think that I would be happy. Well, yes for the first couple of minutes I was more relieved that I survived. The elation of winning was short lived. In fact, a certain darkness enveloped me. Not a depression, more a melancholy. I was quiet as I sat with this feeling.

"What's the matter?" asked Lecky.

"Oh, it's nothing, I'm just tired." But inside I was empty, the thrill of winning washed through me. This feeling was like ... This isn't my path. There is something else and it is close. Something far more important to me. All of this, the fights and winning is just a distraction. It's not the essence of who I am or what I stand for.

Being in touch with this feeling meant that I could see a path forward. The path was fraught with danger. It would take me to a place I had not known or had ignored for so long. It was the internal path, it would give me the liberation that I so desired. But I understood now that I could not 'desire' it; I must become it.

14
MONTIEN

Montien was no doubt the crowd favourite. He was a 190 cm giant who just obliterated anyone who stood in his way. He was a Thai national and also the Lumpinee street fighting champion, and he was fighting a tough Dutch fighter called Jacques, or Jacki as he preferred to be called. He was also a very experienced fighter. As I watched Montien cut Jacques down to size, clinically and professionally, knocking him out cold in less than two minutes, I had my first pangs of doubt and fear. "Jack, are you sure about this?" I asked myself, "Why don't you quit now? You have made enough money..."

My thoughts would just churn away, never ending. For a weaker person they made a lot of sense, but I knew better than to listen to them, you can't always believe what you are thinking is the best option.

Tony Bowman and I were becoming good friends. I really respected him as a fighter and a person. So I arranged a time to meet him for a quick coffee before he took off back to Japan.

"So what are your thoughts on Montien?" I asked.

"Well, his nickname is the baby face killer by the local media as he does not have the demeanour of a top fighter, but who would have known."

"One thing that I did notice was the number of foreigners compared to Thai boxers and other Thai fighters," I commented.

"Yeah, the Thai kickboxers are not so interested in the no rules fighting. I watched Montien devour his opponent at his last fight. Maybe we outsiders are just plain stupid. The money is good, though. I have been avoiding Montien for a while."

"I appreciate your honesty."

"But, if you want to continue to progress in this game you had better fight him sooner or later."

We both sat there as I pondered what he was saying.

"Look Jack, Montien has never gone the distance, he has a one hundred per cent knockout and win record. But I wonder how his fitness is in a longer fight? So my advice to you, Jack, and I am only sharing this with you as we are mates, is to just take his punishment for the majority of the fight and then when – or rather, if – you see him tire, take him out, kinda like Mohammad Ali and the rope-a-dope strategy he used in Zaire against the formidable and undefeated George Foreman."

"Well, that helps heaps, Tony."

"All the best." He got up to leave. "Remember Jack, he is only human and he bleeds like all of us."

———

I got a message through Lecky that Shultz wanted to meet me. He suggested 6 pm at the club the following evening. So I walked to the club and said Hi to Lecky who was in her familiar place on the counter. We smiled at each other and she extended a hand for me to touch as I entered the club.

In the corner in his usual position, I could see Shultz sitting with two other men. They were Thai nationals in smart designer suits. All three were smoking large cigars and the air was thick with the stench of smoke and perfume from the dancers. They were all looking for an edge to get some innocent tourist to pay the bar fine for the evening. Once paid, they were free for the night to do as they please.

Shultz stood as I approached the table. "Hello, Jack, please take a seat. I would like to introduce you to two of my associates." The men did not stand, they just waved a lazy hand in pseudo-recognition of me. That was their first mistake.

"Sit." The older of the two spoke. "Shultz works for us. So, in fact, do you. We are the ones that pick your fights and pay your money."

"Now," said the smaller of the two. "Remember when we first took you on and you attempted to negotiate your contract conditions, which we humbly accepted, there was one condition. We told Shultz to tell you that one day we might need a favour from you. Well, Jack, are you ready to do that favour?"

"It depends on what exactly it is."

"I am afraid that you have no choice, Jack. If you want to fight the great champion Montien then you will do as you are told." That was their second mistake, attempting to boss me around. I was not one of the bar girls, so I expected a certain amount of respect. "Sorry Jack, this is the way it has to be."

I glared at Shultz, and felt the twinges of my old faithful anger start to rise within me. *Settle down*, I said to myself. "What is it exactly that you want me to do?"

"We want you to lose the fight. It will be up to you how you do it, but you must not win. That shouldn't be so hard for you Jack, after all, Montien is the better fighter. The sooner you lose, the more money we will make."

I didn't agree with this, it was totally against everything that I stood for. But I didn't say anything, I didn't want to provoke them or give them an inkling as to what I thought about this. "Does Montien know about this fight fixing?"

"That is none of your concern, Jack," said the associate.

"Who are you men? Where do you come from?"

"We run the clubs and look after the gambling on these illegal events. We are just a cog in a very big wheel."

"Are you Mafia?"

"Yes and no, but our bosses are very well connected and want you to lose this fight. Do we have an agreement, Jack?"

Fuck, fuck, fuck! What am I going to do now?

"... I am talking to you... Jack! ... Well?"

"Okay." I pushed my chair back and walked out of the club. I went straight back to the apartment and waited for Lecky to come home.

When she finally walked in we sat down. Once I had explained everything to her, for some reason I felt better.

"Jack, there is something I need to tell you. I have not been entirely honest with you."

I don't think my day could be any worse, I thought.

Lecky went on to tell me that she had been giving updates about me to Shultz. She had told him everything. At first I was stunned, but soon realised, what did I expect? Was I going to just walk into these people's lives and become a part of them? I was feeling quite raw. I had been so engrossed with my own life. Other than giving Lecky money, had I ever really stopped and thought about anyone else? I knew Shultz was a slimy character who would cut my throat in an instant.

"I had no choice, Jack," she cried. "He said if I don't do this, he would throw me out of my job and apartment. I am so sorry Jack."

"No, it's me who should be apologising." I regained my composure. "I am so sorry for putting you in this position."

"It was Shultz that told me to keep walking around naked in

front of you. He really wanted you to be so busy with me that you would never notice that he was spying on you."

"Well, to be honest, you did a good job."

"It was not hard, Jack. I just wish that we were lovers."

"It is not that I am not attracted to you, because I really am," I conceded. "It's just that I am having trouble with your... manhood."

"But, Jack, so many straight men have enjoyed me, why can't you?" she pleaded. "I do love you, Jack."

"I love you too."

"But what are we going to do?"

"This will need some planning. Can you just keep telling Shultz that I am going to follow their plan? I promise that you will not get hurt. Can I trust you Lecky?"

———

The following morning, I was feeling far more positive.

"Here is what we are going to do. I am not going to take a dive. I never have and I never will. I don't care that I am double crossing Shultz and his bosses or partners or whatever they call themselves. They have chosen to ask the wrong man. The only way I am going to lose is if Montien beats me fairly. I will play along for a bit then I will knock him out in the latter half of the fight. I will rely on you to then cash in our bet with the bookie. You will then need to race to Lumpinee and, just like before, pick me up in a tuk tuk and we head to your place, pick up my gear and then I will go to the airport and get the late flight to Seoul. What do you think of my plan?" I asked. "If we do this right Lecky, I will be able to give you a lot of money. That way, if you have to leave Patpong you will have enough money to set up your own club anywhere."

Lecky sobbed. "So what does that mean, Jack, are you leaving for good?"

"Yes, it looks that way. I have had a dream for a long time, from a young age I have been fascinated by a so called secret martial arts school in Japan. And now I've done enough research and have the contacts to see if this place really exists. So I have to go, and now seems like as good a time as any."

"I will miss you, Jack, I don't want you to go. But I understand and I will help you. You can trust me, Jack, I will help you and look after you."

———

The night of the fight was here at last. I packed my bag and positioned it by the door. I counted all of my money, I gave Lecky every cent that I had, $50,000, and told her to bet on me no matter what the odds were. She knew the bookie and had used him many times. They were always good for the money as he was not run by the mafia. He told Lecky he was taking some huge bets, he had never seen this amount of interest before.

He had an office very close to Patpong Road. There was still two hours to go. The odds on me winning were a hundred to one, with Montien ten to one to win. If I won, I stood to make at least five hundred thousand US dollars. I quickly booked a one-way ticket on a flight to Korea. So my escape plan was set. All I needed now was for Lecky to keep her side of the deal. Would it all go smoothly? I doubted it, but all we can ever do is our best. I really had to focus on my fight.

I took a tuk tuk to Lumpinee stadium because they are fast and efficient; able to cut through the massive traffic jams on the Bangkok main roads and avoid the congestion.

When we arrived, there was a huge crowd waiting for a chance to place their bet and then grab a prime position in the stadium. So the tuk tuk immediately turned around and darted around the side to another entrance.

"Thank you," I said.

The driver recognised me and as we pulled up, turned to me with a wave, "No charge today, Big Jack. You a good man, I hope you win."

I was chuffed.

Everyone was excited about this super fight. I could see why the locals were looking at me to win. Montien was a rich pretty boy and had many sponsors and followers, he was on ads on TV as the nine times Thai heavyweight taekwondo champion and the gold medal winner in the Seoul Olympics in 1988. And he was tall and handsome; a real celebrity.

But I didn't care about any of that. He had been saying that he was going to wipe me off the face of the earth. And I had no power. When I heard that it was strike three to him. I was not going to take a dive and intentionally lose the fight. I slowly strolled through the smaller crowd at the side entrance. There were many pats on the back and well wishes. When I walked into the change room, all the fighters stood up and cheered and clapped. The chant "big Jack, big Jack" went up. I was so touched. Montien thought he was bigger than the people and chose to have his own personal dressing room.

I slipped down to my shorts, took off my shirt, and put in my mouthguard.

"Jack George you are up!" shouted the ringmaster.

I strolled out into the crowd. Some were chanting "Montien, Montien" but to my surprise there was also chant of "big Jack, big Jack". I stopped, held up my fist and smiled at the crowd. This was a once in a lifetime opportunity; to fight the best of the best. It would no doubt be one of the highlights of my martial arts career. As I was walking to the edge of the ring, I made a silent promise to never ever fight again and if I should make it to Japan, I would spend the rest of my days looking for the place where I can dedicate my life to learning about all aspects of body, mind and spirit. I bowed at the edge of the ring. The mud was already streaming with blood from the previous fights. I looked up and could see Thai politicians and high ranking police officers; they all looked like they were having a wow of a time. I should not have been surprised to see Shultz and his two so-called associates, sitting with the local members of government and the police chief. As I entered the ring, I thought of Vic, and what he would be saying to me now.

Deep breaths, son, feel the anger in the pit of your stomach, clench your fists and smash the bully in the face.

I was finally facing Montien. I bowed, he just smiled at me. He was a good 100 mm taller than me and boy, did he look fit! I was not scared, just a little nervous. I had never been knocked down by anyone except on the one occasion I was knocked down and winded by Kit, my younger brother. Strange that I was thinking of my brothers now. We had lost contact since I left to go on my quest and I made a mental note to look them up, just as the centre ringmaster dropped his hand and shouted "fight". I liked this ringmaster, he was fair. He was the ref at many of the top thai boxing fights and looked after the fighters the best he could. A Thai national, but we called him John.

Montien immediately launched a hard back leg kick to my stomach. It sent me flying into the crowd that were right up to the edge of the ring. I did not expect that, I thought I was out of range. Note to self – he has very long legs. I felt the sick feeling, no, it was a twinge that you feel when you almost had the air kicked out of you. Winded. I reckoned another couple of inches up and I would have been rolling around on the floor.

I could see that Montien was looking confident. That was just what I wanted, I launched two punches to his chest. I called them my chest crusher. A very experienced taekwondo fighter from Sydney by the name of Gil Hinchley used to rock me with his heart punches. One day he even put the tough goju karate fighter Dimitri Toposckvi in hospital with a very hard punch to his heart.

Montien sank back and did not look very happy. That was a great shot and my power – which he thought I didn't have –

knocked the stuffing out of him. I had a thought, it was about now that I was supposed to lose. Well, I had news for them, their boy had better find a way to take me out or I was going to win. Montien came in again with his roundhouse attack, I could see and feel that he was starting to tire, I blocked the kicks with my elbows so he would not be so inclined to want to kick me again. I pushed him really hard into the crowd. He rolled about in the front rows and looked quite scared as I waited for him in the ring.

I feinted with a right kick and saw him flinch backwards and pull away. Now I had him, I kicked him with a long sweeping roundhouse kick that gained power and speed as it found its mark, landing hard on his left thigh. He dropped to one knee, I stepped in close and was about to finish him off with a couple of uppercut punches when John stepped between us and allowed Montien to stand.

I knew this fight was deadly serious when John whispered to me, "Take the dive, Jack."

Montien stood up, much to my surprise he was actually moving pretty well. This was not over, next time I would make sure to break his leg. He was showing why he was the champion and I had a real fight on my hands. I chanced a look up at the scorekeeper's video screen; my odds on winning had just changed to 10–1.

He recovered quickly and came at me again with his front leg roundhouse kick to a right back leg kick, both to my stomach. The second kick caught me flush and down I went. This is where Montien could have easily finished me, as I was going down my head was wide open, he had a clean shot with a knee. He hesitated, then I could not believe it, he stepped back giving me space. There I was, struggling to breathe, I was aware of the centre referee counting me out. I was also aware that now, many people would be changing my odds on winning. I timed my stand up perfectly, standing on the count of nine. Now I could say that was part of the plan, but it wasn't. I felt raw and on the verge of losing everything I had.

I could hear Vic shouting at me, *Jack, one step forward!* So I took one step and quickly got my bounce back. I knew what I had to do, so I made him chase me around the ring for the next five minutes. I was recovering at the same time. At last he was tiring and I timed a perfect kick to the right side of his head. This time he dropped and lay there. I did not hold back, there was no standing back up after that kick.

"No one bullies me," I said.

He had no intention of getting up. John and the doctor rushed in. He eventually sat up but could not stand. Though my arm was raised as the winner, I deeply respected Montien, he was strategic and very tough. He let me off and gave me a chance when he knocked me down. He knew in his heart that John had rescued him just before I was about to pepper him with uppercuts. He almost beat me. Who knows what deal Shultz and his cronies offered him. I knew one thing for certain, though this was a very tough fight, as tough as it was, no amount of fitness and fighting would prepare me for what I would encounter in South Korea.

I rushed into the change room, grabbed my stuff and made my way out of the front of the stadium. The crowd was beside themselves and lucky for me the attention of everyone was on the brawl erupting in the stadium. They did not notice my fast exit, so far so good. I finally saw Lecky pull up on the other side of the road. I also saw a large black Mercedes pull out from the curb and slowly move towards us. I jumped into the tuk tuk as I put my cap and sunglasses on in an attempt to hide who I was, and we were off.

As we took off, the Mercedes was waiting to turn around. Now was our chance to lose them. I sat back in the seat and Lecky passed me a small towel. I wiped myself down and asked, "How did we do?"

"All good, Jack, you are now a rich man."

I held her hand and told her how the fight went. She laughed when I told her about the chest crushers. We arrived at her apartment, I jumped out and ran up the stairs, changed into a pair of jeans, a t-shirt, a pair of trainers, pulled my cap back on, grabbed my large rucksack which was almost empty and made my way back to the tuk tuk.

Lecky was sitting patiently, almost too quiet. I was a little hyper as I scanned around for anyone that might be following us. It was quiet, more so than I expected. I was sure we were not being followed, which I thought was really strange.

We raced to the airport. I don't know what Lecky said to the driver, but he was a man on a mission to get us there as soon as possible. We pulled up to the departures and got out. It was then that I saw four nasty looking men get out of a black Mercedes and started running towards us.

"Quick, let's go!" But there was another problem. *This is no good,* I thought. There were what looked like armed security guards and plain clothed police. "Which way, Lecky?"

"I'm so sorry," she cried. "The mafia got to me, and I gave in. So I informed the immigration and police who then told Interpol, in the hope that the mafia would not get you."

I was shattered at the breakdown of trust. "Okay, okay, I get it." I now figured that my best bet was with the police, as the mafia would mean certain pain and a slow death.

We walked towards the police. "Are you Jack George?"

"Yes." I was led away into the airport. The mafia retreated into the crowd of onlookers. I knew they were not done with me yet. Lecky walked beside me speaking in Thai to the security police. As we walked towards their office, people made way for us and clapped and shouted, "Big Jack". I was moved. I did not realise that the super fight had been televised on local TV and Bangkok had literally stopped and watched it.

We made it to the police office. I must say they all looked very friendly and polite. A clean-cut man in a nice suit was obviously the boss. "Mr Jack George?" he asked.

"Yes."

"I am Superintendent Saengkaew, from the Metropolitan Police department, how do you do?"

"Well, considering the circumstances, I have been better."

"Jack—" he paused. "May I call you Jack?"

I nodded.

"You are quite a celebrity, and from what I have seen of you so far you have been a great source of inspiration to the Thai people. My only problem with you is your association with a Mr Shultz, the mafia and illegal betting boss. I learned today that Interpol has been watching you for a while and have been monitoring airports waiting for you to appear. But, they work on capturing international criminals. So they would not know about what you have been up to here in Thailand unless we tell them. As part of my job, I had to inform Interpol of your capture here in Bangkok today, and I am sorry to inform you that they are now on their way here. If we are lucky, your flight will depart before they get here." He smiled. "Oh, well. Where are you intending to fly to this evening, Jack?"

"I am planning on going to Seoul."

"Well, Jack, what should we do?" The superintendent spoke rapidly in Thai to Lecky then said, "Everybody out." The office quickly emptied. "I have decided that for this to all go away and for you to have protection from us right up to your flight it will cost you $1000 US. You can thank your associate Miss Lecky for this as it was because of her that we could organise your safe capture and then release. Are we in agreement?"

"Yes." Wow, what just happened? I relaxed my shoulders and thought, *It is almost over. I will soon be free and flying out of here.* "That will be perfect," I said, with a huge smile.

Lecky had already put the money into a carry bag, which she

handed to the police officer. She had also taken her share, then placed the balance into the rucksack.

"Now have a seat and let's talk about your fight. I had a bet on you, Jack, and you won, so I too made a small fortune."

————

It was time to leave. I held Lecky in my arms, she was being stoic. "I love you Jack and everything that I have done has been for you. Now go on your journey, I will be fine, thanks to you. I am not sure where I will go, but you will always be in my heart, Jack George." She kissed me on the cheek, turned and left with $100,000 US.

Wow, what a rush that was, I thought, as walked through immigration and customs like royalty. I boarded the A300 aircraft expecting to turn right at the door and head to cattle class. But the chief steward motioned to the left. "No, Mr George, you are in seat 1A in first class."

Superintendent Saengkaew took me right up to my seat and looked at me kindly. "You should be safe now, Jack. It has been a pleasure, and I wish you all the best." He hopped off just as the front door closed.

I was handed a glass of champagne as I relaxed back into my seat. *Now, where was I?*

————

I now had some space to think and reflect on the thoughts I had as I entered the ring earlier that evening. I missed my brothers and sisters. I had not been a good brother. I was very close to my brothers and sisters up until the time that I left to go overseas. My younger brother Kit is only twelve months younger than me. We trained in taekwondo together and we sparred a lot. It was often a ferocious stalemate because we knew so much about each other's styles, we would always work on developing strategies that could counter the moves.

I remembered the time we were sparring one afternoon when I tagged him, knocking part of his front tooth out. He did not like that at all. It became very serious very quickly. He started launching bombs into me, and boy, were they powerful! He peppered me with techniques when suddenly he spun on the spot kicking me so cleanly with a shot to my stomach. That was it, it flattened me. I was on my back, trying to get air for at least ten minutes. I developed a deep respect for Kit's power after that.

Up until Montien, that is the one and only time I had been knocked off my feet.

15
SEOUL

I arrived at Incheon International airport. It is not a big airport, and I was surprised by the number of Russians there, arriving on an Aeroflot flight from Moscow. Aeroflot has one of the worst safety records in the history of aviation. The inside of the airport is dark and drab, kinda like how I would expect North Korea, or Moscow, to look and feel.

I did not attract any extra attention, and headed straight through immigration. Stamp, stamp, and that was it.

There is a distinct psyche of the Korean people. They appear highly strung and under stress. I put this down to the fact that they are theoretically still at war. After three years of war, North and South Korea signed an armistice agreement in 1953. So the war has not officially ended. They stand ready at opposite ends of the demilitarised zone between North and South in a ridiculous stand-off. As far as the people are concerned, it is a powder keg ready to ignite at the slightest provocation from either side.

I did have a feeling of impending doom, a kind of sickly feeling in my stomach. I was now turning myself over to people to look after me, I really had no idea what I was in for. Hardly anyone knew where I was. My ex-girlfriend in Singapore, Margaret knew some of the details but all she knew was I was attending Yudo College for two weeks.

Yudo College is in the mountains about ninety minutes west of Seoul. I was introduced to the Professor of the college, Professor Lee, by my taekwondo teacher in Sydney, Master Kwon. He used to run the Taiwan Taekwondo Academy before migrating to Australia. I met another Australian taekwondo teacher just by chance one day, named Master Soh. Soh was a cantankerous man and not well liked, but I liked him well enough as he had always helped me out.

Master Soh introduced me to Master Kwon just after he had arrived from Taiwan. My taekwondo was pretty good, but Master Kwon used to say to me, "You will never fear a kick again after spending two weeks at Yudo College." I used to ask him about hokuto ryu, he said I might be able to find it after visiting Korea. Professor Lee knew these kinds of things, so going to Yudo College seemed like the obvious next choice.

"Shoulders back, chin up." I walked out through the carousels, past the customs officers and ready to meet my pickup. I saw my name – spelt JACK GEOLGE – written on a small piece of cardboard. I had a giggle inside. The Ls and Rs are hard to pronounce in Korean. I walked towards him, waved and smiled.

He was very friendly, as he enthusiastically shook my hand and took my bag, grabbing it off me. "I am Kim."

"I am Jack." And that was the end of the conversation. Kim is a very common surname in Korea. Kind of the same as Smith in English.

We walked up the stairs to Kim's car, a Jeep copy. The Koreans call them Korondo, they look like a cross between a Humvee and a Landcruiser. Once we got onto the freeway, I understood why Kim needed such a sturdy vehicle, the driving was complete madness. It reminded me of a smash up derby where driving was a matter of life and death.

There was no slowing down to pay the tolls so you had to time it right and throw the toll fee into the basket and hope for the best. Once we cleared the toll booths and headed out of the city to the countryside, I could remove my white knuckles from either side of the seat.

"How long?" I asked.

He got what I was asking and held up his index finger and his thumb to signal two hours.

We finally arrived. Yudo College consisted of a large, single dormitory and a hall for training, the size of a double basketball stadium. It was a prominent feature built into the mountainside. Beside the dormitory was a sealed road that disappeared up into the mountain. This road was used every morning to do all kinds of conditioning training. Kim dropped me off at the dormitory entrance.

Oh my God, what am I expected to do now? Where was I supposed to go? One thing that I had learned throughout all of the challenges on my travels, was that things were never as bad as they seemed. As soon as I walked inside, placed my bags down and was about to sit on the sofa, a student who appeared to be couple of years younger than me approached.

"Jack George? Come." He pointed.

To this day I still do not know this young man's name. I asked him all the time, but it was either the way he said it or the speed at which he said it, but I just did not get it.

He took me into a very small room that had four bunk beds. I grabbed the top bunk and realised straight away that I was too big for it. Oh well, it had to do.

From the very first day it was survival of the fittest. At 6 am the next morning, the captain of the team took me off to the side and thrashed me for sixty minutes. It was all a blur and I could not believe how nasty he was. He beat me with such delight, he hit me, he spat on me and the other Korean fighters laughed as they ran past me. I heaved up the fruit that I had shovelled down at 5.30 am just before training started. It was tough and I will never forget it for as long as I live.

I heard that Kim, the captain of the team, and several others were in the special forces during their national service, which all young Korean men must complete. It was no wonder that he pushed me so hard. But I did it, I survived. There was no way that I was going to let this bully break me. The longer it went on, the more stubborn and determined I became.

I was learning that I had something special. I had a real tolerance to endure. This quality would come back to help me time and time again.

The following day I was with the rest of the students on the road up to the top of the mountain. The training was a combination of running, sprinting, piggy backs, bunny hops and light sparring, all on the road heading up the mountain. I seemed to always end up with the giant that no one wanted to partner with.

The intensity is nowhere near as tough as the day before, I was thinking as we picked up the pace again to a sprint, and up came my fruit ... again.

After the morning run up and down the mountain, we stopped at 8 am for breakfast. This slop became my biggest daily challenge. Soup, rice, pickles and a big bowl of kimchi. Kimchi is pickled cabbage, with loads of garlic and chilli. We had this for breakfast, lunch and dinner.

After breakfast, I asked my nameless guide, "Where's the washing done?"

"Oh." He motioned me to follow him. He took me downstairs through a set of double doors, into a large room with tubs and cold-water taps. He left me down there and I did my best to scrub the clothes clean, or at least take the edge off the pungent smell of fighting men. I was careful not to clean my fighting gear too much as I knew the Koreans did not like the smell of me.

At 10 am after breakfast was finished, and the laundry done, everyone gathered in the main hall. I trained mostly with the taekwondo team and a little with the judo team. I didn't do so much judo because of the rate of injury, particularly knee injuries. I saw too many students limping around with knee braces on. The next ninety minutes was pad drills and partner drills. I really enjoyed this training, it was quite technical, and I really improved my foot work.

I could not help looking at the old photos on the wall of what appeared to be people doing moves that resembled what I thought hokuto ryu might look like. I asked a couple of my fellow students, and as I expected, they just grunted and turned away. I made a note to ask Professor Lee about these photos.

After the ninety-minute pad session, we had some free time. I rested in the small room, read a little and dozed a lot. I took this time to write in my journal. It was always peaceful as this was the time when all of the fighters took their academic lessons.

Lunch was 11.30 to noon, and – yep, you guessed it – the same dish of kimchi, rice and pickles.

The 2 pm session was the session that I had been dreading; the fighting session. I may have had size on these fighters – I am 183 cm and weighed 90 kg – but they were fast and vicious. I was just a big white whale that they intended to use for target practise.

In the first session, they hit me at will. They launched into me with pinpoint accuracy and hurt me. Every time they hit me they screamed out with sheer delight. But I was not going down. I was determined to weather this storm. And every one of the fighters that hurt me, I made a mental note that they would never hit me again and I would get my payback before I left.

I certainly found my match in the free fighting. They all came after me, slamming kicks into my body, arms and legs. Lucky I was bigger than most of them so I could weather the onslaught, keeping an eye out and watching for when Master Ko, the head coach, was at the other end of the hall. I would seize the opportunity to get some payback. I would grab my opponent and heave him onto my knees, driving them deep into them and punching them as hard as I could in the face. It was akin to street fighting, but these feisty fighters needed to get into their minds that I did not care and I was just as dangerous as they were. They would scream at me and would give me the death stare.

Make no mistake about it, this was survival.

———

There are many churches and Christianity is quite common, but the Koreans appeared to just give it lip service, as cultivating peace was not high on their agenda. It was easy to see how popular Christianity was, at night there were so many red crosses of the churches illuminated. But I was more interested in the Buddhist and Taoist philosophies.

The training, and what appeared to be just about everything else at Yudo College, was run by the senior students of judo and taekwondo. They bullied me continually.

I am quite surprised by the bullying as I am twice the size of most of the fighters here, I wrote in my journal.

The captain, Kim, was always the instigator of trouble. He yelled at me constantly. Lucky for me I had no idea what he was saying, I kind of figured that so many of this fighting team were just out of the army, and this was the only way they knew how to treat people.

I was not entirely ready for this. I thought I had left this kind of behaviour when I was in school. This was not what I expected. Such an institution as this should be disciplined and control the bullying. But the proof of Yudo College's methods was seen in the amount of competitions they won and the number of international fighters that trained there. So they just keep on doing what they were doing, and the funding kept rolling in.

Fortunately, even the little amount of meditation and mindfulness I had done up until now safeguarded me by keeping me present and not reactive to his brutal onslaught. I thought I may find some solace here in Korea, but boy, was I mistaken. I made a mental note to myself to dig deeper into the meditative aspects of martial arts.

"You cannot hurt me," I said to myself and repeated it like a mantra. Over and over again. I was on a mission to survive and a punk like Mr Kim was not going to stop me.

Yudo College was like the last frontier in itself. An old school establishment. Only the most experienced and hardened students attended. The minimum time for the students is four years. They did a sports science degree majoring in taekwondo or judo.

Many fighters would visit the college from Hong Kong, the USA and other countries. They were not as nasty as me. The Koreans learned that it was best to leave me alone, but they wasted no time hammering any other overseas fighters.

On their first time in the 2 pm fighting class, there were fighters from the USA, Hong Kong ... and me. After about thirty seconds of fighting, all the Hong Kong and USA fighters had been knocked to the ground.

The head coach of the USA team was a man named Billy Joe. Billy was still young enough to fight. "I can't wait to take them on."

"I would not be in such a rush, Billy. There are some formidable fighters here," I said, with a sense of trepidation.

He was from the deep south and had an admirable drawl. "I see they ignore you."

"Yep, just the way I like it." The Koreans knew better than to try it on me. But I knew that it was not over with me yet, I had a real beating coming my way. In nearly two weeks I had not been knocked down.

The next morning, I saw the aftermath of the teams from the USA and Hong Kong. All of the USA team, including Billy Joe were in various stages of being knocked down, knocked out or were limping back to their dorm rooms. Just as I thought. There was too much ego and attitude about them. I had a little giggle at their expense.

Billy Joe could not look me in the eye, but he was a nice enough guy and was humbled by the skills of the Korean team, saying, "I am too old for this, I think I will stick to coaching."

Good idea, I thought.

The captain of the Korean judo team was not your usual shaped Korean; short with the most incredibly powerful legs. Mr Kim was tall with long legs and was incredibly fast. In his broken English, he would walk up behind me and sit so close that I could smell the pungent kimchi on his breath. He would lean in and whisper in my ear. "You will soon be going down," he promised. I was not scared, I was fit and strong after the two weeks of training. The taekwondo team would go on these incredible mountain runs and I would win them, causing even more determination by Mr Kim and his team of fighters. There is no doubt in my mind that the Korean taekwondo fighters are some of the toughest fighters alive, I only stayed for two weeks but that was enough.

Master Ko was a tough brutal man who hid his anger by smiling. He took great pleasure in striking me with his thick bamboo cane. It hurt like hell.

I was often the last one to leave the training hall as the sweeping and mopping was left to me.

———

One day, it appeared that I was in luck. Master Ko walked up to me and asked in broken English, "Why you come here?"

This really surprised me as no one had spoken to me in nearly two weeks. From what I could make out, he used to be an enforcer for the Korean mafia and took great delight in showing me his knife wounds. I quickly took the opportunity to ask about the old photos on the wall.

Ko said he didn't know. Apparently, Professor Lee used to teach a hybrid form of martial arts called hapkido. It used to be quite popular at Yudo College, but once the focus came onto free fighting, the hapkido slowly lost its appeal and eventually shut down.

"Where did Master Lee learn hapkido?" It was only then that I realised that I was pushing my luck.

Ko was a giant of a man, and his big froglike head suddenly got very angry. He stood over me demanding that I now fight him. Not being one to shy away from a chance to test my technique, I did think about the likely result of fighting him and decided that I did not want to be Ko's punching bag.

I stood and said no thank you and rushed back to the safety of my dorm.

I now knew that I needed to meet with Professor Lee. All I needed to do was survive the last fighting session the next afternoon.

———

I entered the grand hall for the last time. I was wearing my taekwondo uniform and my trusty black belt as a good luck charm. I decided to only wear my mouthguard and leave off all the other pads including the head gear. It was all in for me and by not wearing any pads they would feel my bone crushing kicks and punches. The entire team was there, I counted forty of their best fighters. I had been there for two weeks now, and they had never knocked me down, and they wanted to so badly.

From the very beginning, Mr Kim was beside the Korean fighter screaming at him to take me down. But I was having none of it. Out of the corner of my eye, I spotted Master Ko who seemed to be quite entertained by the whole affair. I was on my fifth fighter who came at me hard, I felt his front kick, reverse punch combination that struck me around my liver.

I felt sick momentarily, and thought I was going to pass out. If he knew how much I was hurting, he could have easily taken me out. I just didn't show that I was hurt, he never knew. I quickly recovered, faked with a front kick to his groin and brought my signature roundhouse kick up hard to his temple, knocking him out.

Mr Kim was furious. This is how it went on for the next ten rounds. I thumped them in the thighs and took away their mobility, whenever I could, I would drop them with a groin shot.

Master Ko was getting impatient and called time. I did not dare drink any of the water, so I just had to suck it up. I was up to the last fight. Each fighter that I faced was fresh as they were only there to fight me and not each other. I had seen this last fighter during the daily fighting sessions. His name was Choi and he was tall and very sharp.

Choi moved towards me and faked with a punch to my head, a classic move and I fell for it, for an instant I went to block his punch, at the same time he spun very quickly and planted a reverse side kick to my stomach.

Oh, no, I thought as I dropped to one knee. I quickly stood, but I was breathless and in pain. As I stood, he quickly closed the gap and he kicked me in the head under my left eye, I was seeing double and swimming in a world of pain. Luckily, he did not break the skin, or knock me out. Kim was screaming at Choi to finish me off, I managed to stand and block whatever came at me.

The bell sounded the end of the round, and I had made it. I had survived and fought with courage. I took whatever they had for me. I must say that this had been a test of willpower, more than anything else. I attended every session including all of the morning sessions. Would I do it again? No way. I found the entire experience took me to my absolute limit.

16

KANG

I was all packed and due to be picked up and taken to Seoul for the night. The next morning, I arranged to have breakfast with Professor Lee and hoped to get some answers about the old photos on the walls of the gym. I had no idea where I was going, I only knew that I was being picked up at 5 pm from Yudo College and getting dropped in Seoul, and my flight left Incheon International airport in two days at 11 am.

The car arrived to pick me up and three men got out of the car to greet me. I had not met these men before, yet they greeted me like I was a long-lost brother. All of the taekwondo and judo fighters came out to see me off. I was surprised. No matter how hard we fought, I actually think that in the end they respected me, but were happy to see me go. I left quite an impression and there were a few fighters nursing sore heads.

Again, it appeared that there were no road rules. This guy was driving like a mad man. He reminded me of my father; aggressive with no tolerance for anyone that got in his way.

The other two men were in their mid-twenties, wearing flared jeans and colourful silk shirts. They both smoked continuously, which really annoyed me.

"Where you from?" the taller of the two asked.

"Australia."

He just snorted back at me.

We pulled up outside what appeared to be a gym and walked up the stairs to the reception. We continued through the weights area and out the back into a room that resembled a spare room. No windows, just a locked doorway. One of the men in the colourful shirts knocked, then opened the door. Inside was blaring music, girls dancing and an incredible array of bottles of alcohol from all over the world. It was not what I was expecting. There was an older man sitting at the front of the room on what appeared to be an elevated platform. I noted that all the men had the strangest haircuts, their hair was black and straight, cut like a women's bob style.

The man on the platform motioned me to come forward. "How do you do?" His English was passable. "My name is Kang, and this building is mine. I hear you are a great fighter. I need people like you to help me run my business. Those men that picked you up also work for me. They are graduates of Yudo College and are also great fighters."

What have I got myself into, I thought.

Without a word, Kang stood and took a step towards me. I could see he was muscular and had the confidence of a man who could look after himself. "I have booked a suite for you at the Swiss Grand hotel. It is like a resort. I am paying for you, so enjoy your time there in the spa and sauna. I would like you to come and work for me, Jack." He took my hand and I instantly trusted him. "You can make some good money, at the same time, live the high life. But take your time, no rush, have a think about it. I will see you in two days."

"I am leaving in two days."

"I have cancelled your flight. Just rest and enjoy yourself at the lovely Swiss Grand hotel. There are plenty of flights, so it is no problem to rebook in a couple of days."

Two young women appeared and each took his arm. Korean women fascinate me and these two did not disappoint. The Koreans are quite unique. Not as rough as the Chinese. These two were obviously working girls but they were more than just escorts.

I wondered who this man was. He did not appear cruel, he was more like a father figure. Then it clicked. *He's a godfather.* I would learn later that he also graduated from Yudo College as a champion and worked his way up the ranks of the Yangruni family earning his place in Seoul as Geondal, or godfather.

He motioned towards the men who had brought me there and barked something in Korean. The men and I left, walking a short distance to a Korean BBQ Restaurant. The BBQ is quite unique and a Korean specialty. Each table had a small BBQ and we cooked our own meat.

I spent the rest of the night eating the delicious BBQ with hot chilli sauce, the Bulgogi with a different kind of chilli sauce and the traditional Beebimbop and even the fried chicken, were exquisite. After two weeks of rice and kimchi, I was so ready for something tasty. It was all washed down by bottles of OB Blue, the local beer.

I do not know what time we left the restaurant, I was quite drunk. But the night was still young. We had picked up a number of extra people along the way to wherever we were going, everyone was having a great time.

The two beauties who had accompanied Mr Kang were with us now and were giving me a lot of attention. I could feel their hands wandering. Before I knew it I was in the back seat of the car with one of them, and the party was just beginning.

———

I woke up in a very classy hotel suite, it was way beyond my budget. Oh, my head hurt, and I did not remember how I got there.

The phone blasted to life. It was Professor Lee. "Hello Jack, I am waiting downstairs."

"Oh, I am so sorry, I overslept. I will just be a couple of minutes."

My rucksack was placed neatly on a luggage holder. I felt all of the bumps and bruises from the last fighting session, and my thumping headache from the beer and whisky which I guzzled last night. The last thing I remember is a whisky bottle going to my mouth, before passing out. I am not a party boy. I do not touch any drugs and my priority is living a healthy lifestyle. But I was now wondering why and how I ended up so messy last night and this morning. I was celebrating the end of my internment at Yudo College and just let my hair down. At least that is what I told myself.

It was good to see Professor Lee. I rushed towards him. "Good morning."

"Good morning, Jack." I could tell that he knew exactly what I had been up to. "Please take a seat." We both sat and he ordered coffee. "How was your time at Yudo College?" He was being a little cagey.

"It was tough, but I survived," I grumbled as I emptied a glass of iced water. "I saw some old photos on the wall in the training hall."

"Oh, yes, the good old days. In my prime I used to teach the art of hapkido there but when the World Taekwondo Federation was forcing all martial arts to become members, all the top hapkido and taekwondo schools and masters fled overseas, or stopped teaching all together, like I did."

"I am trying to find a school called Hokuto ryu. But I am not having much luck."

"Well," he paused, "you first need to find the ancient art of daito ryu. I trained for a while in daito ryu in America and Japan. I then went on to develop hapkido – which is an interpretation of taekwondo and daito ryu. Once you find the daito ryu, someone will be able to guide you to the hokuto ryu. But you do realise that the hokuto ryu is just a myth, so it could all be a terrible waste of time for you."

Professor Lee gave me the contact details of a couple of hapkido masters who remained in Seoul and suggested I visit the Kukkiwon, the World Taekwondo Headquarters.

I decided to stay a couple more days in Seoul to check out the schools that Professor Lee recommended and see if I could find out more information about the history of taekwondo, hapkido.

I was also keen to look at some of the newer martial arts that were popping up. One school was kyeok to ki. I ventured to their headquarters in hope of interviewing the founder and chief instructor Master Han. I understood that he could speak English, so a daytime interview and photo session worked out well. We talked a lot about the current monopoly of the World Taekwondo Federation (WTF). He was a member of the WTF and sent fighters to the various taekwondo competitions.

He told me that he also paid quite an expensive yearly stipend to be part of the neighbourhood business group. I assumed that meant a payment to the local mafia group to leave them alone. He did not bad mouth the WTF in any way, rather saying it was progress. Master Han's core movement and technique was very much like the taekwondo that I originally learned back in Sydney. There was also quite a strong kickboxing influence.

I did not have the time to ask him about his ground work and throwing component. When I took the photos, he moved with a smoothness of an expert.

He had an axe kick very much like my own. It was a classic WTF axe kick. He suggested I come back that night and take part in a class. I went back to the hotel and started to write up an introduction for an article that I would post to Kelvin.

I packed my uniform into my rucksack and headed back to the Master Han's dojang. As I arrived, I was almost knocked over by the stream of children running down the stairs. I bowed and found my way to the change room. I loved pioneering these new connections. I had read stories of western explorers that had gone deep into the Amazon and had found tribes that had never seen a white man. I felt like one of those explorers, though not quite as drastic.

I was venturing into new places never experienced by a westerner before. I was a bit of a celebrity, or – I should say – a novelty. My class mainly made up of young men had an exciting vibe about it. I was sent to the corner where I was shown their basic blocks and basic striking. It was interesting as their variations were quite unique. I did manage to see their ground work and throwing. It was very similar to judo.

For the most part I just observed the class. I appreciated the respect and etiquette that was very much a part of the class. It is usually the first thing to go when people start their own system. Once the class was over all the students and instructors lined up for some photos. I was quite surprised to see some of the old cronies appear. They sat on both sides of me and looked to be enjoying themselves. It is funny how the mafia affect every aspect of business in Asia and seem to be involved in as much as they choose.

That was a nice experience. Master Han looked genuinely happy. Why wouldn't he? By having me interview him he would be appearing in an Australian martial arts magazine, and possibly in the States as well.

While I was in the mood for finding new dojangs, I took a few days to explore before I considered working for Mr Kang. Besides, it would be good to get an idea of the current state of martial arts in Korea. So, I headed on the subway to the second place that Professor Lee had recommended. It was not far from the station and the maps were quite good. I arrived at what looked like a martial arts school gone terribly wrong. They called themselves the World Cultural Headquarters of Hapkido Dance. They were surely not serious! This had to be some kind of joke. In the window they had videos streaming of their moves. How far martial arts has fallen; there were men and women doing a cross between ballroom dancing and what I can only figure out were some kind of hapkido moves. On the poster in the window, it was advertising that they had affiliates in countries all over the world. There was even a world championship scheduled. I had seen enough.

Professor Lee, whom I respected very much, must have had a giggle knowing the effect this would have had on me. What was I to expect? It was easy to see that this hybrid monstrosity was no threat to the WTF power mongers. I wrote a short paragraph and sent it to Kelvin, hoping he found it as amusing as I did.

One last stop before I started my work was the famous Kukkiwon, the world headquarters of the WTF. It is a fine-looking structure, situated in lovely gardens and visible from a long way out. I entered the main building and all I could see was one large stadium. That's all there was. I walked outside around the stadium until I came to an office area. I peeked inside and saw a name plaque on the door. It was the office of international affairs. And beside the door was a pile of WTF belt certificates that went from the floor to the ceiling. There would have been thousands of them. I was simply astonished. For me that marked the end of taekwondo.

Taekwondo is now recognised as an Olympic sport and has gone the way that judo has gone. Void of any martial application, totally a sport. I left there knowing I was done with taekwondo. It no longer existed here in Korea as a martial art. I felt the strong urge even more to find the last bastion of martial arts. I knew I was not going to find it here in Korea.

———

That afternoon I took a walk up the steep mountain behind the hotel. The track was not well marked so I was careful with my footing. I was thinking about whether to work for Mr Kang. I gave up making decisions based on logic and trying to think my way through things years ago. What I do is, I find a quiet place, sit and be still. I let go and allow my inner experience to come forward. I then feel in my heart what is right; sitting on this track was perfect. I was away from the humdrum of the city and the mass of people.

I sat, closed my eyes, and allowed the breath to become my focus. Whenever I would start thinking, I would simply go back to the breath. The trees and the breeze worked in unison. It was like the branches would only bend so much and the breeze would only blow so hard. And I was part of that process. I let go and just felt.

I knew that I was walking a narrow line and this kind of work was not good spiritually. Eventually I would have to hurt someone at some time. If I decided to take the job, I would make it very clear to Mr Kang that I am a mediator and not a thug. I learned how to talk to people all those years ago as a bouncer in Sydney. I would also make it clear to him that I have no interest in drugs. I also knew that I was guilty by association with the Korean Mob. The fact that I was now on Interpol's radar was all new to me. I had to tread carefully, watch my back and know when it was time to move on.

———

From where he was sitting, he could get a view of the entire room. Up on his pedestal, Mr Kang looked like a king. He spotted me as soon as I walked in and he looked genuinely pleased to see me. "Jack, thank you for coming back. Please come into my office."

He motioned me to follow him as he stepped down and headed down the hallway and through a large timber door. I was entering into a whole new world, but I was still not sure. After my experience with Shultz in Bangkok, I was a little cautious of what could potentially be the world of the Korean mafia. Being there was kinda like biting on a sore tooth. I knew the pain that this could inflict on me, but I continued to move towards it as the pleasure might just outweigh the pain.

The job was simple enough. Mr Kang was the boss of a small area that included Itaewon, the tourist area. He extorted a monthly stipend from the shop owners in that area. There were quite a few English speakers that traded on the streets. He charged them to run their small pop-up shops. He called it a lifestyle payment, but from what I can see it is plain protection money, money to keep the peace from rival gangs. Mr Kang collected the money then gave the local police a cut, so everyone was happy.

There were often disputes between the traders, and sometimes the foreign shop owners needed to be reminded that this payment is not a choice.

"It would really help to have someone that speaks English, hopefully violence then would not become the first choice." Mr Kang passed me a fat envelope full of American dollars.

I guess I had now made up my mind.

He said he would also pay for my hotel. "You will be picked up at 9 am each morning from the Swiss Grand."

I took the subway from the club back to the hotel, a little chuffed but also somewhat nervous. Taking the subway was a good lesson into the mindset of the Korean salary man, or office worker. Forget about lining up and politely entering the train, it was a free for all, people coming from everywhere and pushing and shoving for the best seat. If you did not push yourself, you ended up back on the platform. The thing was that no one was getting angry or impatient. For them it was just as it is and as it has always been — normal.

———

At 9 am I was waiting patiently at the entrance for my lift to arrive. My lift was a nondescript black Kia with blacked-out windows. The man who was driving did not talk to me, he just grumbled at the traffic. Dressed in a grey suit he looked quite smart compared to me in my jeans and polo shirt, I had the feeling that we were heading to a suit shop. I recall Mr Kang asking me if I liked wearing suits.

A quick trip to the suit shop in Itaewon and I had three new suits, one of which I was wearing. The elderly man that served me refused to take any payment for them. He just said please give my regards to Kang Sajangnim.

We walked to the next block, where there were many pop-up shops. As we passed each one, the shop owner quickly handed over an envelope. It was very discreet and so easy. Or so I thought. We came to one shop that sold leather wear. The owner was very polite but there was no envelope coming our way. With a sweep of his hand my partner struck the man hard across the side of his face, knocking him over. I was surprised, it happened so fast. He just hit him. He then said two words. "Get it."

For three months, the daily schedule remained the same most days. After striking someone, the money was always forthcoming the next day. I thought it was amazing how the money would appear.

Once a week, we would meet Mr Kang at a different restaurant each time. Kang was treated like a king and I really think that he thought he was a king. My partner would pass him a briefcase and he would tuck it away with minimum fuss. Whenever he was away from his nightclub there would be at least four bodyguards with him. Quite often he would also be accompanied by the most stunning Korean beauties. I was always asked to be their chaperone home, but somehow, we always ended up back at my hotel room.

———

Professor Lee said he must meet me, now! I could sense the urgency in his voice.

"Jack, don't ask me how I know, but you are now a person of interest and on the police radar. You really stand out, Jack, and the police cannot help but to notice you and your involvement with Kang and the unsavoury work he does. With connections to the local mafia, standover tactics and prostitution, he is being watched, and that now includes you."

This was not the first time that I had been under surveillance. When I was teaching back in Sydney, I became close friends with one of my students. He would often pop over to my place in the inner city and we would eat and drink together. He was not bashful and did not try to hide who or what he was. I was not aware of his other life, but I heard from the other students that he was into some serious stuff. I should have known better. He was the vice president of an outlawed motorcycle gang. My house was on the same street as a police station, and they had twenty-four-hour surveillance on the street to watch and protect the police cars and bikes. They would have definitely spotted him coming and going from my place, his Harley was so noisy. I feel he was just taunting the police.

One day I arrived home to find my front door ajar and the alarm was off. I thought that was a little strange. A couple of days later, I met my friend, and he was laughing, saying that all of his friends including me were probably being watched. I knew that they had bugged my phone, because there would often be strange pauses and dial tones. It did not matter though, not long after that my friend was murdered in a drive-by shooting.

Professor Lee continued, "At this stage, the police taskforce, where I have many close friends on all levels, are only observing you from a distance. I would not be surprised if your hotel room was bugged and your phone tapped. Jack, I urgently recommend that you go to Japan now, leave South Korea, while you can. I know you are a good man, I am just looking out for you. So please, Jack, do not think that this will just blow over. Now you have a chance."

I do not like this situation anyway, I thought. I didn't need to be warned twice. I had had a good time, earned some money, done some research, and now was a perfect time for me to leave. I knew that I was mixed up with a bad criminal element, and learning so much about myself. It was similar to the lifestyle and situation that I had in Sydney, just a little more intense. I booked my ticket to Tokyo, packed my bag and got a taxi to the airport. I did not say anything to Mr Kang, I just wanted to disappear, and I did.

I am in two minds as to whether I should say that Mr Kang was a good man. If he was not involved in prostitution and strong arming and terrorising the local shop owners, I would probably say, yes, he was a good man. But behind that smile and those clothes and haircut, I think he was more like a smiling assassin. Once you got on his bad side, I would hate to see how that turned out. I had to think of myself first, I realised that I was walking a fine line between getting away from it all or crossing that line and plunging headlong into the dark side.

17
JAPAN

I didn't have a job, I had nowhere to live, and I couldn't speak the language. A great place to start but at least I had quite a lot of money, my winnings from betting on myself in the fights, and my work with Mr Kang. I also had a couple of numbers and contacts.

One was a man called Asoh Sensei. I found a book about his unique martial arts system. It is called SAW, short for Submission Arts Wrestling. It looked quite interesting and included a mix of many systems. He lived in a place called Saitama, north of Tokyo. I will look him up, once I get settled.

I also had Kazoku's number. An Aussie expat that Kelvin Brown introduced me to by way of a letter, she was waiting for my call.

I also had Mr Sumisu's phone number, who hopefully will be able to guide me to the next step in my quest.

I had Listro's testimonial from the Philippines. He was quite convincing as an eyewitness.

And I had a number for an ex-student of mine, Matthew, who was working as a chef at the Norwegian Embassy in Tokyo. He came to live here after the sudden deaths of his mother and father. It was a long shot, as we lost contact quite some time ago which I often regret. He would send me colourful postcards which I really enjoyed receiving. They seemed to be tempting me to come over. Well, I made it, I am here! I planned to try his number when I got settled.

During my years in teaching and training in martial arts, there were two students who I would say were extraordinary. First was Matthew and second was Eddie. I used to kick and punch them with full force, and no matter what I threw at them, they grunted and continued to step forward seemingly impervious to how hard I just hit them. I could not work it out. It did not seem natural. In fact, it was quite dangerous. Some people, no matter how big and muscled up they are, were the opposite, you could knock them over with a feather. But these two were what I called 'unbreakable'.

———

The airport was in the countryside, at a place called Narita. The security around the airport was quite strict. When the airport was being built there were riots and protests about the land grab by the government to make room for this much needed second Tokyo airport.

The town of Narita is quite nice. There is a large Shingon Buddhist temple with beautiful gardens. I walked around Narita in a couple of hours. I didn't want to hang around any longer as I needed to find my way to the skyliner express to downtown Tokyo. It takes about an hour, and it was starting to get dark.

The sun was a bright red as it was setting, just stunning. I sat and watched it leave for the day. Just stopping, pausing and feeling nature. An internal quiet spot that I was learning to cultivate.

The trip on the skyliner was fast and comfortable. The edges of Narita quickly merged into the outskirts of Tokyo.

Tokyo is a massive urban sprawl. From the outside it was not pretty at all, a dense concrete jungle, that went on forever. There was no stop to it. With Tokyo in the middle, Narita to the north and

Yokohama to the south, it marked a metropolis that housed millions of inhabitants.

Tokyo was completely flattened in the fire-bombing by the Americans after the fall of Okinawa. Okinawa was a bloody affair. The Japanese and the local militia were the last line of defence in the Second World War Pacific campaign. The Japanese fought with all their strength but failed as the American war machine, busting to seek revenge for the Japanese sneak attack on Pearl Harbor, gathered their forces to invade mainland Japan.

They unleashed not one but two atomic bombs, one on Hiroshima and one on Nagasaki, as well as the utter decimation of Tokyo. It is recorded that over 100,000 people were killed in the firebombing of Tokyo. This no doubt forced the Japanese surrender.

Tokyo was rebuilt by the Americans. There was not a great deal of planning. The low-rise urban living was built on every centimetre of space. It was a nightmare of narrow streets with freeways being built and constantly updated, superimposed over the top of neighbourhoods; nothing got in their way. Now there is the constant worry of earthquakes that would be disastrous for the population of Tokyo because emergency services would not be able to enter many of the streets.

The skyliner pulled in at the station and I sat there for a moment getting my bearings. The cleaners were quick and had already come on board. I gathered that the train terminated here, and this place was called Ueno. I had heard that name before, but I couldn't remember where.

I left the skyliner station and walked over to the Ueno station on the Yamanote line. The Yamanote line circles the city. This is where it gets a little confusing, all of the directions are in Japanese. Once I entered the station, people were darting off in every direction, all in a rush. They were not rude in any way or bothered by the slowness of the 'gaijin', which means foreigner in Japanese. They just gave me a wide berth. I was heading to a place called Yoyogi, so I needed to go around the Yamanote stations to the eastern side of Tokyo. I spotted a small policeman's booth just inside the main station entrance. The policeman was very polite. I could just manage, "Yoyogi please."

"Ah, wakarimashita, I understand. You come." He indicated for me to follow him. He took me over to what was a long orderly line of people. "I am Satoshi. You have money?" he asked. "Three hundred yen." He showed me what coins to put into the machine. I would have had no idea of how much money to put in. All of the train stations were in Japanese. I only recognised the green Yamanote line as it snaked amongst many other colourful lines, each colour representing another train line or subway. I felt like a lost child. I think that you could get lost and never find your way out of this labyrinth of train stations. I would soon come to learn the Ueno is just a baby station compared to Shinjuku and Ikebukero, each of which has in excess of a million people a day passing through them.

Constable Satoshi took the small cardboard ticket, handed it to me and took me by the arm and set off into the mass movement of people.

As we walked down into the belly of the station, I was amazed at the number of sushi restaurants and donut shops. I was to soon learn that it took a lot of work to find a coffee shop that served a decent latte or flat white. This was long before Starbucks found their foothold in Asia. Constable Satoshi took me right to the bottom of the stairs that went up to the platform.

"Sixteen." He held up his fingers, five, ten, fifteen, sixteen. I took this to mean that there are sixteen stops to Yoyogi. I thanked Satoshi but he never stopped for my thanks. This was one of many acts of unconditional kindness by people out of the blue that punctuated my time in Japan.

I was lucky that there was a small sign at the central exit to Yoyogi Station. Lucky as with most of the stations there are several exits, north, south, east and west. If you got the wrong exit, it would take you miles off track, and totally lost. I traced the path with my finger on the map on the wall. It clearly said Yoyogi Hostel and it looked straightforward. Turn left out of the station, follow the river, past the temple, and there it is, the hostel. I thought it would have taken about five to ten minutes but thirty minutes later I was still walking. Note to self: Japanese maps are not quite accurate.

After a little backtracking, I finally I made it. I stepped across the threshold and into the hostel. I automatically set off a bell that sounded like a bird whistle. It was cute and it made me jump. The Japanese love these brief musical interludes that would be played on the station platforms before they make any announcements. There is everything from an organ player to singing. I thought it was a nice touch. It was now 10 pm and the place was empty.

"Hello. Anybody home?"

"Hai Irashaimase, welcome." A middle-aged woman made her way to the counter.

I was drop dead tired and hanging out for a sleep. The rooms were quite small and old. There was one single bed with a plain sheet and blanket. The pillow was like concrete, at least it was quiet and clean. I had made it, I was here in Tokyo. What a journey it had been.

The next morning, I set off to find some food. I dared not to enter one of the many restaurants until I had a basic grip of the language. There was just no telling what was in the fancy photos of the food that looked so delicious. I found my way into a convenience store. There was a huge selection of various odd-looking food. I grabbed a couple of triangles of seaweed. They were like little parcels, and I was not sure what was inside.

My first attempt to open the package was a disaster. Rice and a really sour plum fell apart as I ravaged the packaging. I made the most out of the rice and spat the plum into a bin, I would learn that the orange tag on the rice package was called umeboshi, sour plum and it had no place in my mouth. What a failure.

I spotted a warm cabinet that had small cans of what appeared to be instant coffee. Luckily for me it was. But far too sweet with added sugar. Through a process of trial and error, I slowly unlocked the food puzzle in the convenience store and was eventually suitably impressed by the freshness and flavour of these delicious snacks. There is one caveat though, I could not stomach 'Natto', fermented soya bean. It is just foul and should never be eaten.

For a modern country I was somewhat confused by the locals. The children would often point at me, like a bear in a cage or at a zoo, it is if they were seeing a foreigner for the first time. I heard their hushed voices – "Look at foreigner." I did not feel discriminated against and there was no malice, but then I remembered a little of their history.

Just prior to the Meiji era, the Japanese had shut their doors to all foreigners and trade except the Dutch and the odd Christian monk. Though the Shoguns and Samurai thrived throughout Japan at that time, the rest of the Japanese froze in a time warp, unable to grow or prosper.

That is my theory why, even now, we 'gaijin' are pointed and laughed at. I learned over time that we were expected to understand their ways of etiquette and the somewhat antiquated rules that restricted spontaneity.

At the same time, I would marvel at the way the young men and women would go out to nomihodai and tabihodai. They are certain bars and restaurants where, for a set fee and short period you could eat and drink as much as you want. This led to insanely amusing drinking games where everyone, yes even we gaijin, played. Once time was up, everyone would spill out onto the footpath and there would be grotesque scenes of these late teens, early twenties vomiting everything up.

After my months of travel and research, I was finally in Japan, trying to find the final frontier of martial arts. Was I being naïve and completely wasting my time? I still needed some tangible proof that this elusive school existed. Otherwise, it would just remain as a dream in the back of my mind forever.

I found a pay phone and bought the required phone card from a 7-Eleven convenience store, though I soon realised that I could use the 10 yen, 50 yen and 100 yen coins for local calls.

It was ringing. "Hello?"

"Who is this?" came a croaky reply.

"My name is Jack, Jack George. Your neighbour Kelvin in Sydney gave me your number."

"Hang on," she barked. "What time is it?"

"It is 10 am, so sorry for waking you."

The phone went silent, I could hear movement and the rustling of paper. "Okay, Jack, right? Can you meet me today at Shinjuku? Take the east exit and find your way to the Studio Alta video screen. You can't miss it, it's huge."

"What time?"

"How about at twelve? Where are you now?"

"I am outside Yoyogi station."

"Perfect. Shinjuku is one stop north. See ya soon." She hung up.

That was that. How on earth would I be able to find my way there?

18

TOKYO

I managed to find the ticket line, and as Shinjuku was only one stop north, I figured out that the cost was 110 yen. Shinjuku station is massive. It encompasses the Yamanote line, in green, the Sobu line in yellow, the Chou line in orange, the Marunouchi line in red, the Keio line and the Odakyu lines, which were down a long walkway and I could not see their colours. Then there was the central east and central west exit, the east and west gate, the southeast gate and new south gate, south gate, southern terrace gate, and then there was the Seibu Shinjuku Station! Oh, no – what hope did I have of getting out of here.

I made my way back to the gate and asked one of the two ticket collectors standing there, "East exit please?"

He pointed behind me to the left. "Mukou."

I had no idea what he was saying, but I figured he was saying 'that way'. I followed his finger and took the stairs up and out of this incredible maze. As soon as I left the station, right in front of me was a huge video screen up on the first storey of the department store called Studio Alta. I could see now that it was quite a popular meeting place in groovy Shinjuku.

Kazoku stood out in the crowd, she was head and shoulders taller than most people. She walked straight up to me. "Jack?"

"Yes. Kazoku?"

"Oh, please, call me Kaz. Let's get out of here."

We walked down a wide walkway to the left of Studio Alta. The fruit shops along the walkway had the largest apples and melons I had ever seen. "They are enhanced by chemicals. But they taste pretty good," Kaz explained. We crossed Yasukuni Dori and headed towards Seibu Shinjuku station. "Keep up, mate." Kaz wove ahead through the throng of people. We passed the popular Dunkin Donuts superstore, another popular meeting place.

We entered Kabukicho, one of the many red light districts around Tokyo and has many bars and restaurants. Just on the border of Shinjuku and Kabukicho there were cinemas that had all the latest blockbuster movies. There is a certain etiquette that one needs to learn when watching a movie in Tokyo. Firstly, there is no limit to the number of people that can be sold a ticket. So don't become upset when you see people sitting and standing in the aisles. You may see people coming into the cinema before your movie has finished and wait at the end of each aisle, as soon as you stand up, they very politely squeeze themselves along the row and try to sit in your seats before anyone else does. Different, I guess.

"I am not working tonight so let's go for a drink." We hopped on the train at Seibu Shinjuku station and got off at the next stop, Takadanobaba. As we left the station and walked along a dark walkway, I followed Kaz down two flights of stairs into what appeared to be a basement. We turned a corner and entered a pumping Izakaya, the Japanese version of a wine bar, except so much busier. There were rows and rows of fresh salads and seafood. The music was pumping the latest rage by the Japanese band B'z. Kaz asked for a seat politely in Japanese and we were soon sitting down with menus in hand. The Izakaya was packed, and very noisy. It was obvious that she was a local here.

She blurted out, "You are very good looking, Jack George," as she motioned the waiter over.

"Ah, Kaz san," the waiter greeted her.

"Two Grolsch beers please Hideoyo san."

The next thing I knew, a beer was put in my hand.

"Campai – cheers." We touched bottles. "So, what brings you to Tokyo?"

I was a little shy after she said I was good looking. "I'm here to interview some of the top martial arts experts, and hope to do some research myself. I need to also get a job. I thought about teaching English but the whole idea of it really bores me. I have done plenty of security work so working as a doorman is more my thing. I also need a place to live."

"I can maybe help you out." Kaz drained the bottle of beer. "Sumimasen," she shouted, "Grolsch Nihon chodai. Two more beers please."

The first plates of food arrived, one was a radish salad with a sesame seed dressing, the next looked like fried dumplings that were served in a chilli sauce. "What are these called?" I asked.

"Oh, you will love them, they are Gyoza."

And she was right, I loved them. There was also a Japanese version of fried rice. This kind of food is called Chyuka Ryori, or Chinese Japanese. Then came the hot noodles in a kind of soup with meat and vegetables.

"It is not rude to slurp your noodles." Kaz slurped a mouth full of noodles, at the same time trying to say that she could help me by introducing me to some people. "As far as finding an apartment..." as she said that, she crossed her legs and I could not help noticing her long legs and her skirt that covered very little! She caught me as I looked down, I turned away slightly embarrassed. "... As I was saying, as far as you finding an apartment, that will be very difficult as you are a gaijin and cannot speak the language. I am happy to have you as my guest until you get settled."

Oh no I have heard that before, I thought. "Just one thing though, the last person that offered me space in her apartment was a transsexual prostitute."

"What do you mean?" She sounded mildly amused. It was hard to read whether she was insulted, or was about to burst out laughing.

"You know, she was a tranny," I explained.

There was an awkward silence between us, luckily more food arrived. This one was their signature dish, Chicken Teriyaki with a shredded radish and Ponzu dressing. There was also plenty of white rice, and the first round of sake appeared. I think Kaz was enjoying seeing me squirm. *How do I explain living with a trans prostitute for six months, and there being no more than a kiss and a cuddle*, I thought.

"Well, would you prefer me if I was transsexual?"

"Lecky is a beautiful person, and we became best friends, and she really looked out for me..." At this stage I opted to leave out that she walked around the apartment naked and I was a no rules street fighting champion, that requires too many details. I also left out the part that I worked for the Korean Mafia and was wanted by Interpol. "No," I conceded, "I am just a straight guy, not looking for any complications."

"That's cool. Well, for the record I prefer men, but have also had a couple of flings with women."

"Oh, really," I slowly responded. *I wonder where this is going?* I thought.

"Do you like me, Jack?" She asked with such innocence.

"So far so good. But I don't know you."

By now it was late in the afternoon. There had been plenty of food, beer and sake. Sake is an interesting drink. Made from rice wine it has a pungent smell and taste, quite sour but unique, not thirst quenching at all. It seems to creep up on you, and after a couple of small hot bottles I was quite drunk.

Oh well, I thought, *I am celebrating. I have not had a chance to stop and really relax since leaving Korea.*

"Okay, Jack. Are you ready to party on back at my place?"

"Sure." I kind of guessed that I would not make it back to the youth hostel tonight. That was okay as I had booked a couple of nights and all of my valuables were in a safe.

We headed out into the evening. There was that large red setting sun again. We both stopped and stood there as the sun skipped into oblivion for another night. It was getting dark now.

Where has the time gone? I wondered. "Kaz, did you pay?"

"They put it on my tab."

"What is it that you do for work?"

"I manage a bar in Nishi Azabu near Harajuku, called Zero Tokyo."

"Oh, what does that mean?"

"I started as an escort a couple of years ago, mainly in the bars of Kabukicho. But this does not mean that I was obliged to sleep with any of the men. It was not much more than pouring their drinks, lighting their cigarettes and making them the centre of attention. They were usually what we call salary men, quite sad actually, mostly lonely men, looking for some company. Zero Tokyo is a great place to work, and I really enjoy it. My apartment is not too far from here, let's walk. It is a place called Shin Okubo. My apartment is quite modern and quiet considering its position. There are plenty of convenience shops and supermarkets nearby. I love the tofu shop where they make the best fresh tofu every day."

Kaz's laugh was quite infectious, and though we had only just met, I think she was slowly growing on me. She had an innocent street smart but was not pushy. She was not classically beautiful, though she was tall, slim with brown hair and green eyes. Not glamorous, quite unique. She had a real gentle side, probably inherited from her Japanese mother. She also had an abrupt manner about her, which could be quite direct, or was it just being honest?

Her height, she told me was from her German father. Both of her parents still lived in Sydney. She was an only child, and by the sound of it, loved and missed her parents immensely. I found her the complete package, quite stunning actually. I was struggling to keep up. She bolted ahead of me not looking back, I was feeling a seedy combination of jet lag and being drunk and would need to rest very soon.

We stopped at a convenience store. Kaz went straight to the beer cooler and put a six-pack of Yebisu on the counter. She also grabbed what looked like dried seaweed and cheese strips and what she called osenbei, which were dried biscuits cooked in soya sauce. There were several different kinds and I enjoyed them all. Lastly was a couple of bottles of water.

"Put it on my tab, Keiko san."

"Hi wakarimashita, certainly," the shop assistant replied.

We then walked down a narrow alleyway to her apartment building and took a staircase to the upper floor. "At last, home sweet home." Kaz opened the door. "Take your shoes off," she barked.

"Whoops, sorry," I apologised.

"That is your room." She pointed to a tiny room with three tatami mats.

"Great, thank you, that will be perfect." I had a quick look then went into the single main room, which had a sliding door off it.

Kaz opened the door. "That is my room." It had a futon, sheets and pillows all neatly folded in the corner. There was also a small kitchen, microwave and a rice cooker. Oh, and not to forget the fridge.

I sat on the low rise sofa as Kaz passed me an open beer. She looked at me with a really sultry look, like she was getting ready to devour me, and I could tell what was about to happen.

"Can I take off my dress?" Before I could answer, the dress was around her ankles and she stepped elegantly out of it, wearing just a red G-string and bra. I just stared at her body. She slipped out of her underwear, and putting her legs either side, she straddled on top of me. How exquisite. She stood up, then took me by the hand and guided me into her room.

The passion continued for what seemed like hours. Finally, we found sleep in the early hours of the morning. We really connected and I realised that there was a lot of pent up sexual tension within me. All those times that Lecky had paraded her beauty in front of me, and would slip into bed beside me. We would just cuddle and I would hold her, unable to go to the next step.

With Kaz, nothing was held back. She felt my muscles and remarked, "You have the body of a warrior." I did, fighting for my life, but she didn't know that part of me yet. She teased me, "Well, do I look like a tranny?" She leant on one shoulder then brushed her hair back from her eyes.

"No," I said. She opened her body to receive me, beckoning me in. So we started again and spent all morning exploring each other's bodies.

Kaz said in a soft voice, "I will ask my boss if they need another English-speaking doorman."

"That is so kind of you."

"We get plenty of celebrities and sports people coming into the club. It would be up you to try and source them for an interview." I had really landed well, and had secured a place to hang out and maybe a job. It was now up to me to source some interviews.

———

The following afternoon I had an interview with the nightclub's manager, Kumisan. She spoke perfect English and as the interview was all in English it was very quick. She was very pleased with my resume, in particular the referral I had from Mark from James Street Nightclub.

"When can you start?" she asked.

"I am ready to start tomorrow."

"Fine. How about I put you on the 8 pm until 1 am and see how you go?"

"Done." I walked into the club and wow! It was huge, very much like the James Street Nightclub. I spotted Kaz who was preparing girls, bar staff and waiters for a busy night.

"How did you go?" She smiled.

"I start tomorrow."

"Well done. So, what will you do now?"

"I might just hang here for a while and have a couple of drinks."

"Let me grab you a mizuwari. This is a popular drink of scotch and water."

I sat and watched Kaz as the DJ warmed up his turntable. I was on my second mizuwari when the doors opened and the crowd came in. The music was blaring 'Blue Monday' which started the crowd off.

I found myself being dragged to the dance floor by Kumisan. "It is my night off. Let's party, Jack." I could see Kaz's face, as this happened right in front of her. But she turned away smiling as Kumisan got us another round of drinks.

"Do you always treat your new employees to a drink and a dance?"

"No, just the pretty boys." Life was about to get complicated, and I just let it happen.

Kumisan and I had a couple more drinks, she leaned towards me and grabbed my leg. "Time to go." We disappeared through a side door and were picked up by a car and a driver. "Take us home," she said. She was quite petite and I would say she was in her early forties, very attractive and she knew what she wanted. The moment I got in the car, she was all over me. In an instant she had my pants off.

We drove for about ten minutes and arrived at a swish apartment block in Shinagawa.

We entered her large penthouse. "This is very nice."

She had my clothes off in an instant, and I had hers off. We touched.

It was soon morning. *Oh no*, I thought, *what would Kaz think*. Kumisan was enjoying the post sex feeling and was snoring like a purring cat. I quietly got dressed and left the building. I got straight into a cab and showed him the address on Kaz's business card.

The time was 5 am. *Wow, I am a bit of a stud*, I thought. *Every woman that I have met so far has wanted to bed me. This is all new to me!* Even in my naïvety, I knew I had crossed the line. I was so stupid and now faced with the distinct possibility that Kaz would kick me out. This was a real coming of age moment for me. I messed up and now had to own it.

I silently opened the door to Kaz's apartment. "Where have you been?" she barked.

Oh no. "I have been with Kumisan. I'm not going to lie to you Kaz, and to be honest, we had not yet set the tone of our relationship."

"Well, I hope you enjoyed yourself." Much to my surprise she did not go on with it, in fact she said, "I hope you have enough energy left as I want you now." Kaz slipped out of her light kimono, and stood there waiting. I did not need to be asked twice.

I was to learn that Kaz did not hold a grudge, or want to go on and on with things that we had already dealt with. I asked her about that, and she said what is done is done and at the end of the day once we had calmly talked it through there was no need to keep bringing it up. I was also surprised at how she would never sweat the small stuff, like complaining that I did not put the toilet seat down, or did not take turns doing the washing, or cleaning.

She did not keep a ledger or checklist to gauge who was doing what. She could see that I was helping where I could and was paying my way with the groceries and helping with the rent. It was all going just fine. In fact, I had never experienced such harmony with a partner before.

———

I was getting on with life and I slipped right in to living in Tokyo. I had a place to live and now a good job, I thought now might be a good time to start researching some interviews for Kelvin's magazine. But first things first. I would call Mr Sumisu san, who apparently lived in Tokyo. I purchased a phone card from the 7-Eleven and dialled the number. It rang once then a recording, "Hai Moshi Moshi this is Sumisu, I am out, so please leave a message."

"Hi Sumisu san, my name is Jack George, and I am here doing some research from Australia, I will call you later tonight."

I walked around the backstreets of Shinjuku. It is an amazing place. I found my way into the incredible Kinokuniya bookshop and climbed the stairs to the fifth floor where there was a great display of English written books. The martial arts magazines there were interesting and from all over the world. The American magazines, while filled with information, were generally a load of bull. I marvelled at the colour of their uniforms and the number of stripes on their belts. So many so-called grandmasters that have never trained outside of their own cities, and never in Asia.

The hardback books were great. I would get lost in Ancient Egyptian history and I loved reading about the Roman Empire. The great Julius Caesar. What a man he was. The reason that we have so much rich accurate history of Julius Caesar is because he kept a detailed journal of his exploits, in particular his time in Gaul, which is now France. He smashed the Gauls and their leader Vercingetorix. Those journals have miraculously survived the centuries and have provided many historians with a clear, though somewhat one-sided, account of Caesar's campaigns.

From Kinokuniya I walked down the main road to the Isetan department store. The smells and the range of food from all over the world was wonderful. I found a café on the ground floor, selling good coffee. A little expensive at 1000 yen a cup, about ten dollars, but it hit the spot. I then made my way back along the main road and turned left at the Yodabashi Camera shop. This camera shop had all the latest camera models at half the price of what you would pay for them in Australia. The video cassettes and blank CDs were also very cheap.

Just out of the station and along a little bit was one of my favourite shops, a copy gun shop. It had just about every handgun, rifle and modern machine gun in stock, made of hard plastic. To access the shop, you had to walk through what is a bogus clothes shop through a narrow doorway and take the hidden escalator to the third floor. Once on the third floor, you get to a security door and are buzzed in. The fake guns are legal in Japan but illegal in many other countries. They look the real deal. They even fire a small hard plastic bullet. Probably about the only damage it would do is you would lose an eye if it was a direct hit. I enjoyed holding and feeling the Smith & Wesson, or the AK47. It would have been fun to have a couple of fake guns when me and my brothers would play wars in the bush that backed onto the house in Berowra.

For the real enthusiasts there was even a fully functional range, albeit a hard plastic bullet, where you could take a gun and give it a go.

For the real mind blowing electronics experience, you couldn't go further than Akihabara, on the other side of Tokyo, accessible on the ever convenient Yamanote line. Akihabara was the place to come when looking for any of the latest electronic items like TVs, cameras and any domestic kitchen products. It had so many shops and high rises, all beaming from the neon lights.

I went down the stairs to the main part of Shinjuku Station. There were a number of pay phones downstairs, just before the station stairs, hidden by a row of luggage lockers. It was quiet there so I called Sumisu san again and this time I was in luck.

"Moshi Moshi..."

"Hi Sumisu san, my name is Jack George, I left you a message before..."

"Hey, man, yes, all good."

"Can I meet you some time? I am wondering if we could chat about your experience and any information you may have on some of the more traditional and a little harder to find martial arts dojos of Tokyo."

He immediately became vague. "Hey, man, I am not sure I can help you." Then there was silence.

"Are you still there Sumisu san? Well, how about we meet at the Lowenbrau beer café, around the corner from Studio Alta in Shinjuku? I will buy you dinner and a couple of beers."

"Okay, let's meet tomorrow at 5 pm, I know the café."

———

I arrived a couple of minutes early and took a prime position at the bar. For some reason, the bar men loved filling the beer glass with at least a third froth. As an Aussie I love my draft beer full to the brim. Oh, well, it was still very cold.

I was looking forward to the meeting with Sumisu san. He used to work as a Sheriff in the dog squad in California. I am not sure what happened, but he was retired, citing PTSD as the cause. I was in for a real treat.

A small, wiry, somewhat intense appearing man entered the café. He stopped and looked around. It reminded me of a predator in the jungle, they would stop, raise their head, listen and sniff the air to sense any danger before proceeding. He looked at me and his smile opened his face, he was beaming with delight. Sumisu san looked every bit Japanese but when he talked, he had a classic

Californian drawl. "I am from Torrance, close to the beach. It's a bit different to Tokyo. I have not been home since my folks passed away, about five years ago."

An avid practitioner of Japanese weapons, he had spent years learning the Samurai fighting arts. I heard that he was accepted into the Katori Shinto Ryu, under Ogawa Sensei. "They make you sign a contract in blood. Wow, man, I could not believe it when they gave me this knife and said, 'Cut yourself and sign.' But it was worth it, I went on to learn kenjutsu, the way of the sword, which also includes sword drawing called iaijutsu, sword fighting called batto jutsu, naginata, shuriken and jujutsu. I even learned some ninjutsu. It's great, I learnt so much. The dojo is in Narita, so it is quite a long round trip.

"I also learnt jodo with Shimazu Sensei, this is in a community hall just off the main drag in Suidobashi, where the Kodokan is located, the world headquarters of the Judo Federation. I have a little history with the jodo crowd. Jodo is with a long stick called a jo and a bokken, a timber sword. I was not much into weapons like the bokken or the jo, but some people love it. The one and only time I went to a jodo class was with Suzuki Sensei. I remember I was sitting there, with my legs crossed, casually chatting with some of the other foreigners as we took a break from class. When this guy, who was Swiss, I think, turned to us and snapped, 'Have some respect, sit up straight in seiza, on your knees.'

"I was not in a particularly great mood and instead of ignoring him, I said, 'Why don't you just mind your own business.' The foreigners doing martial arts used to really annoy me, they would tend to become more Japanese than the Japanese. He was quite offended by my comments and went off in a huff. He joined a group of foreigners that looked special, they wore their hair in the top knot of the samurai and looked ridiculous. That is the reason why I did not have many non-Japanese friends." He prattled on getting uncomfortable with any break in conversation. "So what would you like to know?"

I went dead against my strategy and just asked him outright. "What do you know about hokuto ryu?"

Like everyone that I have spoken with about it up until now, Sumisu san became distant and elusive. Then he blurted out, "What right do you have coming to Japan and expecting everyone to open doors for you?" He lashed out with such anger. "I suggest you grow up, Jack!"

"Whoa, hang on for a minute. I have just met you and you know nothing about me." My tone was slightly impatient. I felt a darkness descend over Sumisu san, I think it was a mixture of the beer and his personality. I felt the old twinge of anger starting to stir deep within me. *Oh no*, I thought, *I must breathe deeply and not let the genie out of the bottle*. I was sure that I would break Sumisu san in two if it became violent. Luckily, I managed to get control of myself. "I am so sorry, I did not mean to upset you."

"Well, I am sick and tired of people just appearing and expecting me to help them out."

I noted that Sumisu san had successfully diverted the conversation away from hokuto ryu. "Well, I am not after any favours, and I have always done it tough. I have been studying martial arts most of my life."

Within a heartbeat he changed back to the Sumisu san that I had met at the beginning. *What was all that about*, I thought.

"Well, there is a dojo on the outskirts of Tokyo. They have a depth about them and might be able to help you." Sumisu san wrote the details on a napkin, and drew a rough map of directions to the dojo.

Oh no, not one of those Japanese maps again.

"It is called the Shinkan dojo and teaches the secretive art of daito ryu aiki jujutsu. Have you heard of it before?"

"Yes, of course."

"Well, I suggest you give them a call and say that you spoke to me. It will make the process a little easier."

"Thank you. This really means a lot to me." I dare not mention hokuto ryu again, as who knows what this guy is capable of.

"You may also find Stanley Morgan interesting." He wrote down his number. That is the second time I have heard the name Stanley Morgan.

We downed a couple more beers and Sumisu san rotated between a real darkness one minute to a sense of euphoria the next. Oh boy, I just wanted to get away from him.

"I've got this." I made my way up to the bar and paid for the food and drinks.

"Thanks, mate, we should do this again sometime."

"Sure." But I actually had no intention of meeting him anytime soon.

———

Kaz called the dojo for me, they were very polite and expected me the following night at 8 pm. I looked up Shinkoiwa on a train map I had purchased at Kinokuniya book shop. It was quite good and gave me the names of the stations in English. Shinkoiwa is on the other side of Tokyo and looks like it is a direct route from Shinjuku on the Sobu sen, the full yellow carriages. Kaz said it would probably take thirty to forty minutes from Shinjuku.

So I set out, found my way easily to the Sobu sen, the train from Shinjuku to Shinkoiwa was quite straightforward. The train stopped at every stop. This is called a kaku eki densha and I was lucky enough to get a seat as the train soon filled up tight. It always amazed me how the passengers on the train would have their personal space entered into as more and more people packed into the train. They commuted for hours every day to and from work. You could really see that space is so important. The longer I stayed in Tokyo the more I missed the sun. The buildings are so tightly packed that it cuts out the view to the sky.

My main concern was how I was going to get out of the train. This would take some tactics. Shinkoiwa was the next stop, so I stood, held my rucksack tightly in front of me and started to apply a slight pressure to the folks around me. This was so subtle, you did not want to push because there was nowhere for them to go. It reminded me of one of my key lessons in martial arts. When aiming to move an opponent you need to create a hole for them to fall into. This was done by shifting your body off line and guiding them very carefully into a hole where you used to be. The key here is for your opponent not to feel my movement as it would then create a reaction. They just end up in the hole and sit there wondering how they got there.

In this case, whilst the train was still moving and packed tight with people, there was literally nowhere to put them. So what I did was position myself as close to the doors as possible then as the doors opened, guide them out of the doors, at the same time saying sumimasen, excuse me and smiling. It worked a treat. I soon found myself on an empty Shinkoiwa station. The silence was eerie as I watched the back of the train disappear. I felt quite alone. Shinkoiwa station is a bleak and nondescript industrial suburb on the eastern outskirts of Tokyo. The platform was soon deserted as the locals quickly dispersed.

I went down the stairs off the platform, there was a mad throng of people all jostling for a way out. I was always surprised how fast the people moved without touching each other. They knew exactly where they were going, like they had a beacon guiding them out of the station. I always imagined what it would be like to get truly lost in one of these large stations, especially if you couldn't speak the language. Would I ever be found? I made my way to the first exit that I could find. I was about to ask in my broken Japanese which way to the daito ryu but the station attendant closed and locked his door before I had a chance to say anything. Oh, well, back to the map.

I found the exit. It was not difficult as I was to take the exit that did not have the mall. The exit I was taking had so many push bikes. There were hundreds of them. People rode to the station parked their bike, locked it up and left it there for the day while they travelled to work on the train.

I kept going left and soon found the main road. I was to take bus fifty-one. Sumisu san said it was about a thirty-minute walk, and the bus was much faster. I got on the bus and was not sure what to do. The bus driver motioned me to drop some money onto a covered conveyor belt. But I had no change. He waved me on, I apologised and made my way to the back of the bus. I was to get off as soon as we crossed the river. So, I sat back and waited until the river and bridge came into view. I closed my eyes just for an instant, I was so tired after being so Tokyo busy. Tokyo busy is when Tokyo sucks you in and you get pushed and pulled along by the crowd. It depletes you of all your reserves. You begin to crave space where you can recover. Usually this is when you stop, on a train or a bus. The next thing I realised I was being rocked gently backward and forward. I opened my eyes with a start. We were parking in the bus depot.

"Sumimasen, are you okay?" asked the bus driver.

"Oh, no." It was already 8 pm and the class would be starting. I could see a river, quite a wide river that ran down beside the bus depot. I pointed to the river. "Shinkoiwa?"

"Ah hai so desu."

I understood hai, meaning yes, so I grabbed my bag and started running down the road. I must have looked a sight, this large man, striding along the road. It is no wonder the Japanese thought we foreigners were strange. I was running fast and soon found a bridge that must have been the one I was supposed to cross then get off.

So I stopped for a couple of minutes to get my bearings. According to the map that Sumisu san drew, I was to follow the river left for one hundred metres, and take the laneway to the right after the third block of units. So I followed his instructions, but I had no idea if this was even the correct river. I turned right as instructed and walked straight ahead looking for the small carpark on the left. Next to the carpark was a narrow four storey building opposite a metal fabrication factory.

When Sumisu san was telling me this, he was going on about the illegal immigrants that were flocking to Tokyo from the Middle East. The majority of them were fleeing Desert Storm, the US war on Iraq. Japan had apparently signed an agreement to allow a certain number of refugees into their country by way of a lottery. The names were pulled out of a hat once a month. So thousands of young men were literally flooding into Japan, and they had started making a nuisance of themselves. There were many reports of them gathering in parks and sleeping under bridges. They were also hanging around supermarkets and shop lifting. There were many reports of women being touched and assaulted inappropriately.

All of a sudden, the immigrants disappeared. The government had ordered the police to round them all up and ship them back to their own country. The crime rate in Tokyo went down almost straightaway. So it quickly reverted back to a very safe city. There were a number of immigrants working at this metal fabrication factory and he had warned me to not talk to them.

I found the building. This was an important step for me as hokuto ryu may be somehow connected to this dojo. I had researched daito ryu in depth as part of my research. I was ready to send off my findings to the publisher Kelvin, and Rainbow in the USA. But I just wanted to hold off. I did not want to create any competition for myself and let someone else be the first non-Japanese to find the hidden ashram.

19
TAKEDA YOSHINOBU

Little is known about daito ryu aiki-jujutsu in the West. Even in Japan, it has long been considered a relic of a prewar era – at best the poor cousin of the modern-day aikido – but nothing could be further from the truth.

Daito ryu has always been a secretive martial art. Its most famous exponent Takeda Yoshinobu, only ever taught people of high social standing such as politicians, teachers, police or military people. He received many gifts from the emperor, all of which had the very famous royal family insignia.

Before that, the art belonged exclusively to the Aizu clan in Japan and was never allowed to be shown to outsiders.

Takeda was probably one of the last true samurai warriors. At the turn of the last century, he spent his time roaming Japan, taking on challengers and perfecting his sword and jujutsu techniques against any one foolish enough to take him on. Although only five feet tall, he was feared and respected as a great martial artist and continued to travel around Japan teaching and spreading daito ryu well into his eighties.

One of Takeda's most famous students, Ueshiba, was the

originator of modern-day aikido. In fact, without Takeda Sensei's teachings, aikido in its present form would probably never exist today. Ueshiba Sensei studied daito ryu for many years and received instructor's certification in the art.

Although it is true to say that there are some similarities between aikido and daito ryu, Ueshiba's aikido is a much weakened form of combat; whereas Takeda's aiki-jujutsu is a method of hand to hand combat, primarily concerned with repelling an attack immediately making ample use of strikes against anatomical weak points, joint dislocation, break, throws and chokes.

Although very small and hard to find, daito ryu aiki-jujutsu has remained remarkably intact since Takeda Yoshinobu started disseminating the art throughout Japan 120 years ago. This is evident in the attendance records that he kept of every single person who attended and the date of the class.

These accurate records are looked after by his remaining family. It is from these records that his wandering can be placed to a mountain retreat. He would disappear for months on end. He never talked about it though. It was all just rumour. It was up to me to make the connection.

Classes were put on hold during the Second World War but the art in its original form is still very much alive in this small industrial suburb on the outskirts of Tokyo.

The moment you lay eyes on the building you get the idea that there is something different about it. Beside the entrance is a bronze moulded name plate, proudly showing the distinguished Takeda clan family emblem, indicating to all who enter that this is a very serious place, and it is definitely no sports or social club.

As you enter the building, you are met by a simple zen garden, water dripping from bamboo into a pond, like a steady heartbeat, indicating life. As you go up the stairs, from floor to floor, the images and sounds of modern Japan begin a subtle change.

The sterile walls of ferro concrete mould into acute angles of age-old rosewood timber, and the glaring neons and sounds of pachinko dull to a hum and are met by the sounds of kiai and the thuds of bodies break falling. As you enter the dojo and step onto the hard tatami mats, your stomach lets out a twinge of nervousness, or is it fear, maybe both.

The daito ryu is an elite school, worthy of its fame. There is no mass production of black belts, and the dedicated student receives instruction from the master and his top students.

The headmaster, Konda Sensei is an ardent admirer of the great swordsman and calligrapher Teshu Sensei, and like Teshu Sensei believes in the concept of shugyo, periods of intense training to strengthen the body and spirit. The walls of the dojo are lined with the calligraphy of Teshu.

I took my shoes off and left them at the bottom of the stairs. It was now 9.15 pm, but at least I turned up. I came to the entrance of the dojo and bowed my head.

The teacher approached me. "I am Sanada. Please..." He motioned towards a small area off to the side of the dojo. He got me some cushions and handed me a large book. It was a visitors' book for me to sign. "Thank you."

Everyone was very polite, all of the senior students bowed towards me. This made me feel very comfortable. It was a far cry from the regular martial arts school at home or in the States. It appeared that all of the students training were doing so with the aim to become a better person. They did not look at me like I was a big foreigner, all they saw was a new student and they were going to make me feel as comfortable as could be.

The class was very traditional, the etiquette was outstanding. I recognised some of the unique techniques from my research. In fact, on the shelf near me was a number of videos including one that I had found in a second-hand bookshop. The name Stanley Morgan immediately jumped out at me. He produced these videos.

Wow, I thought, *I really need to get in contact with this man.*

Sanada Sempai was dynamic. He controlled, manipulated, and choked the students in a demonstration of lethal technique. I stayed until the end of class, thanked them all, and made my way back to the station. I had enough information now to find that there was a tangible reason that the ashram did in fact exist.

———

After doing a lot of research on the martial arts, I was beginning to see a pattern. The term martial arts was first used in the mid-1960s and early '70s in America. There was an influx of Americans now coming back to the US after living in Asia and learning many different styles of martial arts directly from the masters. So styles were commercialised and many so-called schools of martial arts sprang up from nowhere.

Schools had branches, franchises and affiliations. The entire industry began to support many so-called masters, grand masters and great grand masters. Their demonstrations cheapened the last remnants of a proud history as they paraded around in silk uniforms, expecting the public to believe that they were the 39th grand master of a lineage that had disappeared, and – after a little research – never existed.

Yet they still continued to fool the public and people still believe that they are the real deal. One so called grand master of ninjutsu used to be an assistant on a children's TV show. He, all of a sudden, was a grand master of a secret school of ninjutsu. Anyone that recognised him knew he was fake and, at first, did not take him seriously. But the gullible public were taken in by his flashy moves and tales of the assassins. So much so that he went on to create a worldwide following.

From my research I was coming to understand that the martial arts industry was slowly dying. I had trained enough to say that I was not just a beginner, but I was driven to find and learn from a true master untainted by western commercialism. The Sensei's Council, a US based organisation, has taken it upon themselves to recognise the most elite heads of martial arts schools worldwide. All you have to do is look into a couple of the hundreds of members and it quickly becomes obvious that they are a group of almost all men that have created their schools out of thin air. There is simply no regulation and no limit to how far they are willing to go to promote their schools.

I have always said that only the dedicated and pure of heart ever leave their own comfort zones and travel to Asia to pursue a direct path with a legitimate master who has a well known and credible lineage.

―――――

Yoyogi is quite a well-known area. The national gymnasium was used for the 1964 Olympics. I occasionally went to the public gym there which was good for a workout. Yoyogi Park Koen is very impressive. The roads leading into the park are such an iconic mixture of the traditional and the modern. You can also access the park from Harajuku station.

From Harajuku station it is an easy stroll through Yoyogi Park to the Yasakuni Jinja, an amazing shrine and museum for the Kamikaze in the Second World War. In fact, the museum traces the Japanese history for thousands of years. If you take your time you will soon understand that throughout its history there has rarely been any peace; there was constant in fighting amongst the various Japanese warlords and then the Mongols.

The only real time there has been a constant peace has been from the end of the Second World War and it took a drastic measure of atomic bombs to finally stop the Japanese war machine and their taste for battle. Unlike the European feudal era that retained none of their fighting prowess, the Japanese created an artform around their fighting systems that would see it remain intact for many centuries.

Kaz and I would enjoy the walk from her apartment to Harajuku on a Sunday morning. There was an amazing array of live music and dancing. It was incredible, so many characters jamming away with their own unique pop-up performances. We would walk up to Omote Sando and enjoy looking through the gift antique shop on the way with their interesting assortment of antiques and traditional gifts. I would purchase unique postcards that I would regularly send to my friends.

One Sunday we turned left at a huge toy shop and walked around to the street just behind the antique shop. We joined a line, I had no idea where the line went. And it was a long line. In Japan, lining up was so different from lining up in Korea. The lines in Japan were orderly and there was no pushing or shoving. The lines in Korea were like a rugby scrum, a free for all, with no structure at all. We waited and slowly inched closer to a very busy restaurant.

Kaz turned to me with a look of delight. "Do you remember the dumplings we ate when you first arrived in Tokyo?"

"Yeah, they were delicious."

"They are called gyoza, and this has to be the best gyoza bar in Tokyo."

"Fantastic."

It was finally our turn, and we ate and ate and ate these delicious pockets of gastronomic delight.

On the way back up to the station we walked along the famous Takeshita Dori, a narrow street for pedestrians only. As always, there was a sea of Japanese people packed into this narrow street.

Walking home I was reminded of a funny story Sumisu san told me about taxi drivers in Tokyo. I had heard similar from a number of foreigners living in Japan about their ordeals with taxi drivers.

There is a real danger in getting into a taxi at night when you have been drinking. The driver is always polite. Once you have told them where you are going, you had better stay awake or the taxi driver will take you on a sightseeing journey around Tokyo. Sumisu told me he had got in a taxi at Harajuku as he missed the last train. He was heading to his home just up the road at Shinjuku. He fell asleep and woke up somewhere near Haneda airport. It was light outside and he was shocked that he was still in the cab. It was supposed to be a ten minute taxi ride. He had been in this cab for more than three hours, and the meter read 30,000 yen, close to $300. The cab driver then went directly to his home in Shinjuku and expected the entire amount to be paid, otherwise they would keep the doors locked and wait for the police. A valuable lesson.

———

I embarked on a long and tenuous cat and mouse game with Stanley Morgan. I called the number that Sumisu san gave several times, there was no answer and no way to leave a message. I tried one last time, and today was in luck. A man answered the phone in really bad Japanese in an attempt to put me off. In fact, he spoke perfect English. I knew that I did not have long. I explained that I had seen a video that he produced, and Sumisu san had given me his phone number. He said I was out of luck, no video ever existed. I knew he was lying to me, but I pulled back and let him talk. He did tell me the name of a dojo, daito ryu that Sumisu san had already told me about.

"Yes, I know about the dojo, daito ryu."

Stanley rambled on, "Rumour has it, they closed their doors in order to preserve their secrets at the end of the Second World War."

"I am keen to know more about the hokuto ryu."

Stanley suddenly stopped talking. He now knew that I knew that he was lying to me. Stanley started up again, he was adamant that they no longer existed. I was somewhat surprised when he finished the conversation by asking me to phone again in two weeks. When I asked why, he replied, "No reason, just call."

So I waited two weeks and called. He answered the phone after several rings and was quite gruff. He clearly was not expecting to hear from me again. He barked down the line to not waste his time, call again in another two weeks. I did not understand what was going on, but I simply did not have any other leads. This went on for six weeks.

There is something about being driven. Some have an ability to just keep on while others don't. It depends on the person. I am not sure if this comes deep from within or whether you can learn it. It is without doubt one of life's great qualities to be the last man standing. So if Stanley thought I was going to stop calling him, he was mistaken. I had invested a lot of time into this lead, so I was not about to quit now.

The next time I called he cried, "Okay, okay, I give in." Ahhh, at last a breakthrough. "Now I don't know what it is like or how it operates, but I know that the daito ryu dojo has some kind of connection to a mysterious dojo in the mountains. If you do get the chance to visit the daito ryu dojo in Tokyo, you should remember they are also very secretive—"

"I have already been there," I interrupted.

"Well, then did you know that they do not want their association with the hokuto ryu to be uncovered?"

"But, Stanley, I know all of this already. We are just going around in circles."

He knew what he was doing, then cut me off and shouted down the phone, "Call me back in two weeks!" He hung up. Damn, I was getting so close, oh well another two weeks it is. So I waited ... again.

I called in exactly two weeks. "Ahhh, Jack," he chimed, "thank you for calling." Attempting to sound sincere, he did not hesitate, "From my research I am quite sure that the hokuto ryu goes back many decades, and probably hundreds of years. Hokuto ryu is so secret and if they accept you, they make you sign the dojo oath in your blood and you have to swear that you will never leave. Jack, I will tell you what I know. Listen very carefully. I am reading this to you from a small scroll that was given to me many years ago, I have no idea if it's the truth. It is all in Japanese, I will translate best I can."

So it all came out. "You take a train to Chiba Station and change and take the Sotobo line to a place called Katsuura, a small fishing village on the Chiba coast. You leave the station and walk on the right side of the Isumi River. It should lead you up into the mountains; you will pass the Tomisaaki Shrine. Pay your respects to Kami Sama, God, and continue to climb the mountain. You will come to a deep waterfall and a crystal clear pool. But it depends on the season you go. This time of year is the wet season, so the pool will be full. Swim to the back of the waterfall and lift yourself up between the two large rocks until you can then see out the back past the rocks and the waterfall.

"You have now gone further than I should tell you. But I will tell you the rest. Follow the thin track, but be careful as it is not well marked, go through the ferns, it should be quite flat. After about twenty minutes the track will begin to go up. It will be very wet, so you will need to watch your footing. Follow the track and you will come to a fork. Do not take the right side, remain on the left side.

"The entire valley should open up to you once the mist clears. If it does not, continue on the track anyway. By this time, they will be fully aware that there is someone on the track and just leave it to them to lead you in. But, Jack, I cannot warn you enough. It's like a spider leading you into a web, and it is very, very dangerous. I wish you all the best and hope I never hear from you again. You can take these directions as your formal letter of introduction. That at least should give you a chance." The phone line went dead.

I had done it. I now actually had something tangible.

20

AZUMA

I was introduced to Azuma Sensei by Asoh Sensei at a party that he was hosting. I trained a couple of times at SAW in Saitama and was beginning to enjoy it.

There were a few reputable dojos that were creating their own new brand of martial arts. The term MMA, or mixed martial arts was starting to pop up quite a lot. Some very brave martial arts schools were even scheduling events that included – or rather excluded – certain rules around what you could and could not do. SAW was one of these schools. Although it seemed I was distracted from my primary purpose, researching and finding the hidden dojo of hokuto ryu, that was not the case.

The search for the hidden ryu was slow but it was always progressing. In the meantime, I was keen to experience as much as I could. SAW ran an annual competition and it had a SP rule division. This was what I call minimum rules fighting, quite different from the all-out, no-rules free for all that I experienced in Thailand, which suited me as I was not interested in fighting in a blanket 'no rules' format again.

The SAW format appealed to me, it took out the blood sport

potential that had started gaining momentum in the early '80s. There was no widespread competitor format that challenged the fighter in all ranges of fighting. So I did what I do best and signed up for a fight. It was more from a research perspective than anything else.

Kaz was delighted. She would be my photographer and would be ringside to get some great shots. I learned well before that my opponent was a Japanese guy by the name of Suzuki. He was shorter than me and I watched him fight on a couple of videos from previous SAW championships. He was a bit of a pretty boy and was more concerned about how his hair was looking. He liked to do the fancy kicks of taekwondo. Like my teacher used to say to me, once you train at Yudo College where the fighters can really kick, you will never be afraid of a kick ever again. And that was true. I wondered what Suzuki's real talent was. From what I could see, he had never been knocked out or taken down, though he did lose every fight. So I prepared for this fight like I prepared for every fight.

The competition came around quickly. I could not believe how nervous and scared I was, entering into a new format in a new city. Compared to what I experienced in Bangkok, I should have been better prepared. We bowed and the fight started. He was kicking me with pesky roundhouse kicks to my thigh. It was not too bad the first time, but after about twenty, my thigh was starting to feel it. I faked a front kick and easily took him down with an outside reap to his front leg. I landed right on top of him, in a side hold down. The classical name for this hold down is Kesa gatame. I tried all kinds of nasty moves, digging into pressure points and trying to lock his arms. I hit him with quite a lot actually, and he was not fazed.

Oh, no, I thought, *he reminds me of the unbreakable students.*

Whoops, back to Suzuki. We finished the first round and I was five points up, Suzuki zero. I sat in the corner and wiped myself down. My thigh was throbbing. I looked over at Kaz and she smiled, she looked like she was really enjoying herself.

I continued to hit Suzuki and points added up. I was hitting him with some really hard blows, then out of the blue he thumps me with a nasty little knee to my head. Wow, that rocked me. I took him down again and was straddling him in what BJJ called the mount. I slid my elbow backwards and forwards across his mouth and jaw. Elbow strikes were illegal, and he was complaining in between wiping the blood from his mouth.

We stood up, the fight was over, and I had won ten to zero. He took a lot of punishment, which surprised me. He was quite a tough opponent and capable of inflicting a knockout on me if I was not careful.

For the after party Asoh Sensei had booked an entire Chinese restaurant a couple of stops from Shinagawa. I arrived with Kaz. These days I was no longer a single man, Kaz and I were officially a couple. I stopped sleeping with Kumi san a while before. She took it well and was soon with another guy. Kaz and I just clicked, it felt natural, we flowed together and we never argued. I took great pride in having Kaz with me. She was the perfect partner and she fitted right in, understanding all of the etiquette that was required at these Japanese, predominately male, events.

The alcohol was flowing and I could see by the flushed red faces that quite a few of the older men were getting very drunk. There were quite a few of Asoh Sensei's friends, associates and students there. Everyone was so polite and respectful. I think they all knew of my fighting history, as the chant went up "Big Jack, Big Jack, give us a speech". So I stood with a half-filled glass of red wine and with Kaz's help made a short speech. I thanked them for being so nice and thanked Asoh Sensei for inviting me. Kaz quickly translated as I finished up by saying "Campai Cheers" and raising my glass.

Towards the end of the night, I noticed a change in the atmosphere. It all became more serious when two men arrived wearing sunglasses and expensive watches. They sat quietly at the front of the restaurant. I watched as everyone took turns going up to the table and bowing deeply to the men.

Kaz leaned over towards me and whispered, "Yakuza" in my ear.

"Now might be a good time to leave." Just as I said that a strong looking man with an intense gaze and an infectious laugh who was quite drunk, walked over to Kaz and me and introduced himself.

"My name is Azuma." I was surprised he spoke in perfect English. He was a Waseda University graduate in international business. I was impressed.

"I am Jack George, a pleasure to meet you."

"You must come to my dojo, I have many students that want to train with you. You are famous in Japan, Jack George."

He handed me his business card, I knew it was polite and a formality to exchange business cards, but all I could do was to bow my head and apologise to him for not having a business card. He was not put out in the slightest. He happily said for me to call any time and his secretary would look after me. From my research of Azuma Sensei, I could tell that he was the real deal.

So I did. I called and organised a time to go to one of his classes. I had not done any real martial arts training since I was in Korea, and I certainly had not done much sparring. Azuma Sensei had a uniform waiting for me. It was an old style uniform, canvas with the insignia of the dojo stitched on it, I wore it with pride.

The dojo was a well-used building, with a weights gym off to the side. It was a typical dojo with tatami mats. His students were all lined up along the wall waiting and eager. I chose a sparring night on purpose; I just could not help myself.

For my first fight they matched me up against a tall Israeli guy who was quite good. I did away with him after he started to apply some unwanted pressure. The last I saw of him was he was rolling on the ground moaning that I had hit him too hard. This is always the way. Your partner comes in hard then when you respond with a couple of hard techniques in return, they just fold up and complain.

Little did I know, Azuma Sensei had been watching on a closed-circuit TV up in his office. He came bounding into the dojo. "Jack, let's fight."

What an honour. This was Azuma Sensei, a winner of the illustrious All Japan Karate Championship, a gruelling competition. He earned his nickname – The Locomotive – for the way he just steamrolled his opponents.

He was now the head of a large network of karate dojos, that had spread into Russia, and other neighbouring countries. It is full contact fighting. They wear a clear helmet that extends 50 mm out from the wearers face. I had tried wearing head protectors but they seemed to make me more of a target and I got hit a lot more and hurt when wearing them. In this case, they hit these fish tank-like protectors with everything from punches, elbows, knees, kicks and head butts with full force. Add in a ground work and submission component and you have a very robust and very dangerous fighting format.

Fortunately, Azuma Sensei preferred to fight me without the helmet. I knew that I had met my match as soon as we bowed. It was one of those times when I was standing in front of a better man and knew it. So I just rolled on in. He countered my roundhouse kick with a kick to my supporting leg that knocked it out from under me, sending me flying into the gym area. He was right onto me, climbing over the gym gear and continuing the fight.

Now I knew that all I could do was survive, and I so wanted to put up a good fight. So I responded the only way I knew. I kicked his thick head as hard as I could. Umph, he continued to shuffle towards me, like a lion closing in on its kill. I peppered his body with fast low kicks, which seemed to keep him at bay. Seconds later he pushed the weight racks out of the way and slammed hard body punches into my ribs. The fight went backwards and forwards, I really thought he wanted to kill me. All of a sudden, his demeanour changed completely. He stopped, smiled and said, "Great fight."

Wow, he really looked like he was enjoying himself. We bowed off and finished the session.

"Jack, you are a great fighter, I hope we can spar more often." Azuma Sensei was a good guy and teacher. I relished this time with him, and it will be one of the highlights of my career; he was one of the few that kicked my ass.

21
SUMO

I enjoyed working at the club and spending it working beside Kaz. The club was quite tame, really, there was never any trouble, the clientele was mostly Japanese and with the 2000 yen ($20) entry fee most of the undesirables preferred to go to the cheaper clubs. The working escorts lined the bar and could have dinner with their gentlemen upstairs if they were so inclined. I enjoyed watching Kaz, she obviously loved her job and was very good at it. She would catch me looking at her and smile a naughty smile.

All the doormen had to wear black suits with a straight black tie. There were always four of us. Tonight, it was me, Nigel from Manchester, Dimitri from Russia, and Yossie from Israel. I got on with all of them and we had a lot of laughs on the door. They all knew of my exploits in Thailand and had deep respect for the tough format that was.

Suddenly there was a lot of movement on the door. A huge figure strolled up, wearing the formal Kimono of the Sumo, with his hair done in the top knot like a samurai warrior. Following was a huge entourage of minders and women. His bulk took up the entire doorway. "I am Takanoshima," he said quietly. I recognised him immediately, he was a Yokozuna, a Grand Champion, on the rise and one of the most popular sumo wrestlers. "What is your name?" He asked in perfect English.

"I am Jack George."

"Pleased to meet you." He politely put out his ham of a hand and we shook.

Kumi san quickly appeared. "Welcome Takanoshima seki. Please, come in." In one swift motion she opened the partition and let them all in. There would have been in excess of twenty people. "Your lounge area upstairs awaits you. I have my best girls and champagne and whiskey ready."

"Thank you so much." He turned to face me. "Jack san, I have heard much about you, it appears you have quite a reputation. Here is my personal business card, I hope to see you at the next championship. We are both warriors." He put his large hand on my shoulder. He then walked upstairs like a sleek cat.

"Wow," I said, "what was all that about?"

Sumo competitions go for fourteen days and are run the same time each year around Japan. They generate a huge amount of interest, and quite often Japan would literally stop to watch and enjoy the last few fights of the day, this is where the champions and quite often underdogs battle it out to increase the win to loss ratio.

Kaz and I really enjoyed asking friends over to the apartment to watch the last ten or so fights for the day. We would have pizza and beer and it was a party atmosphere. I would catch Kaz watching me, and she'd say, "It is great to see you relaxing, I love your smile. When you are happy, I am happy."

A month later I called the number on Takanoshima's business card. A woman answered in Japanese. I attempted to try and explain that I had met the sumo wrestler a month ago and wanted to meet him for coffee. I thought that this would be a great interview for Kelvin and the martial arts magazine. But it was not happening, she did not speak English. I decided in an instant to get Kaz to help me out.

She loved being included in my plans. She really enjoyed Sumo and would love the opportunity to actually meet a Yokozuna. This is quite an honour, as usually all social activities of a Yokozuna are closely monitored by the Sumo Kyokai, headquarters. So I get her to call his direct line at the stable. Kaz immediately explained that I was given a business card by Takanoshima himself. After what seemed like a lot of pleasantries, finally Kaz got a result. We would meet Takanoshima at his stable near Ryogoku, in two weeks.

I was looking forward to meeting him. Kaz and I set out, and we were both nervous, a little anxious but excited. We arrived at the Takanoshima stables and as we walked the short distance from the train station Kaz took my hand. The Japanese tend not to show affection in public. Kaz and I did not overdo it, but we did enjoy being close. The front door of the stable was lined with beer and sake crates that went from floor to ceiling. Incredible. We had to squeeze our way through what was a very narrow corridor of alcohol. As we snuggled our way through, we entered into what was a hive of activity. When a stable has a Yokozuna they are launched forward and become very famous. Many new recruits that wish to join a sumo stable, strive to be accepted by a stable that has at least one Yokozuna. The stable owners usually are retired Sumo wrestlers themselves and they work very hard with their wives and other family members to run the stable efficiently.

The lifestyle of a Sumo is quite incredible. In between training they graze on a meal called Chanko nabe. It is usually made by the younger junior wrestlers, with chopped fresh vegetables, with meat and fish all boiled in together. They max out on rice and tea, beer and sake. After the morning training session, they then park themselves in the dining room and literally fill themselves with this delicious low fat, protein rich food. They then go to sleep after eating. The aim is to try to put on as much weight as possible. There are some really big units, but I was surprised they don't just pig out on cakes and junk food.

We were shown into a side room that had a large low set table. I wondered how Takanoshima would sit at such a low table. The door slid open and a young man brought some green tea and rice crackers in and left them on the table.

Takanoshima was a tall man, and he was not overweight like so many of the other wrestlers. He slid the door to the side and smiled. "Jack, how great to see you." He rounds his mouth and slows his talking trying to get his voice around the wayward Ls and Rs. He beams his attention to Kaz. "Do you want beer?"

"Yes, why not. My name is Kaz, and I work at the Zero Nightclub."

"Are you Jack san's fiancé?"

"No, no, Jack is my partner."

"Very good." Takanoshima shouted out to his attendant for beer. He soon arrived with a dozen beers on ice and a bottle of whiskey, dried fish and more rice crackers. The attendant poured the beers and we touched glasses, campai, cheers in Japanese.

"Please call me Taka." He downed four beers without stopping. "Umai," he comments, delicious.

We were having such a great time, he knew I worked part time as a journalist and was particularly interested in my adventures in Bangkok. Taka turned to me. "Jack, I may have a story for you."

"That sounds great."

"Okay, I will let you know." He stands, bows and leaves. He had drunk ten beers to my and Kaz's one each. He had also downed at least half of the bottle of whiskey. No wonder there is so much beer in the entrance corridor.

———

Kaz was up early. She tapped me on the shoulder and I rolled over complaining that I was still tired. But she persisted. "Jack, get up and come with me, you will love it."

The morning was still as the sun was only just rising. Kaz reached out and took my hand. "We are finally going to Shinjuku Park."

Kaz had been on to me for ages about taking some time out and going to her favourite place. Shinjuku Park was unique as it showed all of the seasons separately. In Australia, especially in Sydney, we tend to see just two seasons, winter and summer. In Japan, especially in a good garden, you could clearly see the four seasons which are punctuated by the cherry blossoms. They are stunning around the large ponds and walkways, with many people sitting and having parties, celebrating with sake. In autumn, the Japanese maples turn a fiery orange as they shed and welcome the change of season. I always enjoy walking on the dead leaves, the sound resonates right through me. Winter is usually very cold, and it may snow – the entire park blanketed in a white lining – it all looks spectacular.

As we got near to the entrance she veered off to the side and down a short cobbled pathway. "This way is better." She went directly to a bamboo gate. There was a sign that I could not read but I guess it was saying 'No Entry'. "Oh, don't worry about that." She marched straight in.

Right in front of us was a pathway that led to a large pond. Along this pathway was the largest and fattest black bamboo that I had ever seen. It lined both sides of the wide path. I heard a deep moan. It was as if the bamboo was alive, crying – no, singing – or was it talking?

Kaz stopped mid step. "Isn't it incredible, Jack? When Tokyo gets too much for me and I yearn open space, and just need to escape the Tokyo throng, I often find a sense of peace here in this park."

We stopped and sat for a moment on an old timber bench in the corner of the park. There was a small bridge across the pond into the tea ceremony house. It was very small, and hidden from the main path. From this position you can see forever. It is amazing that this open space exists in what is one of the most heavily populated cities in the world. It was not so long ago that the samurai used this ground for hunting and training.

As we sat, Kaz leaned across and whispered in my ear. "I love you, Jack."

Wow, I went all tingly! I had never been in love before. But I could feel something really special with Kaz. "I love you too, Kaz," I kind of mumbled. *Am I really in love?* I asked myself, *I am just not sure what that feels like.* My mother and father loved me, but they never said it, so I was left in a quasi-wonderland, not really understanding or knowing about love. I had had relationships, but they never lasted long. Some would say that they loved me, and I would ruin it and manage to squeeze my way out of it. Yes, so here we were again. I am sure that love is not supposed to be complicated. So I made an agreement with myself; although I do not understand love, I will act with love, kindness and tenderness with Kaz, and just see what happens.

I saw a tear slide down her cheek. "You are a decent man, Jack. I never thought I would ever experience love again. But it happened, and I am so happy." She turned towards me and looked very serious. "Jack, do not trust Takanoshima, he is not an honourable man. I know that you can look after yourself but please be careful."

A couple of months later, as I was working at the club, Kumi san approached me. "Jack san, you have a phone call."

"Oh." I had never been contacted in the club before. I picked up the phone in Kumi san's office. "Moshi Moshi, this is Jack." On the other end of the line there was silence. "Hello, is there anyone there?"

"Jack." I felt the tension in the voice on the other end.

"Yes, this is Jack."

"This is Takanoshima."

"What a surprise." I was quite shocked to be speaking with him as I had not spoken to him since Kaz and I had visited him in his stables.

"Jack, I need to meet you."

"Okay."

"As soon as possible."

"How about tomorrow?" I was fully aware that he would be spotted by the media the moment he left his stable. He could not just come and leave as he wished, particularly someone as popular as Takanoshima, especially as he was recently engaged to a Japanese supermodel and actress. So I knew this wasn't good. "Where can we meet?"

"Away from the stable; how about I pick you up at the entrance of the electronics shop; Laox on Chuo Dori at Akihabara at 11 am."

"I can do that. See you then."

———

Kaz always began her morning walk by grabbing a hot can of sweet coffee from the convenience store. I enjoyed the hit of caffeine but found the canned teas and coffees too sugary. This morning there was an urgency in her step. Late last night Kaz had overheard some of the bar girls talking after their shift at the Zero Nightclub. She was thinking it was just gossip until she heard my name and Isamu Koboyashi, a brutal henchman, in the same sentence. Koboyashi worked for the Kōdō-kai, one of the largest and most dangerous yakuza, mafia groups in Japan.

Kaz ushered the bar girl to come to the side. "Wait, what did you say?" She lowered her voice to a tense whisper. "Tell me again."

"Jack san is in trouble." The bar girl went by the English name Monica.

According to Monica, Koboyashi, who visits her when she works at one of the other clubs, asked casually if she or any of the other girls knew anything about Jack.

The bar girls at the Zero Nightclub were all carefully vetted. Getting a job at Zero could be quite difficult. The kind of women they looked for was not someone who just tease the men and baits them with their bodies. No, the management wanted women who were educated and could entertain the men with their wit, sense of humour and general knowledge. They were not to give an opinion or judgement, or engage in competition with the men. They must learn about them and encourage them, gain their trust and not spread rumours or hearsay. So Kaz was quite taken aback when Monica told her these things. Monica was not a dummy and worked hard; Kaz liked her.

So Kaz had warned me as best she could. I was adamant that I would be okay. Leaving early for my meeting with Takanoshima, Kaz tried to talk to me as I was getting ready. "I will be at the park when you are done, meet me there." She needed to be out of the apartment where she would be able to take her mind off it.

She walked out of Shinjuku station through the smaller east exit, not through the larger south exit that took you past the large police box; and took the short walk past the kaiten sushi train shops and game parlours to the little known side entrance to the park. She walked through into the park, careful that she was not followed. This was our special place, where we had declared we loved each other.

In the six months we had been together so much had changed. I knew that if she had to leave Tokyo she would miss the hustle and bustle of Shinjuku. I hoped we would be okay.

As the creaks and groans of the overgrown bamboo swayed in the light morning breeze, she sat and waited, wondering with a sense of dread if I had survived the meeting with Takanoshima.

———

Running late as usual and out of breath, I had to rush to make the meeting – too many late nights working on the door and drinking at the bars, smoking now and a bad diet. It reminded me that I must take better care of myself. I called Takanoshima to check and confirm the meeting from a public phone. Why was I getting the feeling that I was being followed?

He barked down the phone. "Change of plans, meet me at Ryogoku station in the carpark at the back of the stadium. Get there as fast as you can."

That was not far so I made a quick change of direction and was soon heading towards the new location. It was only eight minutes by train, so just a short distance to walk.

I felt like a pawn in a chess game. I thought that was strange as he was now a grand champion, a Yokozuna. Usually, getting anywhere near him as a foreigner was impossible. The Yokozuna were just too well protected.

As I was nearing the carpark, I straightened myself up and walked directly towards the lone black Mercedes. The car door swung open and out stepped the great Takanoshima. He moved his incredible bulk from the car towards me. As he extended his thick hand out, I stepped back and bowed with respect.

"I do not have much time, Jack."

"Okay, what's up?"

"I have some information that will ruin the reputation of the great sport of Sumo. This may also be the end of my career and possibly my life."

"That's a bit severe, isn't it?"

"Stop messing around, Jack, I need you to pay attention. My only course of action is to go to the media for help. The yakuza have integrated every level of Sumo, and the police are like a toothless tiger, also infiltrated by the yakuza. Will you help me?"

"This is terrible! But what exactly does it have to do with me?"

"Sumo is now run by the Yakuza with betting and payoffs. Kōdō-kai head Katsuyuki 'Toddy' Takawawa is responsible for putting the pressure on the Sumo leaders, and the fighters have had enough. I have gone to the Japanese press so he will not be happy when he finds me." Takanoshima paused. "I blamed the leak on you, Jack." He dropped this like a bomb. I could not believe what I was hearing. "I told the media that you are the whistleblower, Jack san. I am sorry! I simply did not know what to do."

Though this information is not entirely new to me, many of my expat friends, and me included, had long suspected that the bouts at the highest level were fixed. But of course we had no proof. Tachiyama, a foreigner, was the only Champion Yokozuna, the Japanese hierarchy were desperate for a Japanese champion. Akashibono, also a foreigner who was winning the championship and was looking really strong, must lose so that Takanoshima would be the next Japanese champion.

I had watched the bout along with millions of Japanese. Akashibono put up no resistance and just let Takanoshima push him out of the ring. It was obvious the match had been fixed, but up until now no one had been prepared to speak up. The thing was, the match fixing was now beginning to affect every level of Sumo and people could see it. Takanoshima was in the thick of it, and had tried to keep it under control for years. But the pressure from the mafia had consumed the sport. They were now controlling more and more.

If it continued the sport would implode. But the Yakuza were right in with many politicians and police, paying them with the predicted organised wins from the Sumo. Their deadly tentacles were into everything.

"I never considered for an instant to write about this or tip off the media. I always knew that it would be too dangerous. Damn! What have you done?" I yelled.

But Takanoshima just casually got back into his car, his driver closing his door. He rolled down his window and said again, "Sorry, Jack."

It was going from bad to worse. I ran to the Chuo line and took the express to Shinjuku. I stopped briefly at a baiten, a small shop that sold magazines and newspapers. Oh, no, my photo was on the front page of all the Tokyo newspapers. I put my sunglasses on and bought a face mask so I was unrecognisable. The Japanese used face masks as a courtesy to others when they had a cold or flu. Luckily, I had my cap in my pocket. I needed to get to Kaz at Shinjuku Park.

———

"What does this mean?" Kaz asked, desperately hoping to hear from me that it would all be okay.

"He has told the press that I am the whistleblower. And I am going to name all of the wrestlers and Yakuza involved, going back many years." I was speechless; that bastard had set me up. I was a dead man. I had to move quickly, there was no use trying to clear my name now. The yakuza would get me way before I could ever hope to be free. The police were no good either. The strong links of the mafia were in every level of society.

"Oh my god," Kaz whispered, as she reached for my hand. "What will you do?"

"We are both in danger Kaz."

"The Yakuza will kill us both then wipe out our families."

"Kaz, I know a way to keep you safe." I am not a brave man when it comes to living and dying. My reaction has always been to just flee as fast and as far as I can. "I love you with all my heart, but I need you to let me disappear."

"No way, we are in this together." She was pleading with me to take her with me. But I could not, it was impossible to include Kaz in where I was going. Kaz would never forgive me if I chose to run by myself. I knew that I had been pushing my limits for too long. It had to catch up with me somehow and this was it, my life was collapsing in front of me. Kaz, her family and my family were now in danger! What had I done?

We made it back to the apartment. I just managed to see a figure in a dark suit slip into a side street as we raced home.

The apartment was okay, it had not been broken into or ransacked. I turned to face Kaz. "Go to work. Just go. I'll be okay, I will sort this out." But that was a lie. "Just remember that I love you and will always love you."

She knew from somewhere deep inside her that I was leaving. She dropped to her knees and let out a long primal scream. I was distraught and could not hide my grief. I was Jack George and I ruin people's lives.

22
LEAVING TOKYO

I fled, and from the moment I left that apartment, there was no trace of me. Losing my tail was easy, I just ran into the crowded Shinjuku station and disappeared, it was as if I never existed. I was prepared but not well enough. I needed more time. I knew that was impossible.

I did not blame Takanoshima, he had been playing a deadly game, and he stood to lose much more than I did. That would now play out as it must.

The only way I could survive was if I found the ashram. The only way Kaz would survive was if I removed myself thoroughly and completely. I had never given up on the search for the hidden ashram but I understood that I had to do this without anyone knowing. Secrecy was what protected them from the murky world I had created around myself. So it was either now that I try to find the ashram and take on all that encompasses or I would leave Japan for good and take my chances back in Australia. Either way, I had to leave Kaz. It was a no brainer, I was staying in Japan, and I was going to give it my all to find the holy grail, as I called it, of martial arts.

So I just left, I did not say goodbye. In a way I was happy, which was strange. I had an exit plan and I was free. I felt like a huge weight had been taken from my shoulders. I was preparing myself to give my life over to a path that was good. I just had to find this hidden place.

I had the details from Stanley. I had deposited all the money into the National Australia Bank when I arrived in Tokyo. It was $400,000 US into a long term deposit at a high interest rate. It did not matter as I would never use or need that money. But who knows the machinations of life. I was always someone that would plan for the worst and hope for the best.

I left all of my other belongings in my backpack in a locker out of the way at Shinjuku Station.

Kaz, I heard later, spent a number of months trying to find me, but I was gone and did not leave any trace.

The police visited her a couple of times, but they were sure that she had no idea where I was. It was true, Kaz had no idea. And it ate away at her.

The yakuza followed her for a couple of weeks, and she kinda knew her phone was tapped. So she had only one path left available to her, she knew that she now had to leave and go back to Australia. She was heartbroken, so much of her life had included me, and she could not stand all the memories that came flooding in. She packed her bags and said goodbye to me forever. "I do love him," she told her friends when she left, "and part of me will always hope that he finds his way back to me."

———

No one knew where I was heading. Stanley just got sick and tired of my constant pressure, the phone calls, the stalking. But I was not going to fail. He either told me or he had to kill me. So he told me.

"Do not tell anyone that I gave you directions to what is the best kept secret of martial arts and has remained in its pristine beauty for hundreds of years. Passed down from menkyo kaidan, the highest certificate, to dairi soke, the keeper of the scrolls to simple sensei, the teacher, the headmaster." Stanley had been precise.

I moved quickly, wearing sunglasses and my hat low. I had no belongings or bags weighing me down. Once I reached Katsuura station I knew I could not relax, I kept my hat and sunglasses on, and avoided going near the police box as I left the station.

Following Stanley's instructions was quite easy really. I was soon following the river and it was becoming more and more remote with every footstep. I was really doing this. I felt quite bad that I did not contact my family to fill them in on what was happening. But I couldn't, no one was safe from the mob, even in Australia.

By the time I reached the large pool, the road had narrowed to a track. I jumped into the pool fully clothed. The waterfall was gushing down. I easily found the two large rocks and pulled myself up. Then I walked on the track for what seemed like hours.

As I walked the silence became deafening. The shrill of the cicadas gone. There were no birds and everything was very still. It reminded me of the bush that my brothers and I used to lose ourselves in. It was so quiet as I would sit and get taken over in the stillness, feeling any movement.

There was movement, a shift, or was it just the rustle of leaves, only the most adept would pick it up. It was like a ripple in consciousness that disrupts the ever-present stillness. I could sense danger, a vibration ever so subtle.

I knew that I could find a safe haven at the ashram but getting there was proving to be no easy task. Maybe I had missed the fork in the path; it seemed too long, maybe it just doesn't exist. What was I doing there? I had no place there, I wanted to run back to Tokyo and take my chances, but I knew that was not an option now, this was the only place that I could completely disappear from my current life. It was the only way that Kaz and I could survive.

It was far too late now, they know I am here.

23
THE ASHRAM

The sun slowly brought life to the droplets of morning dew as they fell, caressing the leaf as they departed, all in perfect harmony with nature. There was an eerie silence as the damp mist gently enveloped the hidden valley. It was almost as if all life was sleeping. You had to be sharp and pay attention to the silence, to pick up the ever so subtle movements. The monks know the narrow trail well.

The only sound I could recognise was a swoosh swoosh of the cotton training pants, heavy after the thin sleet had made everything wet and slightly hindered visibility. I was being led along the track, all I had to do was follow the feeling. I had almost made it. They led me with their movement. Then out of nowhere an open doorway appeared in front of me. In complete silence, I removed my scandals and entered what looked like a main room, dojo. My senses cascading with the sweet smell of lavender and jasmine incense took me back years to my time with Vic. There was row after row of bald heads sitting motionless.

I walked to the back of the dojo. One of the monks turned to me. "Sit here."

So I sat and settled, legs crossed but not uncomfortable, back straight, but not rigid. They all took a deep breath and when they were ready, they simply closed their eyes and commenced their meditation by repeating the ancient and deep guttural chant "ohm". I must admit that the way they seemed to guess what I was thinking and how they moved around me, surprised me.

This sound "ohm" is an ancient sound that brings down the senses, not dull them as remaining alert is essential. Just sitting, chanting and watching the thoughts arise and disappear.

My legs began to hurt, and my back quickly stiffened up. The head monk that oversaw the morning training struck anyone losing attention across the back with a bamboo cane to bring them back to the Ohm sound and the breath. I was not exempt. My back was red and raw from being struck.

Once the bell sounded and everyone was getting up, Amano walked straight up to me. "Jack, follow me." He took me by the arm, ever so gently. "Come, Jack, it is time to meet our headmaster."

Amano Sempai is the most senior of the monks and had spent the last forty years running the ashram. Standing at five feet tall, he was a force to be reckoned with. He was not a patient man, but was not cruel either. But he had a terrible temper and ran the ashram with an iron fist. He often attempted to speak English and we all giggled when he mixed up the words. Now he walked with me up a narrow path, to a simple yet beautiful temple at the top of the hill.

Sitting there in a white hakama and loose white top was Watanabe Sensei. He opened his eyes and spoke quietly, "Sit down, Jack." He sat there and watched me. Finally, he asked, "Why are you here Jack?"

I felt like I had been preparing my entire life for this day. "The simple answer is, I want to find the truth, and from that truth, wisdom."

"Well, maybe that is one of the reasons, Jack. I have been expecting you and knew you would be coming very soon. Now you have arrived, and as you probably know, once you sign and are accepted into the ashram you are here for life. You cannot leave. How do you feel about that, Jack?"

"I feel this is my life's work. I became interested in martial arts from a young age and I have been struggling to find my place and fit in for many years. I have had a certain amount of success with the physical aspects of martial arts, but I have had a lot of trouble finding a teacher that could take me on the next part of my journey."

"So how do you feel about never leaving?"

"I will do whatever it takes to find myself and to learn how to join the mind, body and spirit through the expression of the body."

"Ah, Jack, that sounds wonderful, but we will see."

On the walls of this temple were many photos. Ah ha! I now understood the connection between daito ryu and hokuto ryu.

Sensei saw that I was looking at the old photo of Takeda Yoshinobu. "He was a student and teacher at the ashram," he confirmed. "Very good, Jack san."

There were so many great masters with their photos on the wall. No wonder the techniques looked familiar. Many of the hokuto techniques and training methods are the backbone of the daito ryu.

Watanabe Sensei was a tall man with a presence and distinct charisma about him. He did not look typically Japanese. I could feel his kindness but there was also an incredible strength coming from deep inside him. "Here, Jack, read and sign this form."

"Umm, I cannot read Japanese."

"So sorry." He searched about for the contract in English. "I see, well you will need to learn the language, but you will start by learning dojo Japanese. Here it is. I translated the rules into English, when I heard that you might be joining us. But there might be many errors; please read and sign this one, Jack. I will get you a knife so you can sign in blood."

Sensei then took me down and introduced me to the monks. They all lined up and one by one, came towards me, took both of my hands in theirs and shook and stated their names. "Kamiya to moshimase, yoroshiku onegaishimasu" which is a polite way of saying I am Kamiya, nice to meet you. It was all over in a couple of minutes.

There were about fifty monks ranging in age from early twenties to early sixties. One of them stepped forward. "Come, Jack, first we cut your hair."

So, off it all came! I had never had my hair so short. They then took me to a dormitory, which was very clean and fresh. Here they motioned towards a small pile of clothes and a futon with a sheet and blanket. I guessed that this is where I will be living.

The clothing that we wore as warrior monks and the shaved heads was not because we were part of some religious cult. It was much simpler than that.

Sensei would teach us that everything we saw, and everything we said would create a reaction within us, and others. A response or a comment, a need to be heard. This was the function of the ego, he would say. So we needed to reduce the amount of input we experienced, remove any catalyst that could create a habitual response. This was why all the structures like the dojo and the dining room and kitchen were all bland; neutral.

This carried on to the clothes we wore, they were simple and plain, nondescript, and did not evoke an opinion. The trousers were hakama, loose and baggy. The tops were simple crossover cotton jackets, cool in summer and warm in winter, just perfect.

The hokuto ryu monks can move without evoking a sound from that movement, and from the senses of a lay person, move amongst them without them realising it. This is why monks learn to walk the way they do. Toes first, then slide the rest of the foot down, gently putting the heel down. When they move, they want their opponents to feel them before they see or hear them.

The following morning was my first official session. The sun broke through the shutters, the meditation finished and the movement commenced. The seemingly still monks commenced their disciplined warm up. We stretched and warmed up the body. This routine never changed, using movements called hikiotoshi and hizajime designed to move and warm up at the same time. It was not long before the distinct sound of the students' bodies hitting the hard, old and tattered tatami mats filled the void. When the student steps onto the mat there is a flicker of anticipation. Each mat could tell a long story, hand crafted and then tempered and moulded to take a life of its own. The mats were washed down every day, but there is a distinct smell that was neither pleasant nor unpleasant. Once the mats have softened, they smell of courage and determination. A mixture of sweat and blood.

I joined the training session. *Here we go, I must get a good start.* I put my left leg forward and tried to strike my partner with a move that resembles the use of a sword. I'm launched through the air. If I am thrown correctly, I will be able to roll and spin mid-air and land safely. A lapse in concentration and death would be instant. This ukemi training is one of the hallmarks of the hokuto dojo. You are thrown as hard as possible and have to roll with the throw.

The essence is for the person being thrown to be totally aware throughout the entire process so even whilst being thrown through the air, you can adjust and re-position yourself no matter what is happening to you. When the senior monk throws the students with no power, just movement and Ki, he enters the students' space and uses his power against them, launching them into the air and landing with a thud. The throws of the hokuto dojo are all designed to break, dislocate or kill.

I stand up, and am thrown again. Over and over again. Anywhere between fifty and a hundred times. Around the fifty mark, my mind and body were screaming for me to stop. But I kept raising myself up onto one knee, then I stood and just let go. I did not resist in any way. I tucked my head into my shoulder and rolled in the air, thinking, *I must remember to tuck my head.*

I was the first foreigner to feel this vicious ritual. Every day they would all try to break me by lining up and each having a go to throw me. This went on for months. At first the harsh surface of the mats tore the skin off my knees, elbows and abdomen. I was shredded and all I could do was just keep showing up, the blood from my injuries seeping through my uniform and staining the mats. Eventually the broken skin was replaced with a hard callus.

It would be too easy for me to crawl from the mats and curl up in a ball, but I was determined. My will to keep going – and sheer stubbornness – eventually wore out the seniors throwing me.

When Amano Sempai screamed "Suburi" we all lined up and took a wooden sword, bokken, from the sword rack. The last bokken was always the heaviest and it was left for me. The timber swords could be lethal when moving towards each other with such power. You could feel their lethal intention. I lost all track of time when we practised the sword cuts with a partner. I joined the count and just let go. We usually did at least 1000 cuts a day.

We did the same thing every day. It was so boring. That's what the teachers wanted; they wanted it to be boring. To give in to the monotony and quit. At least I knew what I was in for each day at the same time.

No one in their right mind would choose to enter the hokuto dojo. And those that did choose did not last long. I often wondered what their stories were and made a promise to myself as soon as I had learned enough Japanese, I would get to know my fellow monks.

There were many fallen yakuza that came looking for the lethal edge at the dojo. It was usually the last straw and an act of final desperation by the Mafia Oyaban leader; to instil discipline and purpose into these seemingly no hopers. This was long after they ceremoniously removed their little finger with the tanto sword for disgracing themselves. They oozed a bad element, and they were all the same, always looking for a way not to train or contribute to the running of the ashram. I suspect that most of the ongoing running costs of the ashram were paid for by well off patrons connected to the local yakuza family.

This base element relished in hurting me whenever possible. In the early days I did not understand enough Japanese to push back. The senior teachers just watched and assessed my reaction and attitude to the obvious bullying. It was just as well, as many times I wanted to bury their heads in the mud. As the seasons came and went, the training was a constant, day in and day out. And slowly, every day, one more bully disappeared. But the yakuza were not the only students to attempt to push me around. At first the other monks made it very clear that I was not liked or wanted. I could crush these students, but I restrained myself. One student, only just senior to me, took great delight in pissing all over the toilet floor and then throwing the bucket and mop at me to clean the mess up.

During training, Amano Sempai would entertain the monks with his stories. From what I could make out, he was a gambler and had four children and a wife that did not work. Long after he lost this job, he would dress in his suit and act as if he was still going to work, only to catch the train in the direction of his company and get off a few stops before and go to a casino and try to win back the money he had borrowed from a loan shark. The shark was really putting on the pressure to pay back the money he had borrowed and lost gambling. Eventually he had no more money and told his wife everything. She was shattered and left with the four children for her parents' place. Amano Sempai then left his house and, like me, made his way to the ashram. He now lived and made the ashram his life.

Amano Sempai often talked about one of the most famous

students at the school. Back when it was still okay to dress as a samurai, Takeda Yoshinobu spent many years roaming the hills and valleys of Japan. Upon one such trip, he visited his hometown. At the time, the outskirts of the town were being terrorised by bandits. One morning after Takeda Yoshinobu left the village the villagers found the bandit with his head buried in the mud. Dead. Takeda never admitted to disposing of this bandit, but he probably used obiotoshi, a famous hokuto technique.

———

"Who do you think you are?" Watanabe Sensei asked me.

I responded by telling him my name.

He scoffed. "Try again. You have meditated, as you say, for many years and you do not know who you are?"

I had nothing to say. His eyes looked through me and I could not move. I was absolutely stumped. I thought I was pretty special, a pretty important guy. But here under the gaze of the master I just withdrew and all of who I thought I was, was just an illusion. Within the first thirty seconds of sitting opposite Sensei, I was left with a feeling deep within me that I was in the right place.

"Let us meditate." He then guided me through a basic meditation. He opened with, "Jack san, you are not who you think you are. Now focus on the breath and release everything. Let go of all thoughts and preoccupations. Just let it all go."

This simple meditation was similar to what I had done in the past with Vic, but doing it under the guidance of Sensei, I was really able to trust in him and release everything.

The gong sounded and seemed to reverberate right through me. We had been sitting together for an hour, I did not realise. Sensei instructed, "For the rest of the day, Jack, I want you to stop believing that your thoughts are true, release from the cycle of habitual thinking and breathe deeply into this new reality."

For the rest of the day, I was more confused than anything else. What had I got myself into? Who am I? What a question. I am Jack George, and I am a tough dude. I have proved myself over and over again. So I continued to resist and so the beatings continued.

———

One morning, as I was walking towards the dojo, blissfully in my own world, Amano Sempai pulled me aside and gave me a small brass bowl. "You will need this today. Today you do 'Takuhatsu'. You will beg for your food."

I was given special clothes that resembled medieval Japanese wear. *I have reached a new low*, I thought. *Why me?* It was all to try and break me down. They were not interested in my experience or any of my history for that matter. I sought them out after years of looking and asked them to teach me. What was I doing? I still wanted the lessons but the ancient way in which they taught me was frustrating. So I resisted.

Amano Sempai could see my dissatisfaction. "Leave. If you are not happy here, go. But I warn you will never be allowed in again."

I sucked it up, put on my happy face and the baggy gown and hid my face under the wide brimmed hat. I joined the end of a line of fifteen monks. This was going to be quite an experience. I was hungry so I was motivated to do this. We walked single file and chanted "So hum".

The novelty soon wore off, especially after I only received a meagre amount of beans and weak soup. The food at the ashram was basic, but having to beg for my food was a whole new experience.

In the ashram, the days seemed to mould together. There was no use trying to remember what day or date it was. Time was irrelevant and I learned to tell the time by watching the sun. The physical difficulties, I was starting to see with a sense of nonattachment. I was beginning to embrace them. The exercises where still very tough, just as demanding, but somehow I no longer felt the need to comment.

Amano Sempai could see the change in me. I was starting to embrace the difficult, so he continued to ramp it up. All to no avail. The more arduous they became the more forgiving and, I am astounded to say, the more loving I became. When it was my turn to be thrown, I would yell out "onegaishimasu if you please," as loud as I could and I would see the smiles and laughter on everyone's faces. I did not resist this, I just went with it. I would ask Sensei about it, and he would just say, "You are doing well, Jack san."

Sensei asked me the question again. "Who are you, Jack?"

I simply replied, "I do not know, Sensei." That was a significant jump in wisdom.

"To not know who you are means you are transcending the body identity, which we all go through. I am my body, I am my name, I am my job, I am a father, a son, a martial artist.

"All the labels continue to go on and on and on. We are wearing golden chains that imprison us in our own thoughts of all the various identities that we continue to spiral around in our thoughts, never moving past this habitual pattern. By you not knowing who you are, Jack, you are beginning to break these chains that only restrict you. My advice to you is to continue to let go, do not align with anything. Just like the freedom of the cherry blossom. It knows that its life is over yet in all its beauty it just enjoys the present moment, not thinking about what comes next. Jack, we all want answers to everything but to be able to sit still in the midst of all the movement of the mind and just radiate from still awareness, is the key." Sensei's wisdom resonated with me.

I thanked Sensei as I left and headed towards the kitchen to help prepare for the evening meal. I must admit that I felt at peace and one with the physical movement of the technique, but I found that trying to retain that attitude outside of the dojo was a challenge. So that was my work, my spiritual work. To sit with all of the emotions that come up, not to comment or give them life, just smile and watch them float way, just like the cherry blossom.

———

My body was toughening up, the bulk of my muscle had transformed into strong sinew. The last of the body fat I was carrying had disappeared. The first months were tough. They really tried to break me. I was a blond-haired foreigner, and they did not want me there. Why? Because they feared me.

For those first six months, I resisted and fought back any way I could, and the beatings continued and got more intense. Amano Sempai just sat in seiza with other instructors and shook his head. They threw me hundreds of times until the day when Sensei stepped onto the mat and said "enough". He gently picked me up and let me wipe the blood and sweat from my knees and elbows. He turned to me. "Daijobou? Are you okay?"

"Yes."

"Yosh, come at me with any technique as hard as you like."

I was not expecting this. One part of me wanted to lay him out, really take it up to him and give him a good thrashing. The other side of me just wanted to walk away. Even having this choice inside my head was for me a cause for concern. I had never hesitated before, I always went for it and finished the fight very quickly. But this was my chance to show them how good I am. I'm Jack George, martial artist, never defeated in combat. I was not going to let this old man defeat me.

Initially I pulled my technique short. Sensei could see that I was pulling my punches and yelled at me to come at him with all I had. So I did. I went at Sensei with my signature step up side kick, he simply shifted his weight very subtly to the left, stepped around behind me and just for an instant disappeared from view. The next thing I knew I was being eased backwards and gently placed on the floor on my back. I was not hurt, just confused. *How did he do that?*

He had a smile on his face. "Mou ichido. Again, Jack san, do you know judo?"

"Yes, Sensei. I trained in judo for five years with the Sydney University team." I didn't go to uni, anyone could train at their dojo. I can hold my own and thought I was pretty good.

He stepped towards me and put his arms up motioning me to take the traditional judo stance with him. I fell straight into his trap. He grabbed my extended arms, spun me around, stepped behind me and flung me like a wet sheet taking me back and choking me out. I briefly lost consciousness and woke up with Sensei gently caressing my face. It was not a malicious act; he was genuinely caring for me.

This went on for a good hour. I threw everything at him, and he put me in so much pain but I did not get close to him. He would pull his technique short, limiting my ability to break fall or roll out of his move. I crashed into the mat shoulder first and had all the wind knocked out of me. Sensei would adjust the pictures hanging on the wall while he was waiting for me to stand.

As I stood, usually after a couple of minutes, he would slam me down again. But I kept getting up. I was exhausted, but Sensei was enjoying himself. At one hour, Sensei put his hand up to signal the end. I bowed deeply on my knees clearly understanding the lesson that had just been beaten into me. Sensei simply nodded his head and walked off the mat retiring to his quarters. I then had to sweep and wipe the dojo down. This in itself took me a long time.

All of the students and teachers were fanatical about keeping the dojo spotless. I thought it was just a Japanese obsession, but it was all tied in with the spiritual essence of the ashram. I asked Amano Sempai why the obsession, and he replied, "You will learn in good time." I would walk on the mats in my sandals on purpose just to annoy the other students. They would run after me and forcibly remove my sandals. I continued to play these games for as long as I did not commit fully to the ashram.

The beating that I suffered at the hands of Sensei was a turning point for me. I realised that everything I had learned in martial arts up until now was useless here. All the break falling that I had been doing and taking the throws was preparation for Sensei to receive my technique and show me that my techniques had no place here in the ashram. I was a little lost.

Everything that I believed about myself was built on shifting sands. I was now faced with a choice. To commit fully to the teachings of the ashram or quit. I could easily revert back to my previous life and travel the world in ignorance, or I could stay here and study in depth the ways of the martial artist. It was a no brainer. The ashram was my destiny and my salvation.

I really took time to consider what had happened. The strange thing is that throughout the brutal display of deadly technique, I did not feel any malice or anger from Sensei. He moved and dealt with what was needed perfectly, just the right amount of effort needed. No more and no less. I felt deep within me that it was never anything personal. And it was not routine either. Somehow, Sensei would transcend the outer body and he seemed to resonate from within me, this is hard to explain as it is all feeling. To put it plainly, he touched my heart, and transferred a deep knowing from within himself. It raised me and enlivened me.

The training was always the focus of the day. The ukemi, breakfalls, the suburi sword cuts and the waza techniques, were trained every day. Often, Amano Sempai along with the assistant trainers, would give ukemi only and we would be thrown for an hour or more. This way we would not become complacent and established a rhythm. The mind and the ego would then nudge into our awareness, *this is getting easy* or *I have got this*. We just never knew what was coming.

During the hour-long session of being thrown, the instructors would add in a new texture of changing the standard way of throwing us. They would add in shihonage and kotogaeshi, two of the now well-known moves that are signature to the hokuto ryu. They would also change the suburi around and we would cut the bokken against each other, that seemed to go on many hours.

We knew it was a long session when the hands started to blister from the skin rubbing on the timber swords. I experienced the same feeling when I was reaching my limit doing ukemi. I felt my body take over and the mind shut down; for the briefest time I became one with the timber sword and my opponent. I was totally empty, as if time had stopped. Pure bliss. Then bang! I was back in my body feeling the pain of the sword as it struck my partner's sword. But I want that feeling again, I pleaded but too late, it had passed.

We knew we were in for a long session when Sensei would do just one technique for the entire session. It was usually ippon dori, the first technique we learned when we entered the ashram. Again and again and again he would say that all the understanding of the entire system was in the first technique.

Sensei would often choose me to demonstrate a technique or a point because I was larger and stronger than the other monks. He would never stop working on perfection of his own moves. We were always learning when training. Just when we would think that we were getting it, Sensei would say or do something quite profound. One day really stands out for me as to his unbridled brutality and how he would turn it off in an instant and show a compassionate side. In the midst of an intense session, there was a small moth that landed on the mat between me and two other monks. I was about to squash and remove the moth, when Sensei stopped the entire class, got down on his hands and knees and ever so gently picked the moth up and walked it outside. "We all have a right to exist, even a moth." Sensei smiled.

————

I noticed there were never any visitors to the ashram. It was totally self-contained. We would spend hours in the gardens. All the food was grown here and the farm animals provided eggs and what little meat we needed. The chickens and pigs were kept in open pens, and fruit was plentiful. There was solar electricity but usually ran out so we used candles and had cold showers. No luxuries here and I did not miss them. Days were spent in quiet contemplation or training. This was basic, and I was ready and waiting for the challenge and difficulty. We worked and trained so hard, there was never any question about what we were doing.

I studied the language for hours. It was unlike English in many ways, far more direct, one word conveying so much meaning. It would take a whole sentence in English to convey the same meaning. The other monks were always correcting my Japanese. I soon picked it up and was talking and in turn understanding more and more about the history and details of this wonderful ashram.

I had changed and was far more friendly to everyone. I think I was even happy. The bullying stopped and I started to joke around with the other monks. They even started to teach me the first series of techniques. Every counter to an attack was incredibly painful. "Jack," they would say, "if your opponent is in pain, their balance has been broken. No one likes pain."

Sensei would add his comments as well. "Jack san, power down, touch and unbalance, what does this mean?"

We spent all our time in the ashram, the only connection I had to the outside world was when I was out in the community, begging. Contact with anyone outside was forbidden. Sometimes people would try and make conversation, but we never responded.

Once accepted in the ashram, they watched and monitored your progress, they then chose a plan for you which included the physical training, the meditation, and then your help on the grounds, in the garden, the laundry and in the kitchen. So everyone was kept very busy, all the time. We all took turns in the kitchen, we followed a strict

Japanese diet and had many recipes to follow. Some would cook and some would clean. There was always something to do. Keeping men active was the key to a productive life, Sensei believed. "The mind is a fickle beast, so much that we think about we believe to be real."

This part of the mind is best called the 'ahun kara' in Sanskrit or, in layman's terms, the ego. In fact, the ego is everything that we think about. The ego had no part in the techniques of the Hokuto ryu ashram. It causes us to hesitate whilst we choose the correct response. We need to have the answer as to whether we act or not immediately and in a split second, go from zero to one hundred per cent in the blink of an eye. In all movement, you must be trained to deal with the action not the reaction. If we are dealing with the reaction, we are too late.

The scrolls of the dojo gave detailed explanations of the techniques and the spiritual path that we studied. Japanese people are usually Shinto or Buddhists, but we at the Hokuto Ashram had a completely different philosophy, born in combat and honed on the meditation cushion. But meditation is only a vehicle to take you so far. There comes a time when you need to release from the meditation and just let go of everything and become one with all that we see, hear and feel.

Sensei was very patient with me. "Do you understand Jack san?"

This was all new. I needed to assimilate it slowly.

"Ah," he would snap, "a little at a time, Jack. Now is time to train." And he would set off towards the dojo with me following closely behind.

When Sensei was teaching in the dojo everyone attended, usually the morning session would commence at 11 am, and go for at least one-and-a-half hours. Today, Sensei was lecturing on the importance of "breaking balance".

There were fifty monks when I was first there, including the one chief trainer Amano Sempai, and three assistant trainers,

Motchuzucki Sempai, Kazu Sempai and Yamada Sempai, each of them on their own path.

"Kazu Sempai, what does it mean to break balance?" he asked.

"Well, it's hard to explain, Sensei."

"Just try."

"It is the feeling I get when all thought subsides and all sounds cease to burden me. There is only me and my opponent. I am totally focused on his movement and the rhythm of his breath. It is complete."

"Very good. Now practise the moves with that same intention." We all bowed and commenced the sitting movement.

The sound of the hakama was all we heard as we all moved around the dojo walking on our knees. Then the silence of the dojo was shattered by the explosive kiai, yell and "todome no atemi," or big strike in English which would symbolise a sword strike to finish off our opponent.

Once training was over, we would make our way down the well-trodden path to the kitchen and dining room. There was a feast of fresh salads and brown rice, which we rolled up in nori seaweed and some furikake sprinkled on the food. We then poured ourselves a small bowl of miso soup. There was always what we called mouna at mealtime then after 9 pm when the last class had finished. Mouna was silence. I would brew up a cup of green tea and take it back to my dorm where I would join the others in silence, meditation then lights out at 10 pm.

At 5 am the sound of Ohm chanting would gently invade my sleep. One by one we would get up and meditate on our futon for an hour. Then at 6 am we would walk up to the main dojo and sit together.

At the dojo we would rotate all parts of the syllabus. Considering that I was the most junior, and the average time the monks had been here was ten years, I was allowed to do the ikajo, nikajo and sankajo series of moves, which I picked up quickly. I would move on to yonkajo as soon as they thought I was ready.

There were no women at the ashram. That is just the way it was. I cannot give you an explanation other than there was nothing sexist about it. Sensei had a tremendous respect for all women. He often reminded us of the fantastic Egyptian civilisation that was one of the most incredible empires for well over 3000 years. He would say that women were able to vote, get an education and divorce if need be. An incredibly advanced culture.

I wondered about Lecky. Is she okay?

And that always led me to start thinking about Kaz. There is pain there. I would sit in stillness and watch the cherry blossoms fall, its time over. They would bloom so beautifully for such a short time. It took me to another place. A time when Kaz and I started to feel deeper feelings for each other. We would walk the paths around Shinjuku Park together, holding hands intensely. We would lie on the soft grass and watch the cherry blossom, sakura, take their last short journey. Moving aside and allowing the new growth to come. They were quite beautiful how they floated so elegantly and came to a perfect rest on the white cobblestones.

I would marvel at this simple act of love and took everything out of that moment. Then the next moment and then the next moment, giving Kaz my total attention. She said that she could feel my love. How I missed her now. I knew this would do me no good, thinking about her and wanting to see her again only brought me pain. So, I had to shut it down, and not let her enter my thoughts.

In the temple where I often met Sensei, he could sense that I was not myself. "What is the matter, Jack san?"

"Why do we leave our loved ones and disappear without a trace?" I asked.

"Everyone's reasons are different, Jack. But what is it exactly that you are asking?"

"I was in love, Sensei. And I left her without a word. I just left and never looked back."

"Why, Jack?"

"I am hesitant to say, Sensei, as I took your oath to forget about my past life. So is it okay to think about it, even talk about it?"

"Tell me," Sensei prompted.

"I was in trouble with the yakuza. A very famous Sumo wrestler set me up as the whistleblower for fight-fixing all the sumo bouts."

"Go on, Jack. What has this got to do with your love?"

"She never really knew the details, I kept it to myself so that if she was ever questioned she would have no idea what I was up to. It got desperate, and in order to protect her I had to leave without a trace. Now my heart truly hurts."

"Yes, Jack, affairs of the heart are difficult. You cannot change what you have done, and it was a true act of love to fall on your own sword, as we say. But I can feel your love lost. Just think about your love in meditation and practise the loving kindness meditation. For other religious traditions, this can be translated as prayer. Whenever your heart gets heavy, think deeply about your loss and bring them into your mind and say to yourself, may you be happy may you be well and free of pain and misery. Breathe, focus deeply on your lost love and repeat that process over and over again.

"Then what I want you to do, Jack, is to bring yourself into mind and say silently, may I be happy, may I be free of suffering and pain. This is important as we cannot change the past, but we can forgive and let go of the pain that is making us sad right now."

I bowed deeply. "Thank you, Sensei, as usual your kind wisdom makes so much sense."

"Let us sit for a while now, Jack." We sat for thirty minutes when the bell was rung for lunch. "Yosh iku zo, let's go." He jumped up and started making his way to the kitchen. I stood up, and was in deep gratitude that this man had my back.

———

Once a month, the entire ashram fasted from the finish of the Sunday dinner until Tuesday lunchtime, about forty hours. We only drank fresh water from the well or weak green tea. At first, I was not accustomed to missing one meal let alone several and I really suffered. The simple task of missing a meal was so different from anything that I had ever encountered. I was used to just grabbing something to eat whenever I felt the slightest bit hungry.

Eating for me had become a habit. It was the sensation of the food in my mouth, the feeling of chewing, that came the addiction to taste. Amano Sempai would say, "You are weak, Jack, how do you say in English? You are a pussy cat, Jack san." We would both laugh, but I felt weak. I drank water to try and alleviate the hunger pains. I had no other option. All food was kept under lock and key. My stomach slowly shrank in size, so I ate less. Which in turn stripped off more weight.

At the end of the fast we would drink delicious bone broth and eat a small amount of fruit and nuts. It was important to not go and graze and fill up on the wrong food. It takes real discipline to fast with just water. This is the kind of mindset that is important to become a warrior and monk and be able to overcome the discomfort of being hungry.

The reason that we fasted was to cleanse the body. Prevention of disease was the key. Not fasting when you were sick. I always felt much lighter and healthier after the fast. Sensei was sure that by fasting, coupled with our low fat almost vegetarian diet, we remained disease free and heathy for many years.

———

One day as we were all going about our various duties the gong in the dojo was sounded. The gong was never used except in the case of an emergency. There sitting in the middle of the room, on his knees with his arms tight in a painful position behind his back was a man that I had never seen before. He was sobbing and complaining about the pain in his shoulders and elbows.

Sensei walked up to him and sat on one knee. "Who are you?"

"I am not talking to you," he spat. He was not a homeless person that would sometimes find their way into the ashram.

"Why you don't tell me who you are, I want to help you. Maybe you need a little more time to think about it." Sensei turned to Amano. "Tighten the knots."

Two of the senior students tightened the knots, pulling his shoulders back and then they tied his feet to the knot in his back.

Sensei then turned to Kazu Sempai. "Massage his shoulders." Kazu started massaging the intruder's shoulders. As he went deeper into the exposed pressure points the man let out a deep groan. Kazu Sempai was a shiatsu master and knew how to massage the pressure points. He continued to work the same spot. The man was now screaming.

"I can make it stop," said Sensei.

"Please, please make it stop." The pain was now excruciating.

"Okay I will make it stop."

Kazu ceased his digging and the pain stopped immediately.

"Thank you, thank you," he whimpered. "My name is Nakamura."

"What do you want, Nakamura san?"

"He had this knife." Amano Sempai held up the weapon. "Were you planning on using it?"

Nakamura sat there in silence.

"Okay leave him tied up here for the night."

The groans continued all night, they got worse and worse.

At 4 am, Sensei visited the man again. He got down low and said in the kindest voice, "What do you want, Nakamura san?"

The pain was slowly increased until he was groaning long and deep. Finally, he had had enough. "I was sent by the Kōdō-kai to find and kill a man called Jack George."

"Who is that?" Sensei asked.

"I do not know, I don't have the details. I just work for the Kōdō-kai. I was looking for a secret martial arts school, somewhere in Honshu. I had no idea where it was. I stumbled across this place, I was lucky I guess."

"Do you see any gaijin?" he barked. "You have interrupted the feel and life force of our ashram." Sensei was now raising his voice. All the monks looked the same with their shaved heads and clothes. "I will let you go, but if you or any other of your assassins come back, you will all die a very painful death. Untie him."

He breathed a sigh of relief, as the tight knots were slowly loosened.

"Take him out of here." Four of the monks came forward, one of them wrapped a black cloth over his eyes. They then duck walked him out of the ashram and dumped him into the pool where he could find his way back to civilisation.

Sensei was not an angry or aggressive man, but he had a job to do and he did it with a conviction that he would protect everyone within the ashram. After that intrusion, Sensei started a roster of guards that would stand silently hidden from view twenty-four hours a day, until he felt that we could relax. We all took turns rotating every two hours. As it turned out, we never had any intruders again.

I was due to have my meeting with Sensei a couple of days later.

"I really appreciate you protecting me."

"You are a very important member of this ashram, Jack."

"When you were questioning that man, you said that he disrupted the feel and life force of our ashram. What did you mean by that?"

"That is a good question. According to the ancient scrolls, there are three states of consciousness. Consciousness is a generic term many people use for awareness, even mindfulness. They are satwa, rajas and tamas. Tamas is heavy, thick and depressed. It absorbs the flow of consciousness, rajas is fast moving and energetic, it reflects the flow of consciousness and satwa is light, still and calm and conducts the flow of consciousness."

"So, what does this have to do with the dojo and martial arts?" I asked.

"Well, nothing at all, actually. Jack, have you ever heard of self realisation?"

"Not in detail. Is it enlightenment?"

"Exactly," Sensei nodded. "Self realisation and enlightenment are the same thing. It is just a state of mind that sheds all of its limitations and the ego dissolves, letting go almost completely of the ingrained identity and we refer to as I, me, or mine. I say almost completely because more often than not there can be many different stages of self realisation. Everything from a partial realisation that may only last seconds, to a full realisation that can stay with you your entire life. So you see, Jack, we use the words of the wise to guide us.

"This ultimate aim of the ashram is to be able to use the martial arts and all of the supporting practises and train to transcend violence and leave a peaceful life. The words of the wise have been a part of the ashram advanced teachings for hundreds of years. But we really have to choose the best and right time to start to give you the next stage of your development, your spiritual development. Just as Christianity has the Bible and Vedanta has the Bhagavat Geeta. We too have fine-tuned the teachings of Christ, Buddha and Krishna to form our own customs and rituals such as meditation that then align with the practise of martial arts so that we can reach the ultimate freedom and wisdom of self-realisation.

"I know this sounds a bit much, Jack, are you keeping up, or have I lost you? I must tell you now that the hokuto ryu's spirituality is a far cry from the dogma and stylised antiquated rituals that many of the religions get so caught up in. Rather our spiritual practise is vibrant, and creative, quite simple really. The three gunas are an easy way to give words and life to feeling the states of being. They are all the same, not one is superior in any way to another. If we observe, we can see the way they interact in ourselves. In the dojo, we clean it diligently every time we train. When we wipe down the floors and walls, what are we doing, Jack? Let me tell you, we are removing the rajas, the energy and movement that has accumulated during the class so that we can return it to satwa, still and neutral it now conducts the flow of consciousness, enabling us to have a blank surface for us to then train and grow physically and spiritually. If we do not regularly remove the build up of rajas, the space will become tamas, and continue to build up absorbing the flow of consciousness. That then repels all growth. Can you now understand why we are so tidy?"

I would sit for hours deep within the thick bamboo, listening to the silence punctuated by the gentle breeze bringing the bamboo to life. It's funny how these seemingly random interests and desires move us forward to the uniqueness of our lives and destiny.

———

I had been a part of the Hokuto Ashram for ten years, and had made incredible changes in my life. I had completed all of the requirements up to the advanced 8th Dan black belt.

In the beginning sets, you are only allowed to wear a white belt. Then when you graded for 3rd Kyu, 3rd level, you are allowed to wear a brown belt. When you get to 1st kyu and graded for first dan black belt and from that time as long as you are entitled to wear a black belt. All the coloured belts do not exist, they were an unnecessary distraction on the journey invented by modern martial arts. In fact, in the western countries they would put so much emphasis on black belt, they would act like the black belt is the pinnacle of their training. But we knew that it was just the beginning.

As the years went by, I was teaching most of the classes. Amano Sempai was getting too old, and his joints could no longer take it. His once jet-black hair had turned completely grey. He would sit at the back of the dojo in seiza and watch the classes. I could tell that he loved every part of it. He was older than Watanabe Sensei.

"What will happen to Amano Sempai?" I asked Sensei.

"So desu ne." Sensei considered the question. "Well, this is his home, he has nothing in the outside world. All of his children are older now and there was no way that they would look after him, and we must make him comfortable as can be. When he can no longer walk or look after himself, he may choose seppuku."

"What is that?"

"It is a ritual suicide, and only the most courageous will take this path."

One morning a couple of weeks later the sun was rising very slowly. We were all summoned to the courtyard just in front of Sensei's quarters, beside the temple. Amano, who has been steadily declining the last couple of months, sat in seiza, he was wearing a brand new white hakama and white top. He looked resolute. Behind him stood Sensei with his best sword out of its scabbard.

"What is going on?" I whispered.

Kazu, who was now junior to me, explained, "This is seppuku, or ritual suicide. It is a great honour for Sensei to be the one to assist him."

I could feel myself go weak at the knees. This just seemed absurd. How could I stop this?

Kazu put an arm around me. "Jack Sempai, please do not make this any more difficult than it needs to be. Amano Sempai has chosen his time. We cannot, must not, interrupt this important time."

I was to learn that the whole ceremony is an honourable way to die. Amano Sempai had chosen this path as he did not just want to waste away and be a burden to us all. It was a gift of love to us all. It was the warrior way. Watanabe Sensei only allowed the most dedicated of his students to leave this world this way.

Amano Sempai picked up a small tanto sword from beside him. It was incredibly sharp. He wrapped the blade of the sword in paper, then he took a short sharp breath and raised the knife above his head. I was stunned. Some of the senior students shouted out, "Ganbatte, Amano san." They were already grieving. He plunged the knife into his lower left abdomen, he then drew the knife right across his abdomen to the right side. Still alive he dropped forward exposing his neck. It was time and without hesitation Sensei struck with force, removing his head with one lethal strike. It was over so quickly. Four of the monks knew exactly what to do next. They rolled up the body in the paper and carefully placed his head alongside it, then lifted him ever so gently onto a funeral pyre, which was immediately lit and his body was turned to ashes. Then, according to his wishes, the ashes were swept under the cherry blossom trees, where he would join with the earth and be and give life to the cherry blossom.

Wow, what a rush, I thought, *now I have seen everything.*

Sensei remained stoic, but he had lost a friend. They had been together for many years. "Shikata ga nai," he would say. That is life.

———

We were sitting in his temple, sipping sake when Watanabe Sensei suddenly opened up to me about his own life. He was a farmer and worked very hard for his family. He inherited their very profitable farm from his father. He studied kendo and judo at a local community centre. He found out that his wife was having an affair. He went into a red hot rage, his honour had been broken and he lost face. His wife pleaded with him to not hurt this man, who was the local baker. His son was only sixteen at the time, and he knew what had to be done. One night, it was late and his wife was out, and he was drunk, the same as he was every night. He just couldn't deal with it. His son took it into his own hands. Determined to restore his father's honour, his beautiful boy silently lifted his best sword and made his way down to the baker's house. He broke in through a back door and burst into the rear room, only to see his mother naked and making love with the baker. He was disgusted, but did not hesitate. He brought the blade down again and again on the two lovers. It was over very quickly.

Watanabe caught his son bringing the blade back home. "What have you done?"

"I sorted it for you, Papa."

He instructed his son to support his version of what happened, and he will take the fall for killing them both. Reluctantly, the boy agreed.

Watanabe went to the local magistrate and told him that he had committed this heinous crime. So he was locked up. Back in those days, the judge was quite lenient for killings of wives and husbands that were having an affair. So he was turned over to his brother who knew about the secret dojo, but he was not to tell anyone about it. He left his dear son with the farm. He knew that he would be able to cope.

"He will be fine as he is strong. I love him. The price we pay."

Sensei needed to appoint a successor, his health was failing him. I spent many hours with him talking and learning as he gently entered the twilight of his life. "Don't be sad, Jack," he would say. "You are like a son to me."

"And you have been a father to me. I love you." I would say it to him over and over again.

"It will soon be my time, Jack, I will soon sit up and meditate, I want to be totally present throughout the death process."

All of the monks came in one at a time to pay their respects. Sensei was so happy as he closed the door on each of his students. I must say that all of the ashram students and teachers were well trained and stayed present as they turned their total attention to their much respected and loved Watanabe Sensei.

"It is time, Jack, can you please help me onto my mat."

Sensei was totally ready, so dignified. He knew that how you died was a reflection of how you lived. He sat up in seiza, his back straight, chanted for a couple of breaths then focused completely on his breath. There was so much love throughout the ashram. Sensei sat there for five days, I watched and waited. On the fifth day he simply took one breath in, then without a breath out, he simply dropped his chin to his chest, and he was gone.

Sensei sat bolt upright for a further three days. We rolled him onto a stretcher and amazingly his body was still supple and warm. All of the monks walked behind the stretcher as his body was placed on the top of a funeral pyre. As were his instructions, we were to burn his body and then scatter the ashes throughout the beautiful garden. Some of his ashes were placed in a vase in the dojo on the Shinzen, the structure that sat above the front of the dojo, that we bowed to at the beginning and end of every session.

Just before he died, Sensei had revealed to me the land the ashram was on was bought outright by Takeda Yoshinobu Sensei and was the property of each headmaster as they lived and eventually died.

"So, Jack, all of this will be yours."

24
CHANGE

When it was announced that I was to be the new headmaster, all of the students clapped and shouted 'banzai' three times.

"Tomorrow it will be business as usual," I said. "We must remain strong in body, mind and spirit and retain the vision created by Sensei and all the great teachers that have gone before him."

I ran the ashram just as Sensei had; I was fair and just. I continued to deepen my own spiritual practice. There were many lessons written by Sensei about his experiences and teachings in the scrolls. They were so rich in knowledge and wisdom. I would spend many hours studying and practising his lessons. They remained a valuable source for me for many years.

Over the last couple of years, we had been getting numerous enquiries offering large sums of money to buy the property that the ashram sat on. We had heard the noise of construction slowly creeping up on us. Our beautiful hidden home would soon be a secret no more. These developers wanted to swallow it up and use it to build houses and condos, making the absolute most of the land.

On top of the pressure from the developers we faced the

extinction of what is being called a monster from a past era, that does not know when it's time is up; branded a relic from the past by the developer's propaganda machine enticing the buyers by promising them a share of this beautiful part of the world. A warrior haven that had survived the decimation of the samurai, cruelly hunted down, beaten, and their top knots hacked from their heads.

I agreed to relax the rules and allow some of the monks to go home. They no longer had the patience required to put up with the noise of the heavy machinery, getting closer and closer every day. No students had entered the ashram in over six months. As the numbers started to dwindle, many of the classes were cancelled. I was seriously considering what to do as more and more left the ashram.

Watanabe Sensei had said to me, "The world is changing Jack, one day in the near future you will have to make some hard decisions. Do we keep up with the world or do we become an ancient relic? The teachings will always be relevant, we just need to teach them. It will soon be time to take what we know and teach the masses that violence and conflict are not the source of happiness. If we do not act, then we are just as bad as the tyrants and dictators. We must show how non-violence and peace can be the chosen path by all human beings. And you do not need to run to silence in an ashram. You are the ashram and peace and love is inside of you just waiting to come out. It will be up to you, Jack san, to close the ashram down."

So the time had come. I decided to shut the ashram. "The winds of change are all about us, it is time for a new era." It was right that we now chose our time to acquiesce, with our heads held high.

I felt that I was in more and more danger of being recognised. At one stage before I entered the ashram, my photo was everywhere. I felt like public enemy number one, responsible for the downfall of the great and very popular sport of sumo. Now I am the sensei of the ashram and may soon have to become the voice trying to save its teachings. I now knew it was time to act. It was time for me to go home.

Some wanted to stay. I could understand this as the ashram was their home. They had no money; it was very sad. So I would let them stay. Those who stayed became caretakers and security, keeping the place clean and watching for trespassers. I would allow monks that had left to return one day if they chose. No ex-monks were to be turned away, including me. New students or vagrants that somehow found their way to the front door would still be turned away. All of those who stayed behind must keep the place locked up. Only a few monks remained.

I was feeling a deep well of love. I had so much gratitude for how the ashram had shaped me. Prior to entering the ashram twenty years before, I really struggled with love. Through the teachings, I learned to find love in the smallest actions and was bewildered at how I found a love and acceptance of myself. I just let go and went with it. Now I led with kindness and forgiving. I was not sure how that would manifest with the yakuza, who no doubt would seek me out.

25
THE LAST WARRIOR

After my twenty years at the ashram, it closed. The place was deserted other than the handful that were staying. Most had gone to their homes. Before they left, I instructed them to not lose the lessons they had learned and to become a beacon of peace to everyone in their family and groups of friends.

I was the last warrior and was determined to take the secret teachings to the world. I closed the thick heavy door behind me and made my way to the train station, unperturbed by the obvious changes to everything, I fitted right in. I was dressed as a monk as they were the only clothes I had left. Before leaving, I'd grown my hair long but tidy, pulled back into a ponytail, and I had a full beard. The bamboo brim hat was drawn down and I lowered my gaze. I walked smoothly with purpose, and though I must have looked a sight, people politely moved aside as I walked through the crowds. I felt pretty good, considering I was leaving my home of twenty years.

I had left the ashram quite often over the last six weeks or so to beg for food and to gently acclimatise myself to the outside world. I would stand where I always stood, people knew me and would talk to me, give me food, ask me to say a prayer for them, and I would just politely nod my head.

I continued my journey to Shinjuku. No one seemed to recognise me, and no one stared. Shinjuku had completely changed, gone was the building at the south exit where Tokyu Hands was on the fifth floor, but I could still find my way around. I spoke the language, in fact I was having some trouble remembering English. I made my way into the belly of Shinjuku station; everything looked the same. I found the locker and it was open. None of my belongings were left. What was I to expect, it was no wonder after twenty years the station would want their locker back. The problem was all of my identification was in my wallet. I made my way to the lost property and made an enquiry. Everything was archived and there were records going back decades. I must have looked strange, a gaijin dressed as a monk, looking for a wallet.

To my delight, the counter staff disappeared out the back and soon reappeared with my bag and belongings. *Only in Japan*, I thought. I made my way to the restroom and found a corner to get organised. I cut my hair right back and shaved off my beard. *Wow, a new man.* I slipped out of my hessian pants that were kept up with a drawstring and put on my jeans, they hung off me. I was hard and lithe, after years of intense training, not carrying a gram of fat.

I folded the clothes neatly and placed them next to the garbage bin, slipped on my cap, a face mask, and my timeless sunglasses. I made my way to the National Australia Bank in Shinjuku where I had deposited the money prior to fleeing to the ashram.

"Can I transfer the money to the National Bank in Australia?" I asked.

"Yes, no problem."

They gave me the details I would need including my account number to be able to set up an account in Sydney. They then transferred the money from a term deposit to a regular saving fund, so I could access some of the cash now. I had the money invested and re-invested for twenty years. The total was almost $1 million US. I took out some money I would need for living expenses. I had lived for so many years where the only currency was blood, sweat and tears. I was sure the money would come in handy in the future.

What I was trying to get my head around were all these strange boxes that everyone was either talking into or doing other stuff on. It had their entire attention. The Shinjuku crowds in and around the station – that I had admired twenty years ago and would marvel at the way they seemed to have an in-built radar to avoid collision – now continually ran into each other, it was total havoc.

I became quite nervous as I was heading towards Kaz's place. It was a long shot, but I had to at least go and try. I was able to observe with ease the long latent emotions, so I just went with them, not becoming them. Wow, Kaz's apato was still there. But the whole block looked like it needed a good wash. I made my way to the door and gently knocked. The door swung open, there was a young mother standing there with a child wrapped around her leg.

"Sumimasen, does Kazoku san still live here?"

"Ah, sou desu ne," said the woman in Japanese. "Let me think. My mother lived here for many years, and when she passed away, I moved in here. I do not know who lived here before my mother. Sumimasen, I am sorry."

I knew there and then that going back to Australia was my best option. If Kaz was there, I would find her. First things first, I booked into the Shinagawa Prince Hotel. The concierge said something to me about Wi-Fi. I had no idea what they were talking about. They asked for my mobile phone number and something called an email address. I just nodded politely, "Sumimasen."

I started to gradually put my life back together. I was in no rush and I knew it would take time. I went for long walks around the area, there were coffee shops on every corner, called 'Starbucks'.

Just amazing. I stumbled upon a quiet park where I could be still and contemplate. I found this very refreshing. I was lucky as years of the basic Japanese diet had prepared me for any food that was available. I ordered room service, re-introducing meals like Caesar salads, club sandwiches and steaks. I ate sparingly as I was used to restricting my eating.

The following day I made my way to the Australian embassy and filled in an application form for a passport. Everywhere I went they asked me for a credit card, it was as if cash no longer existed. I signed up for a MasterCard, which was handy. I booked my ticket to Sydney with Qantas airways. As I recalled a promise I gave myself in another life, I bought a business class ticket.

It was quite refreshing to walk around Tokyo being totally anonymous. Training at the ashram had prepared me to be able to blend into my surroundings. This was hardly the mountains or the forests, though the concepts were the same. I gradually reintegrated back into the masses. It would only be a matter of time before someone recognised me on one of the many cameras that watched over us.

In fact, it was sooner than I anticipated. I was waiting in line in one of the many convenience stores. I had a couple of onigiri in one hand and a sweet canned coffee in the other. A man in his fifties who looked like he was a gang member, stepped out of the incessant noise of the pachinko parlour next door and walked right into me. I did not see it coming, I think my urban surroundings had disorientated me for a second. I managed to hold my rice and coffee, but the man swore at me in Japanese, "Hora koitsu kuso jiji… ketto…" but in the process of spitting out these expletives he stopped dead in his tracks and pointed at me. "Jack George," he whispered. How on earth had he recognised me? It had been twenty years!

Before he started yelling and made a scene, I took his jacket lapel in both hands about 200 cm apart, pulled him abruptly forward wrapped the jacket lapel around his neck and used his jacket to choke him out. This choke when done properly will render your opponent incapacitated within ten to fifteen seconds. Then the idea is whilst they are sleeping soundly you throw them with all your might, this would usually kill them as their head would hit the concrete first.

Instead, I lowered him down onto the ground, put him in the recovery position put my mask and sunglasses on, turned the other way and quickly walked back to the hotel, where I stayed for the next couple of days until I could take the limousine bus directly to the airport.

It was a night flight to Sydney. The cabin crew were very nice, polite, and attentive. A couple of the female staff were being just a little bit too friendly. I enjoyed the banter; it had been so long since I enjoyed female company.

As soon as I landed, I called Kelvin's number but the phone had been disconnected. So I looked up and rang his photographer David Newland, who I knew quite well. He answered the phone and I immediately asked him how I could get in contact with Kelvin.

"He is in a nursing home in Narrabeen on the northern beaches."

———

"Jack, my God." Kel said. "You just disappeared; where the hell have you been?"

"I will explain everything to you as soon as I get settled. Remember when we met up all those years ago and you gave me a contact in Tokyo?"

"Yes, Kazoku," Kel remembered. "Her parents used to be my neighbours when I lived in Bilgola Beach."

"Do you remember which place? Can I get Kaz's parents address, please?"

"I don't know Jack … it was so many years ago."

"Kelvin, I need to get to them, they may be in danger, I can't stress this enough." I sounded desperate, and I meant to.

Kelvin looked up the address for me. "They may have moved years ago, Jack; here it is anyway, and you owe me a coffee."

26

KAZ

I walked down the steep driveway and made my way up to what looked like the front porch. I could not help but notice the men's shoes and thongs lined up inside the doorway. I did not allow myself to comment. I tried knocking but there was no reply. I could hear music coming from the back of the house. I stopped and listened, I felt movement so made my way around the back. I took off my mask so my face wasn't covered in any way.

"This is not good, I don't know what I am expecting." To Kaz, I probably died years ago. But I couldn't help it. It is the fighter in me, and I just had to know. It was quite selfish, and I was feeling a great compassion for Kaz. Let's face it, we were in love, Kaz was my soulmate.

———

There is a woman in the back garden. It looks like Kaz, but I can't be sure. I don't want to sneak up on her; I was now a master of stealth, I had spent the last twenty years studying how to be quiet and go undetected.

I called out, "Kaz?"

She stopped and looked up. "Can I help you?" She walked gingerly towards me. "Who are you?" She stopped and looked again... "Oh, my God ... Jack, is that you?"

"Yes."

She brought both hands up to her face. She then stood up straight. "I waited and searched for you, Jack!" she screamed.

"I am so sorry. Let me explain."

"I am not interested, Jack; you broke my heart."

"Both of our lives were at stake," I said softly. "All I could do to protect you was to just disappear. That damned sumo wrestler set me up and blamed me for the downfall of the sumo association and the mafia was closing in on us, fast."

"I warned you so many times, Jack... You broke my heart..."

"I know and I understand, it must have been so difficult for you. But I have never stopped loving you."

"All of my energy has gone into my family. It took me years to get over you, Jack ..." Her voice became shallow. "And now you just turn up on my doorstep? What now, Jack?" She moaned. "What do you want from me? Where have you been?"

"I was a coward, Kaz, I ran and ran to get away. Remember the hidden ashram that I told you about? Well, I found it."

"Kaz, are you okay?" An older couple came from a back gate, walking up the slight incline towards us. The woman was a spitting image of Kaz, tall and elegant, and looked quite concerned.

"Oh, hello," said the woman, who was obviously Kaz's mother. She could feel that I was no danger, it was my calm and contained resolution that kept this all together. "We have not met before, I'm Kaz's mother."

I could see that her face was flushed and she was playing with her hair.

"Oh, I'm so sorry for the intrusion, I think I should leave." *Oh don't be a martyr*, I thought to myself. *You have to suck it up and take what's coming.* I went to step on to the side veranda up the stairs and through the garden to the hire car parked on the street. My way was blocked by a solidly built young man. The man was in his early twenties, I guessed. He had an intensity about him, and something that I just could not put my finger on.

"What do you want?" He had a conviction in his voice that I recognised but was not sure how or why.

An older man, who was Kaz's father, put his arm around the young man. "Don't be scared, my boy."

I felt like I was losing it. There was an intensity about this situation that I had not felt for many years. I started to get angry. I could feel it like a wave dropping over me. I hated this primal feeling and I felt ten years old again. "Just stop," I said, probably a little loud.

Kaz's parents took a step back and shied away. Kaz stopped and stood there in silence, and the young man looked stunned.

Kaz softened. "Jack, relax. When I was at my worst, I would talk to you and tried to feel you. I knew that you were still alive, but I did not understand why you did not come to me."

"I just couldn't. It had nothing to do with not wanting you, in fact it was the opposite. I wanted you to survive. I wanted you and your family to keep on living."

"I thought you didn't love me anymore," she cried. "I tried to move on, I cannot explain it," she pleaded, "I could not work out what was wrong with me, we were so close and we loved each other so much. You really loved me, Jack."

"I know, and I still do, but I too had to work out how to not crush myself by thinking about you. I spent twenty years in an ashram, tucked safely away from everyone and everything. I was broken. After researching the holy grail of martial arts for many years, I found it. I finally found it. I knew that as long as nobody else knew I was there, you would be safe. In the end there was just me remaining. I had all the lessons I needed and grew so much as a human. I was promoted to the sensei of that wonderful space, so I had an obligation to stay there. But developers were pushing hard buying up the surrounding land, so I thought it was time to close the ashram."

Kaz walked towards me. "Jack, you are the same man, but I can feel you are different. I'm not sure if I still love you."

With that my heart sank. "I have never stopped loving you."

"I had to let you go, Jack. It was the only way I could survive."

"Mum, who is this man?"

"Jack, you have a softness and an understanding that is new to me. It will take time to get to know you again."

"Mum, stop this. Who is he?" He was screaming.

Kaz's mother was also crying, beside herself, hating seeing her daughter and grandson so upset.

"Jack please be calm. Say hello to your son, Drew – Jack – George," Kaz whispered.

I was completely blind-sided. I had no idea.

Drew shook his head. "My father? I don't believe you. My father was killed twenty years ago. Prove to us that you are who you say you are. Mum, have you been lying to me? I can't believe it. Where have you been all this time?"

Drew is tall with my broad square shoulders. He has a shock of strawberry blond hair, like my grandmother. With his mother's green eyes. There was just no doubting that he is my son. A tear fell down my cheek.

Drew was crying. "Dad? I can't believe it, you are alive."

I walked towards him and opened my arms and we hugged each other and cried together. There was nothing else to say.

I found my Northstar and it guided me home.

ACKNOWLEDGMENTS

A huge thank you to Linda Diggle for your kind patience and fine expertise in working with me to bring this book to life.

Thank you to Vaughan and May Lai for your great support.

A huge thank you to Liz, you are my rock and my lighthouse that would always gently guide me back to what is real.

Thank you to Jack George and all the other players in this epic adventure. By bringing you all to life, I learned so much about myself.

Thank you to Mark Dapin for your help and guidance.

Thank you to Valerie Khoo, boss at the Australian Writers' Centre, for your suggestions and guidance.

I thank all the editors, type setters proof readers and cover artists.

ABOUT THE AUTHOR

Andy Dickinson is the founder and head of Northstar Ju Jitsu. He has spent over forty years training, competing and researching all aspects of martial arts and personal wellbeing worldwide. He is passionate about teaching martial arts as a legitimate path to understanding oneself and helping his students to see the link between training in the dojo and living a courageous life.

He has written and recorded a thorough online academy that adds a new dimension to the quality of how martial arts is taught and allows Northstar Ju Jitsu to be studied anywhere in the world.

Andy is the author of *Stand Tall, Ancient Tradition Modern Warrior* and *Warrior Upgrade* as well as several eBooks, and is a prolific blog writer. Andy presents and educates on a multitude of topics related to martial arts and life. Above all else, Andy finds his greatest inspiration teaching all levels of students and nationalities on his online academy and at his beautiful dojo in the heart of the inner west in Sydney.

www.facebook.com/Andrewgeorgedickinson
Instagram/andydickinson
www.andydickinson.com.au
www.northstarmartialarts.com.au

OTHER BOOKS BY THE AUTHOR

Stand Tall: A Journey from Boy to Man to Master

Andy Dickinson: Ancient Tradition, Modern Warrior

Warrior Upgrade: Twenty Ways to Upgrade to a Warrior Life

AN EXCERPT FROM THE SEQUEL
THE SEVEN WARRIORS

I stand and put down my sword, open my hands to show I am not armed and start a slow walk towards the dojo.

"Who are you?" I ask the lone figure as he walks up behind me, stopping exactly two tatami mats distance from me. I notice his walk, very controlled, no arm swing, and the placement of the toes down before his heals, making his walking movement silent.

"I can see that you have killed one of my students." He says. "He was a very experienced fighter. You and your team are very good. But I and my team are here to take your lives."

"So you are a ninja group, the lowest of the lows, gutter rats that work for the highest price. Now you work for Takakawa. Whatever code you follow we will cut you down and dispose of you as petty criminals."

"We are not ninja. We are a small group that follow a very old and traditional way of living. We are not unlike you, and this ashram—"

"What is your name?" I ask.

"My name is Inoue, and I am the leader of this group. We are simply following orders from our master who was hired by Takakawa."

A group of ten men appeared at the dojo entrance. At about the same time, my men appear behind me, spreading out, appearing very menacing. I noted that Vik was absent.

The two groups stood opposite each other, sizing each other out. The men standing opposite us all looked very calm. We, as a group, started walking towards them. I step forward towards Inoue, I note that he shuffles back, maintaining and controlling the distance between us. All of my men assumed a ready stance, the Zanshin was thick in the air.

Inoue flicked out a long knife which was concealed. He came at me fast and hard. I only had enough time to put something in the way of it finding my belly, the outside of my forearm the bony part, it grazed my arm but it was enough to draw blood. We were at quite a disadvantage, as the three archers were covering the front of the ashram.

Scott let out a piercing kiai and focused on the two in front of him. He launched a high round house kick which sailed past the man as he leaned back. A knife appeared and was thrust towards Scott's heart. He shifted his weight and stance side on, catching the blade hand with both of his hands, slamming an elbow into his temple. He then grabbed the man by his hair drawing his head to his knee, knocking him out cold. Scott then moved onto the second man.

www.ingramcontent.com/pod-product-compliance
Lightning Source LLC
Chambersburg PA
CBHW030620120726
47904CB00006B/1970